Charles R. Haines

A Complete Memoir of Richard Haines

1633-1685 - a forgotten Sussex worthy, with a full account of his ancestry and

posterity

Charles R. Haines

A Complete Memoir of Richard Haines
1633-1685 - a forgotten Sussex worthy, with a full account of his ancestry and posterity

ISBN/EAN: 9783337399450

Printed in Europe, USA, Canada, Australia, Japan

Cover: Foto ©Andreas Hilbeck / pixelio.de

More available books at **www.hansebooks.com**

A COMPLETE MEMOIR OF

RICHARD HAINES

(1633–1685),

A FORGOTTEN SUSSEX WORTHY,

WITH A FULL ACCOUNT OF HIS ANCESTRY AND
POSTERITY;

*[CONTAINING ALSO CHAPTERS ON THE ORIGIN OF THE NAMES
HAYNE AND HAYNES, AND THE VARIOUS COATS OF ARMS
ASSOCIATED WITH THEM];*

BY HIS SEVENTH MALE DESCENDANT,

CHARLES REGINALD HAINES, M.A. Camb.,

AUTHOR OF "VERSIONS IN VERSE," "INDIA AND THE OPIUM TRADE,"
"EDUCATION AND MISSIONS," "CHRISTIANITY AND ISLAM
IN SPAIN," "MOHAMMEDANISM AS A MISSIONARY
RELIGION," AND OF A SCHOOL EDITION
OF THE "'PROMETHEUS' OF
ÆSCHYLUS."

WITH ILLUSTRATIONS.

" *Dos est magna parentium Virtus.*"—*Hor.*

1899.

TO THE MEMORY OF MY ANCESTORS,

ESPECIALLY OF MY

FATHER AND MOTHER,

TO WHOM I OWE, WITH LIFE,

ALL THAT HAS MADE LIFE WORTH THE LIVING,

I DEDICATE THIS

LABOUR OF LOVE.

NAMES OF SUBSCRIBERS.

*W. Barnes, Esq., Common Side West, Mitcham, Surrey.

A. Ridley Bax, Esq., F.S.A., Ivy Bank, Hampstead.

J. P. Bickersteth, Esq., Grove Mill House, Watford, Herts.

*Mrs. Bradstock, Bank House, Waltham Cross, Herts.

W. Lumsden Byers, Esq., 29, Thornhill Terrace, Sunderland.

E. Godwin Clayton, Esq., 10, Old Palace Lane, Richmond, Surrey.

*Miss Clayton, 62, Elizabeth Street, Eaton Square, London, S.W.

F. A. Crisp, Esq., F.S.A., Grove Park, Denmark Hill.

E. H. W. Dunkin, Esq., Rosewyn, 70, Herne Hill, S.E.

*Mrs. Fanny Grave, 26, Oakley Flats, Oakley Street, Chelsea, S.W.

Everard Green, Esq., Rouge Dragon, College of Arms, London.

*Major R. L. Haines, R.A., 2, Pentillie Avenue, Plymouth.

*H. A. Haines, Esq., The India Office, London.

*Captain Gregory S. Haines, Governor's House, Military Prison, Dublin.

*The Rev. F. W. Haines, Bromley Common, Kent.

*Christopher Haines, Esq., Bacon's Farm, Bramfield, Herts.

*Edwin Haines, Esq., Brookers, Paddock Wood, Kent.

W. Haines, Esq., 2, Marine Parade, Worthing, Sussex.

W. T. Sanden Haines, Esq., Lavant, Chichester.

The Rev. Francis A. Haines, Bosham, Sussex.

Charles Singleton Haines, Esq., Rock House, Ulverston.

A. Montague Haines, Esq., Wellesley Lodge, Sutton, Surrey.

The Rev. Willoughby Charles Haines, Chaplain to the Forces.

Hubert B. Haines, Esq., Victoria, British Columbia.

Miss Evelyn Haines, 110, Belgrave Road, S.W.

Basil J. Haines, Esq., Manor House, Queen Charlton, near Bristol.

Robert T. Haines, Esq., Hawthorne, Bickley, Kent.

John Haines, Esq., 24, Hampton Place, Brighton.

*Miss Mary J. Haines, Manor House, Cliftonville, Margate.

*Mrs. Hare, St. Boniface, 32, Westwood Road, Southampton.

*Mrs. Ireland, Cowfold, Sussex.

J. Leopard, Esq., Wycombe House, Hurstpierpoint, Sussex.

J. Lister, Esq., Basil Grange, West Derby, Liverpool.

*Mrs. Richard Moline, 13, Burlington Street, Bath.

Mrs. Peachey, Seacroft, Sandown, Isle of Wight.

* Descendants of Richard Haines.

Hugh Penfold, Esq., J.P., Rustington, Worthing.

The Rev. H. Palmer, Sullington Rectory, Sussex.

W. M. Rhodes, Esq., Hill House, St. Leonard's-on-Sea.

R. Garraway Rice, Esq., F.S.A., Carpenters Hill, Pulboro', Sussex.

*Mrs. Rippon, Broadway, Hanwell.

John Simmonds, Esq., Church House, Godalming, Surrey.

Miss Simmonds, Church House, Godalming, Surrey.

Sir Harry Stapley, Bart., Holyport, Bray on Thames, Berk

The Rev. W. Tringham, Longcross, Chertsey.

*Mrs. West, Clysma, Granville Road, Scarboro'.

Percy Woods, Esq., 50, Widmore Road, Bromley, Kent.

* Descendants of Richard Haines.

ILLUSTRATIONS.

CONTENTS.

West Sussex.

(From Speed's Map, 1610.)

INTRODUCTION.

In 1891 the late Mr. A. M. Haines, of Galena, Illinois, seeing my name in *Notes and Queries*, wrote to me on the subject of my ancestry. For forty years he had been investigating the origin of Haines (or Haynes) families in the New and Old World. I was obliged to tell him then that I knew nothing of my ancestors beyond the third generation, nor was there any one else who did know. Since then I have spent a great deal of time and a considerable sum of money in searching for information, with the result to be found in this book.

The work is intended, primarily, as a memoir of Richard Haines, the real "founder" of our family, but it has been my wish to make the book as complete as possible by including in it anything connected with the subject which was likely to interest outside readers. Thus Baptists will find in it a full account of an episode of great importance in the history of their church, and one which is nowhere else described in detail. Students of the social and economic life of England in the reign of Charles II may glean something of interest under that head. There is a chapter that may be of use to the compilers of the N. E. Dictionary.[1] Farmers and fruit growers—more especially the promoters of a revival of the cider industry—may learn some "wrinkles" from the experience of a practical Sussex farmer two hundred years ago. There are two chapters on the origin of the name Haine and the various coats of arms borne by different families of the name, which will not fail to interest any member of the many existing Haines families who wishes to know something of his past history. May I add that I have a vast quantity of information of all sorts relating to the name Haines, especially in the West, South, and East of England, which I shall be happy to search in reason and without charge for any one who applies to me ?

It will perhaps be useful to future searchers in the same field, if I state here, generally, what sources of information I have more or less exhausted.

---

[1] My contribution to this has been a search through 16 vols. of De Quincey's works.

Registers searched[1] : Sullington,* Storrington,* Washington,* Thakeham,* Wiston, Findon,* Burpham, Arundel,* Binsted,* Petworth,* Wiggenholt,* Parham, Ashington,* Kirdford,* Warnham,* Pulborough, Wisborough Green,* Tortington, Rudgwick, Billingshurst, Shipley, Beeding, Lyminster and Warningcamp, Horsham, Angmering, Greatham, North and South Stoke, Rumboldswyke, Cuckfield, Fittleworth, Bramber and St. Botolph's, Stopham, Ford. Egdean, Balcombe, Cold Waltham, Walberton, Clapham, Patching, East Dean, Madehurst, St. Peter Major Chichester, All Saints' Chichester, St. Olave's, St. Martin's, St. Andrew's, St. Pancras, Chichester.

Bishops' Transcripts (only) searched : Duncton, North Chapel, Farnhurst, West Grinstead, Sutton, Bognor, Ferring, Lodsworth, with Kingston, East Preston, Selham, Graffham, Midhurst.[2] All the above parishes are in Sussex. In Surrey have been searched : Godalming, Elstead, Puttenham, Witley, Ockley, Abinger, Wotton, Alfold, and Shere.

At the Record Office : All the lay subsidies for Sussex that seemed likely to be of use; Sussex fines from 1558 to 1760; a list of all occurrences of the name (*a*) in Chancery Suits from 1558–1750 (of which only a tithe have been examined), (*b*) in Close Rolls Catalogues, (*c*) in I. p. m. indices; the Board of Trade South Carolina papers; original records at Somerset House relating to the sea fight of 14 October, 1747, off France in lat. 47°.

Most of the wills catalogued under the name Haines in the P.C.C. have been examined down to 1800. They amount to nearly a thousand ; also many from the counties of Essex, Herts., Berks., Kent, and Surrey.

At the British Museum : All early magazines and registers, and the whole of the Rolls Series, County Histories, periodicals such as *Notes and Queries*, New England Historical Register, Reports of Historical MSS. Commission, Harleian Society publications, and all the genealogical magazines, the early numbers of newspapers such as the *Oxford* or *London Gazette* ; and, in the MSS. room, indices of all the Charters, Seals, etc., the MS. collections on Sussex, and the copies of Visitations.

At the Bodleian : This library I have only partially explored.

[1] Those marked with an asterisk have had their Bishops' Transcripts searched as well as the Parish Registers.

[2] I have since searched the registers of this parish also.

At Chichester: Besides the Transcripts most of the registered wills, many of the MS. ones, the Bishops' Diaries, Attestation Books, inventories, lists of churchwardens, marriage licences, Probate and Administration Bonds.

At Lewes: Most of the East Sussex transcripts, marriage licences, old Poll Books; also some of the parish registers, at Seaford.

Almost everywhere in my searches I have been shown the utmost courtesy. The clergymen of the parishes named above, with scarcely a single exception, have afforded me every facility, and I must especially thank the Rev. H. Palmer, of Sullington, and the Rev. George Faithfull, of Storrington, in this connection. Many landowners in Sussex, and in particular R. M. King, Esq., of Fryern, near Storrington, have allowed me, with extraordinary kindness, to inspect title deeds and other documents. More especially I wish to thank Lord Leconfield for permitting me to get information from his manor rolls and deeds at Petworth, and the Duke of Norfolk for letting me have his manor rolls at Arundel searched.

I am indebted for much generous assistance in my task to R. Garraway Rice, Esq., who, being engaged on similar work in Sussex, has given me the benefit of any notes he has come across relating to my search. I have also made considerable use of the unrivalled knowledge of the Chichester records possessed by E. W. Dunkin, Esq.; but the two persons without whom this book would never have been written—alas! both dead since the work was begun—are the late Andrew Mack Haines, of Galena, Illinois, U.S.A., and the late C. E. Gildersome Dickinson, of Edenbridge. The former inspired the search and was always ready—till his eyesight failed him—to communicate to me any information he had gathered in his forty years of investigation, and to write constant letters of lively interest and encouragement. As to the latter, I can scarcely overrate the assistance given me by him, professionally and otherwise, in my researches. His keen sympathy, accurate judgment, and untiring enthusiasm were always at the service of a genealogical beginner like myself, while his wonderful knowledge of record searching, his extraordinary diligence and acumen made him an invaluable coadjutor in my work. It is a matter of the deepest regret to me that neither of the two who would have best appreciated this book will be able to see the results of my labours.

No one can hope to trace a yeoman family beyond 1500, as no parish registers, or wills (as a rule), go beyond that date, and I consider it no mean feat to have carried our pedigree back so far without a break in the chain of evidence. What has surprised me is, that no branch of the family seems to have preserved any documents, letters, pictures, books, or relics of its ancestors. Putting aside the Bible in Mrs. Hare's possession, and the very interesting marriage certificate and naval warrants in the possession of Mr. Edwin Haines, of Paddock Wood, no single line of writing earlier than 1800 has been brought to my notice. Where are all the copies, not to say MSS., of Richard Haines's books? Where are the letters he received from many important persons? Where is the "silver bowl" mentioned in the will of Gregory Heine? I cannot help thinking that some strong box, or some plate chest, contains things which would be very interesting to all readers of this book. May I entreat any one who can light upon any fresh evidence of this sort to communicate with me? The most insignificant fact or the vaguest tradition often proves a valuable clue.

That there are many errors in this volume I do not doubt, but let those who discover them remember that the work has been done in the midst of much pressing business. I shall be grateful to any one who points out a mistake or suggests an improvement.

I have to thank my brother Hermann A. Haines of the India Office, and the Rev. Francis A. Haines of Bosham, Sussex, for kindly correcting the proof sheets of this book; and my brother, Major R. L. Haines, R.A., for assistance in describing the sea fight of 14 October, 1747.

Uppingham, Oct. 1899.

West Wantley House (built 1656.)

(From a photograph by C. R. Haines.)

CHAPTER I.

ORIGIN OF THE NAME.

"What's in a name?"

THE proper surname of Richard Haines, the subject of this memoir, was Hayne (or Haine). The spelling *Haines* does not occur, as far as I am aware, in Sussex before the seventeenth century, except in the registers of Beeding, though *Haynes* is found at Petworth, Tortington, Billingshurst, and Wiggenholt before that date. There is no evidence that any earlier ancestor of Richard than Gregory, his father, could write his name. He spelt it Heine in 1633,[1] and Heines in 1638.[2] The form Haines has been used by every known descendant of Richard.

It was a common name in the South and West of England during the sixteenth and seventeenth centuries. Camden suggested Ainulph[3] as the derivation. Another supposed derivation is from Hainault. As Edward III married Philippa of Hainault, it is possible that some Hainaulters may have come into England in the fourteenth century, but there is no proof that they founded any families of the name of Hayne or Haynes. The ancient and honourable family of de Hayno, who held lands in Southampton and the Isle of Wight from the thirteenth century to the sixteenth century, may have taken their name from Hainault.[4]

The form Haynes probably arose in three distinct ways :— firstly, as in our own case, by the mere motion and will of some bearer of the older name Hayne[5] ; secondly, by a corruption of

---

[1] Witnessing that year's transcripts of Sullington parish registers as church-warden.

[2] Witnessing his mother's will.

[3] Based apparently on the change of Ainulph's town into Haynestown, and then into St. Neots.

[4] They became extinct with the marriage of Mary de Hayno to Willm Pound, of Drayton. See Herbert Haines : *Manual of Brasses*, Part II, p. 174.

[5] Gregory II. may have added the *s* because he believed himself descended from some family whose representatives used that spelling ; or (most likely) because he wished to distinguish himself from another branch of his own family.

B

Hayne-son; thirdly, from the Welsh word "Einws." About
1100 A.D. Einion, prince of Powysland in Wales, had a son of the
same name, who, according to Welsh custom, was called by the
diminutive Einws, pronounced Eins. His son John, strictly John
son of Einws, became John Einws, or Eines, or Eynes, and finally
Heynes. From him descended a flourishing family that spread
over Montgomeryshire and Shropshire.[1]

Mr. J. H. Mathews, of Cardiff, suggests[2] that in the West of
England, Hayne may safely be derived from Welsh, or Cornish,
hên, *i.e.*, old, or the elder (Irish sean, Lat. senex); while Kelly's
Directory for Sussex (1898) says Henfield is derived from *hean*,
Anglo-Saxon for "poor."

Many of the Haines families of the present day have doubtless descended from ancestors named Haine. The word *hayne*
is found as a place name in compounds, such as Woodhayne,
Willhayne, especially in the West of England, while Hayne and
Higher Hayne are found in Devonshire and Kent during the
sixteenth century. There was a castle of Hayn[3] in France, 1516,
and land in Pembrokeshire in 1530 called Le Hayn. Haynes Lees
appears in Warwick as early as 1575,[4] Haynes Green was in Essex,
Haynes Park in Bedfordshire, Haynes Hall (now Haines Hill) in
the parish of Hurst, Berks, Haines Hill near Taunton, Haynestown in Leinster. Bedfordshire can also boast a parish called
Haynes, and Kent a hundred of Hayne.[5]

The word *hayne* and the participle *hayned* are found in several
provincial dialects, for instance those of Gloucester, Somerset, Norfolk, and the North of England. The words appear to mean land
reserved, or enclosed, for some particular purpose, and are doubtless connected with *hay*, plural *hayne*, meaning hedge. Allied
words are *haw* (Yorkshire *haigh*), French *haie*, German *hain*. If
hayne in the sense of "hedge" be the origin of the name, we
should have expected to find such forms as *William atte hayne*,
but amongst thousands of references no such instance has been

---

[1] See Botfield's *Stemmata*.
[2] Notes and Queries, 8 Ser. xi. January 9, 1897.
[3] Cal. Letters and Papers, Hen. VIII Rolls Series, 1530.
[4] Cal. State Papers, Dom. Ser. 3 August 1575.
[5] Old maps of Africa gave a Haines river in Somaliland, but this name has been
dropped in favour of the native name, Juba. It is said to have been named
after Captain Stafford Haines, of the Indian Navy, who died at Bombay in
November, 1855. His crest was a demi-stag in front of a rising sun, with motto
"Deo non sorte."

found, though de Hayn[1] occurs once, and Hen[2] (perhaps Heyn) once at Shoreham.

It is just possible that, as Heane in Anglo-Saxon was pronounced Hayne, the name is purely Saxon, the original meaning having been long forgotten. If so, it can boast a very respectable antiquity, as a certain prince named Cissa, lord of Wiltshire and Berkshire, had a nephew[3] named Heane, a rich and influential man who founded the monastery of Abingdon in 675.[4] One family at least uses this actual spelling, Heane (pronounced Hayne), viz., that of Dr. Heane, of Cinderford, Gloucestershire.

Besides the possible forms de Aine,[5] Ayn,[6] Hean, Henn, Hene, Hyne, the name occurs spelt in various ways as Heyne, Heynes, Heyns, Heygne,[7] Heynis, Heyncys,[8] Eyn,[9] Eynes, Eyns, Eynns Eynnes, Heane, Hein,[10] Hane, Hayens, Hayne, Haynes, Haine, Hain,[11] Hains, Haines.

---

[1] Rot. Claus. Tower of London, 1203.
[2] Lay Subsidies, Sussex, 6 Ed. III.
[3] Nepos.
[4] See Dugdale's *Monasticon*.
[5] Close Rolls, 1224, Eustace de Aine.
[6] Patent Rolls, Ed. II 22 April, 1333, William Ayn, of Kent.
[7] Brit. Mus. Charters, 52 A. 5, 1413. Also Cal. Anc'. Deeds, I, c. 238.
[8] Registers of Arundel, Sussex.
[9] Cal. Anc'. Deeds, I, A. 835, Robert Eyn, of Bromfield, Essex.
[10] An Essex family. Arms, Brit. Mus. Add. MSS. 5524.
[11] A present Essex family.

CHAPTER II.

EARLY OCCURRENCES OF THE NAME HAYNE IN SUSSEX.

"Look unto the rock whence ye are hewn, and to the hole of the pit whence
ye are digged."—Isaiah i. 51.

It is at Horsham and Warnham that we find the earliest traces of
the name in Sussex. In the reign of Henry III, a certain Martin
Heyne[1] granted to Richard Neel of Horsham rent from a tenement

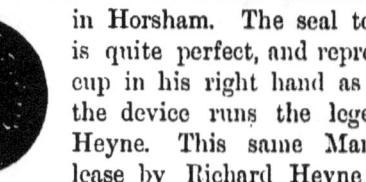

in Horsham. The seal to this Latin document
is quite perfect, and represents a man holding a
cup in his right hand as if for a toast. Round
the device runs the legend S(*igillum*) Martini
Heyne. This same Martin also witnesses a
lease by Richard Heyne of Horsham of rent
from land in H. held by Peter le Horl.[2] Of the same, or suc-
ceeding, reign is a sale by Richard, son of Reginald Haine, for 8
marks, of half a mill and pond at Caldecote to Richard le Erl
of Warnham.[3]

Curiously enough this, perhaps the earliest of all, is the only
instance I have discovered of Reginald as a Christian name to a
Haines surname before my own, unless the Reginald Hane[4] be a
different person, who appears as fourteenth on a list of fourteen
jurors, "honest and lawful men of the bailiwick of Hastings," that
sat (about 1318–9) on an inquisition concerning the state of the
King's free chapel of St. Mary in the castle of Hastings.

A few years later the subsidy roll for Sussex, dated 1 Ed. III
(1327) contains the name of William Hayne of Horton in Burbeache
(now Beeding parish) as paying 16s. Five years later, he appears
again with William le Hen of Shoreham and John Heyne of
Iwhurst in the hundred of Wyndeham.[5] In 1379 (2 Ric. II),[6] we
find William Hayne sen^r. and William Hayne jun^r. and John

---

[1] Brit. Mus. Charters, 18563: the date is conjectured from the writing.
[2] Charters, 18565.   [3] Charters, 8795.
[4] P. R. Office Miscell. Chancery Rolls 4/23. The late Mr. C. E. Gildersome
Dickinson kindly sent me the reference.
[5] Now Ewhurst in the parish of Shermanbury, Hurstpierpoint.
[6] Lay Subsidy, Sussex, 189/42, villat de Horton.

Hayne taxed under the Poll tax. As the church registers of Beeding from the middle of the sixteenth century are full of the name Haine, we may take it that these were descendants of the above progenitors.

In 1401 we come again upon traces of the Warnham family, for in that year Richard Haine sen[r]. of Warnham made a grant of lands to Richard atte Strode of Slinfold.[1] Eighteen years later, William Hayne of Warnham granted to John Bradbregge lands called Chykynnys, Brokelonde, and Palmerstonnys[2]; while in 1421, John Hayne was appointed attorney to John Bradbregge for the transference of certain lands to the vicar of Warnham.[3] In 1433, William Hayne of Warnham granted to John Bradbregge and others all his lands and tenements in Horsham.[4]

In 1451, Thomas Holborn and Rose his wife settled 54 acres of arable and 6 acres of meadow land on Richard Hayne and his wife Matilda.[5]

Twenty-five years later a Richard Hayne was witness to a grant of lands from Margery Gorynge of Dorking to Stephen Cokke and others.[6] In 1482, Richard Hayne of Warnham granted lands and tenements in Warnham, called Haynys, Chekynnes, Brokelonde, and Palmerstonnys to Richard Whitehead, clerk, and others, "yeldynge to the forsayde Rychard Hayne at the feste of Saynt John Baptyst next comyng a reede Roose yef hyt be axed."[7] The broken seal attached to this document, which is beautifully clear and legible, has for device a big I, with above it the semblance of a crown. In the next year (22 Ed. IV) Richard Hayne and Isabel his wife and William Brown and Isolda his wife sold for £40 to John Michell of Stamerham and Margaret his wife 80 acres of. land and 6 of pasture in Warnham. (Ped. Fin. Sussex, 13–22 Ed. IV, No. 34.)

The only other occurrences of the name in Sussex prior to 1500, that I have found, are Thomas Hayne, M.P. for Chichester in 1400, and Richard Hayne M.P. for the same city in 1437, the

[1] Bodleian Charters, 205.
[2] Brit. Mus. Charters, 18704, dated 6 January, 1419-20.
[3] Bodl. Chart. 219, dated 10 November, 1421 (8 Hen. V).
[4] Bodl. Ch. 288, dated 1 June, 1433.
[5] Ped. Fin. 30 Hen. VII. See Cartwright's *Rape of Bramber*, Dallaway II, 369. The indenture was dated at Warnham.
[6] Brit. Mus. Charters 8905, dated 15 March, 1475-6.
[7] Brit Mus. Charters 18771, dated 24 March, 1482-3 (22 Edw. IV).

latter being described in the original return as a citizen of
Chichester. Thirdly, in 1404 there is record of a fine levied, by
which Sherman Greene and others settled on Richard Hayne al's
Grassyer of Chichester, and on Clementina his wife, 3 messuages,
5 cottages, 2 shops, 12 acres of arable, and 4 of meadow land in
Horsham and Roughway.[1]

In 1518 we find Elizabeth Hayn, widow, with her son Thomas,
leasing lands called "Cradils" in Warnham;[2] while in 1527
appears a Thomas Hayne, al's Cocks, of Warnham, receiving from
Thomas Beckett of Ockley and Warnham an acquittance of £14
for land and tenements in Warnham, called Wylbeckets, to which
deed a Richard Hayne is witness,[3] and in the next year the said
Thomas receives in tail a grant of lands called Byrchetts from
Thomas Maye in Rudgwick.[4] In 1537 Thomas Hayne, husband-
man, of Warnham, bought from Richard Pylfolde of Warnham,
yeoman, land called Ferthingmede, al's Gendensmede, in Horsham.[5]
It seems probable that this Thomas Hayne, and the Thomas, son
of Elizabeth Hayn, widow, were both identical with Thomas Hayne,
al's Cocks, above mentioned.[6]

The will of Thomas Hayne, al's Cocks, is registered at Chichester,[7] as made 1 September, 1548, and proved 4 June, 1549, in which
appear lands named Byrchetts and Wylbeckets, but no Ferthingmede. His brother, Richard Hayne of Ockley, in Surrey, who died
at Rudgwick in 1570-1, was head constable of one of the hundreds
of Surrey and "reputed a very honest man."[8] From Thomas
descended a flourishing family that gradually dropped the name
Cocks, and finally became Haines. They lived at Ockley, Wotton,
Abinger, Ewhurst, and Rudgwick, and their pedigree is directly
traceable down to Evershed Haynes (or Haines) of Wotton and

[1] Cartwright's *Rape of Bramber*, Dallaway II, pt. 2, p. 345; Sussex Arch. Coll.,
xviii, 112.

[2] Brit. Mus. Charters 18801, dated 10 April, 9 Hen. VIII. Five days later
John Caryll, serjeant-at-law, gives Eliz. H. and Thomas H. a receipt for 40 marks
for lands at Warnham.

[3] Brit. Mus. Charters 18811, dated 9 April, 18 Hen. VIII.

[4] Brit. Mus. Charters 18812, dated 22 July, 19 Hen. VIII.

[5] Brit. Mus. Charters 18820, 3 October, 28 Hen. VIII.

[6] Thomas Hayn of Warnham appears in the Lay Subsidies of 1524 and 20
February, 1524-5, as taxed for goods worth 60⁵, and in June, 1546, as taxed for
lands worth 60⁵, and so on 15 April, 1547.

[7] Consist. Court Chich., vii, fo. 62ᵇ.

[8] State Papers, Letters and Papers, Hen. VIII, date 1 March, 1538-9, a
passage which gives us an interesting peep into ancient rural affairs.

Horsham, gentleman, who, dying in 1776, left no sons but a brother Henry.[1]

Contemporary with Thomas and Richard were others of the name at Rudgwick, the earliest of whom, mentioned in the church registers, are Abraham Hayne, born about 1550, and a Walter Hayne, buried in 1600. Descendants of the same name are still to be found in the neighbourhood, and there is some unclaimed property belonging to this family, the present representative of which lives at Guildford. Miss Frances Haines of Eureka, Illinois, U.S.A., whose ancestors migrated from Alfold, co. Surrey, near Rudgwick, probably belongs to this family.

All the above spelled their name Hayne or Hayn. The only traces of Haynes in Sussex, previous to 1600 (apart from occasional misspellings of the other form), are these: (1) Christopher Haynes,[2] one of a number of brothers well known in Queen Elizabeth's reign as holding offices in her household, who lived at Arundel, and left his nephew Richard of Hackney his heir. Richard left only a daughter, who married Edward Hopkinson; (2) Robert Haynes, clerk, of Wiggenholt, who died in 1574, leaving a son Christopher, from whom descended the family of Haynes, living at Billingshurst; (3) John Haynes,[3] constable of the Castle of Arundel, whose will, 4 February, 1551–2, was proved 30 October, 1552, by William Haynes, proctor for the relict Jane; (4) Richard Haynes, a bricklayer, of Tortington, near Arundel, whose daughter Agnes was born 1598 at that place; (5) John Haynes[4] married at Petworth 24 June, 1578: (6) Ane Hayens married Thomas Sprincke at Midhurst 30 September, 1677, and Thomas Haynes married Alice Allen at same place 27 July, 1593.

[1] See will P.C.C. 126 Bellas. Whether Henry left descendants I do not know.

[2] He was brother of William and Nicholas Haynes, see below p. 138.

[3] He left no sons.

[4] This may be a mere mistake for Hayne.

CHAPTER III.

ANCESTRY OF RICHARD HAINES.

"The glory of children are their fathers."—Prov. xvii. 6.

THE ancestors of Richard Haines are traceable with practical certainty five generations back in the male line to Thomas Hayne[1] or Hayn, who died between 14 November, 1557, and 12 January, 1558–9, as we know from his will being written on the one date and proved on the other at Storrington.[2] As this is the most venerable record touching the family, I transcribe it literatim from the original copy at Chichester :

. . . . . probatum apud Storrington xii die mensis Januarii.

In the name of God Amen/ the xiiij day of November yn ye yere of our Lord God 155ʌ[3] I Thomas Hayne of Clayton wˣyn the pysche of Sullington yn good .7 pfett remembrance make my testament 7 last wyll under thys forme folowynge : fyrst y bequethe my sole unto almighty God 7 my body to buryed (sic) wˣyn ye churche yarde of Sullington : also Y geve to ye mother church of Chychestʳ vjᵈ : also I bequethe to thomas hayne hayn (sic) the son of Jhon̄ hayn when he ys xii yers of age a flocke bedd a payer of Shets/ a payer of blancketts a bolster 7 a coveryngⁱ wˣ a gret caldren after the dyscesse of hys father 7 a calve of iiij yers olde. Item I bequethe to the foresayd thomas halfe the farme wˣ hs mother/ yf hs father dey before hs mother/ 7 ij oxon a good horse or a mare 7 halfe a houndreth of ewys 7 wethers/ Item y geve to Rychard hayne the son of Jhon hayne v ewys 7 a heffer of iij yers olde : item y geve Wyllyā alley helfe a quarter of barly : item y geve to Jhon̄ hayne ye son of Wyllyā hayn a colve of iiij yers olde/ item if so be that thomas hayn or Rychard do dye won before the other y will that the lengyst lyve of them shall have both other bequeysts of goods 7 halfe ye farme wˣ ther mother after the dethe of ther father : 7 if so be that the foresayd thomas 7 Rychard do dye before ther lawful age : then y wyll yᵗ my son Wyllyā sonnys Jhon̄ 7 Rychard shal have halfe the farme wˣ ther aunte Item y bequethe to An hayn the dozgtʳ of Jhon̄ hayn vi shepe : the resydue of my goods not bequethyd y geve to Jhon̄ hayne my

---

[1] Whether our Thomas was descended from one of the Hayne families established in Sussex, or migrated from some other county it is impossible to say. The Wases with whom they seem to have had some connection came from Berkshire. A tradition recorded by Mr. William Haines of Worthing says " the Sussex Haineses (presumably his own branch) came from Devonshire " ; another tradition (recorded by the same) ascribes their origin to the Isle of Wight.

[2] The entry in the Consistory Diaries at Chichester gives the date of Probate, which the original will does not give. There are no signatures to the will.

[3] The original copy of the will gives the date thus.   [4] Query, this word.

Clayton Farm, the earliest residence of our Family in Sussex.

(From a photograph by C. R. Haines.)

Sladeland, built 1712, sold 1804, the last residence of our Family in Sussex.

(From a photograph by C. R. Haines.)

son whom y make my whole executor 7 Wyllyā hayn my son ov⸏sear y⸏ my
last wyll be pformyd and for hs labor I geve unto hym vi⸏ viij⸏ 7 hafe a
quarter of barly these beyring wytness Rafer Massye curat of Sullyngton
James Wayse Wyllyam hayn w⸏ other.

On 6 February, 1539–40, Thomas Hane—no doubt our Thomas
—witnessed the will of John Crossingham of Sullington. But we
find still earlier mention of him in the "Lay Subsidies" for
Sussex. A Thomas Hayn of Thakeham[1] parish was taxed 5s.
16 April, 16 Hen. VIII (1524) in goods worth' £10, and again to
the same amount the following 20 February. His worldly
prosperity increased, as in 1540–1 (32 Hen. VIII) his name appears
under the Eswrythe half hundred (in which Thakeham is situated)
as assessed at 10⸏ for goods worth £20. Five years later, John
Hayne[2] is taxed 16s. for goods worth £16, while in the following
year Thomas's name occurs again as taxed 2s. 8d. on goods worth
£16, while John's name does not appear. Similarly 1 April, 1547
(1 Ed. VI) and 1549–50 (3 Ed. VI) Thomas Hayn is taxed 12s.
for goods worth £12. In these subsidies for 1546, 1547, the name
of Thomas Hayne, or Hayn, of Warnham also appears, as taxed on
lands worth 20s. and goods worth the same.

The wife of Thomas[3] is not mentioned in his will and therefore
no doubt predeceased him. We have no means of knowing who
she was, but perhaps a Wase or a Crossingham. There was some
connexion between the Hayne and Wase families, as on three
occasions wills of the former family are witnessed by members of
the latter. Once as above; again on 26 March, 1561, the will of
John Hayne, son of Thomas, is witnessed by James Wase; and a
third time on 24 May, 1610, the will of John Hayne the younger
of Sullington was witnessed by Mary Wase, wife of John Wase.
This John Hayne was the son of William, a grandson of Thomas.

The two sons of Thomas, John and William, became the
progenitors of two flourishing families. The elder branch, descend-
ing from John, kept the proper spelling of the name, and its
members were always known as Hayne or Haine. They were

---

[1] Which adjoins the parish of Sullington.

[2] Probably son of Thomas unless, as I am inclined to think, John is an error for
Thomas.

. [3] A Thomas Hayne, householder, was buried at Sullington 18 March, 1561-2,
whom I cannot fit into the pedigree. The original will of Thomas Hayne has no
date of probate endorsed on it. Can the date given be wrong, and this Thomas H.,
householder, be our Thomas? If not, it is curious that the burial of Thomas
Hayne is not recorded in the Sullington Register.

settled for many generations in Washington parish, which adjoins Sullington and Thakeham, owning or tenanting the farm houses named Clayton, Chanckton, and perhaps Chantrey, all of which are still standing. One of the earliest members is even spoken of[1] as "of Rowdell," which is now the most substantial mansion in the parish. From Washington about the middle of the seventeenth century some members of this family migrated to Broadwater near Worthing, where a branch (as is most likely) of the younger stock joined them or intermarried with them. The only living representative of this elder branch, who has so far come to light, is Alderman Charles Hugh Haine, Esq., of Eastbourne.[2]

The living descendants of William, the younger son of Thomas, number at least 250. This William must have been born about 1520-1525. His first appearance in the "Lay Subsidies" is on 5 January, 1544-5, between which date and 18 April, 1551, he is taxed under Storrington for goods worth £11; by 1568, or thereabouts, his goods had become £15, and on 30 September, 1572, he is returned at £18. Besides these facts we know that on 12 November, 1555, he witnessed the will of Joan Callow of Storrington.[3] In 1557, 1558, 1561, 1564, he stood sponsor[4] in Storrington Church to children of parents named Belchamber, Cosyn, Cressingham, Duppa, Byne, Benet, and Emery. The Court Rolls, again, of Storrington,[5] for 5 April, 1571, tell us the interesting fact that on that day a white cow (strayed) was in the custody of William Heyne, and on 13 October of the same year a stray pig, on which date, and on 4 April, 1572, he was a juror in a Court Leet for frankpledge. That is all we know of his life's history, but from the incidents of the stray cattle we must at least write him down an honest man. He was buried at Storrington 19 February, 1575-6, being followed to the grave on March 2 of the same year by his wife Joan. Of her we only know that she stood sponsor from 1557 to 1568 (and perhaps in 1573 also) to children whose parents were named Benet (twice), Clement (twice), Wilkine, Donat, Duke, Browne, Bishop, Byne, Reeve, Duppa, Pytter, Rickman, and perhaps in 1573[6] Callow and Elphecke.

---

[1] In the register of the parish.
[2] See pedigrees.   [3] He was churchwarden of Storrington, 1566.
[4] The Register of Storrington contains the names of Sponsors from 1556 to 1592. The recording of the names was then discontinued as savouring of Popery!
[5] R. Office, Portfolio, 205, No. 55.
[6] The Joan Hayne of this year may have been wife of William's son John.

William Hayne's will was proved 17 March, 1575–6, by his son and executor, Richard. This we know from the entry in the Consistory Diaries at Chichester.[1] But neither will, nor registered copy of will, is forthcoming, though indexed. William had three sons. The baptism of John his firstborn is the opening entry in Storrington register. He is probably identical with John Hayne of Barnes farm, who was buried at Sullington 19 August, 1612. Richard, the second son, was baptized at Storrington on 9 June, 1551.[2] On 30 January, 1582–3, at a Court Baron held at Storrington, Richard was, with his son William, admitted to seisin of lands in Storrington called " Brownes " and " Wiltons," which he bought of Thomas and Ann Brakepole. This property is described in the Manor Rolls[3] as " one tenement and certain customary lands in Storrington with appūrts, formerly Browne's, and one toft together with one cottage and five acres of land with appūrts called Wilton's." On this transaction the Lord of the Manor received the very substantial sum (for those times) of £16 13s. 4d. Richard did fealty, and was admitted, " having seisin by the rod." He further appears at courts held 14 December, 1584, 5 April, 1585, 12 April, 1588, as juror, and on the first of these dates he obtained licence " to demise and farm let to an honest person one messuage, one barn, and 15 acres of land for five years." He is not mentioned as present' at Courts held on 9 November, 1583, 1 October, 1584, 9 October, 1587, 7 October, 1588, while on 7 April, 1587, he is fined for default, and on 22 September, 1589, 11 November, 1591, 11 November, 1596, 3 May, 1597, he " essoins," i.e., sends an allowable excuse.

If there is any truth in the family tradition, mentioned to me by Field-Marshal Sir Frederick Haines, that an ancestor made his money in an expedition under Drake, it seems probable that this Richard was the man, and the above record of his attendance at Court Leets shows that he was unable to attend 1585–1588, and again from 1588–1597. On the other hand he had. at least three children born after 1584, one being baptized 23 March, 1592–3, and he was present at Chichester in 1590,[4] and sequestrator of Binsted Vicarage. 8 November, 1592.[5] His death occurred at

[1] Vol. A, 1575–6. The name is given as Haynes.
[2] See also Attestation Books, Consistory of Chichester, V, 1590.
[3] Now in the possession of the Duke of Norfolk, who very kindly allowed me to have them inspected.
[4] See Attest Bks. quoted above.
[5] Consistory Diaries, Vol. A, f. 113.

Binsted near Arundel about 16 September, 1597, and his dictated will was made 14 September,[1] and proved 26 September in that year by his widow Elizabeth. He left to his sons Richard and Adam the lease of his farm at Binsted, which he held of William Shelley, late of Michelgrove in Sussex, for the rest of its term, adding that during that period his wife Elizabeth should be responsible for their tuition and government. To his daughters Joan and Mary he gave a money legacy of £11 apiece, declaring that his other sons William and Thomas were already provided for.

Richard migrated from Storrington to Binsted about 1585, and next year was churchwarden of Binsted. The last occasion when he acted sponsor at Storrington was 4 December, 1584. Previously to this he had performed that office eleven times (as recorded), beginning in 1565, when he was only 15 years old. His god-children were of parents named Sclater, Leedes, Bosworth (twice), Filder, Duke, Wase (twice), Gravet, Emmett, and Penfold.

His wife Elizabeth was born at Wiggenholt,[2] but we do not know her maiden name. She appears to have been married before 2 November, 1572, as on 2 November, 1572, Elizabeth Hayne stands sponsor to a Filder child. She stood godmother on four subsequent occasions to a Penfold, a Holstock, and twice to a Benet. The marriage most likely took place at Wiggenholt, where she was afterwards buried. After her husband's death, she married Gregory Hurst of Kirdford, Sussex.[3] About the same time, Agnes, the daughter of Gregory Hurst, married Richard, the son of the above-mentioned Richard Hayne. Hence came into the family the name Gregory, which stills runs on in it. Elizabeth Hurst survived her second husband, and died at Wiggenholt in 1628–9.[4]

The pedigrees appended to this volume will show the ramifications and emigrations of the descendants of William and Thomas, the sons of Richard and Elizabeth, who founded families at Storrington and Wiggenholt respectively. From one of them,

---

[1] Chichester, XIV, 478.

[2] See Attest. Bks. Consistory Court at Chichester, V, 1589; from which we find that she was born xxx years before and had lived 4 years at Binsted and 12 at Storrington. She must have been married very young, unless xxx is a mistake for xxxx.

[3] Lic. to marry at Binsted dated 30 January, 1599–1600 (Chichester).

[4] See Consist. Diaries G., f. 95. Admon. of her goods granted to Thomas Haynes 30 January, 1628–9.

probably from William, I believe to be descended a family whose eldest living representative at the present time is William Haines, Esq., late of Putney, but now of Worthing, well known in antiquarian circles as a collector of tokens. The Thomas Haines of Burpham, in Sussex, and afterwards of Broadwater in the same county, who stands at the head of his pedigree, was born about 1660, and may have been son of William Hayne-of-Thakeham's grandson William. This William may have removed to Thakeham, where the birth of Thomas, son of William Haine(s), is recorded 4 December, 1648. Or Thomas Haines of Broadwater may have been the grandson of another grandson of William of Storrington, namely, of Thomas Hayne, who was baptized 28 December, 1639. That the family of Thomas Haines of Broadwater was in some way connected with the Sladeland family is probable because (1) the children of William Haines of Broadwater, grandson of the above-named Thomas, were legatees with their father under the will of Mary Greenfield (niece of the subject of this memoir) in 1755; (2) one of the aforesaid children was named Gregory, evidently from the Gregories of the other branch; (3) Mr. William Haines of Worthing has informed me that the actual connexion between the families was well known to his aunt Hester Trill, and there was a MS. pedigree, setting it all forth, which was burnt by its possessor in a fit of temper. Moreover Commissary-General Gregory Haines, C.B., was always considered by the Broadwater family as a real, though distant, cousin. Tradition has it that an estrangement took place relative to some land, either called Stroodland, or at a place called Strood, which may be the Strood in Wisborough Green, a parish adjoining Kirdford.

Richard Hayne, third son of Richard and Elizabeth, succeeded to his father's farm at Binsted, where he lived and died, and was buried 18 February, 1638-9. It was he who bought the Sladeland property in conjunction with his wife and son Gregory on 20 September, 1619,[1] from Edward King.[2] He acted as churchwarden of Binsted Church in 1604, 1616, and 1630, and set his mark to the Transcripts of the registers for that year, as he also did in appraising the goods of John Racton of Binsted, yeoman, for an

---

[1] Richard's father-in-law Gregory Hurst died 7 April, 1619.

[2] There is a fire-back in Wephurst house, which was built by John Haines, with a K upon it. This, Mr. H. F. Napper, of Laker's Lodge, thinks refers to the name King. It may have come out of Sladeland house, when Gregory Haines rebuilt it in 1712.

inventory taken 16 June, 1634. The mark resembles a rough loop of string with the ends "in the air."[1] His marriage with Agnes Hurst took place about 1600. Husband and wife died within a few days of each other, and they were buried together at Binsted. The wills of both remain, and also the account given by Gregory, the son and executor, of his administration of their goods. In it the total value of Richard Hayne's estate is given at £671 6s. 8d. The document which is dated 1 March, 1638–9, is as follows :—

THE DISCHARGE.

Inprimis for the funerall Charges of the sayd Deceased and his wife whoe Dyed within fewe Dayes after him.	iiij^{li}		

Inprimis for the funerall Charges of the sayd Deceased and his wife whoe Dyed within fewe Dayes after him. } iiij^li

Itm̄ for the letters of adm̄stracon wth the will annexed the bonds Inventoryes and other thinges therunto incident. } xxxij^s iiij^d

Itm̄ this accountant Desireth allowance of the rent of the lands of the sayd Deceased untill Michaelmas next in regard the Corne now growinge upon the sayd land is valued in the sayd Inventory. } xliiij^li xij^s iiij^d

Itm̄ for the taxacon to poore Due for the sayd lands and for the tax to the Church. } ij^li

Itm̄ for the Charges of this accountant and his suerties and friends in Cominge to this Court to take adm̄stracon to passe this account. } xx^s

Sum ... ... lij^li v^s viij^d

LEGACIES GIVEN BY THE SAYD DECEASED BY HIS LAST WILL & TO BE PAYD BY THIS ACCOUNTANT.

Inprimis to the high Church of Chichester ... ... v^s[2]

Itm̄ to Gregory Hayne sonne of the Sayd Deceased ... v^li

Itm̄ to Elizabeth Chambers daughter of the sayd Deceased. } v^li

Itm̄ to Agnes Gruggen daughter of the sayd Deceased... v^li

Itm̄ to Rachele Hayne another daughter of the sayd Deceased. } c^li

Itm̄ to Mary Hayne another daughter of the sayd Deceased. } c^li

Itm̄ to Jane Hayne another daughter of the sayd Deceased. } c^li

Itm̄ to the overseers of the sayd will five shillinges apeece. } x^s

Sum̄ ... ... cccxv^li xv^s vj^d

---

[1] See facsimiles facing p. 17.
[2] The will says vj^d and v^s to the poor of Binsted.

ORDINARY CHARGES.

Inprimis for Drawing this account and the proctor's fee.			v⁵.	iiijᵈ
Itm̃ for examining this account	... ...		iijˢ	iiijᵈ
Itm̃ admission therof				·viijᵈ
Itm̃ for the apparitor's fee				xiiᵈ
Itm̃ for double ingrossinge this account			viˢ	viijᵈ
Itm̃ for the Quietus est under seale			xvijˢ	

Sum̃	xxxiiijˢ	
Sum total shewn and to be shewn ... ... ccclxixˡⁱ	xixˢ	ijᵈ
Thus remain in the hands of this accountant to be distributed and divided according to will ... ccciˡⁱ	vijˢ	vjᵈ

Eighteen days later Gregory Hayne sent in a similar account of his administration of the goods of his mother Agnes Hayne, charging himself with the sum mentioned in an inventory of her goods which amounted to £301 7s. 6d.

THE DISCHARGE.

Whereof this Accomptant Desireth allowance and abatement as followeth, viz. :—

Inprimis for two oxen seized by the lord for herryotts.	xjˡⁱ		
Item for two funerall sermons and for two mortuaryes.		xlˢ	
Item for twelve Dozen of bread		xijˢ	
Item to the Clerke for making the graves and ringing the knells.		iiijˢ	
[Item] for two Coffins		xvijˢ	
Item paid to Xp̃ofer Horley for goeing on a message...		xijˢ	
Item paid for wyne and sugar		xjˢ	
Item for meate spent at the prising of the goods ...		viijˢ	vjᵈ
Item for tenn payre of gloves		xˢ	
Item for writing the wills and Inventory		xˢ	
Item for servants wages Due		xiiijˢ	
Item shee (sic) Craveth allowance for five sheepe whereof foure had lambes and the other was a barren ewe wᶜʰ were prised in the Inventory but were Disposed of before the Death of the Testatrix.		lˢ	
Item paid to Mr. Johnson vicar of Binsted for the allowance of ground in the Churchyard there to place the monuments of the Deceased and of her husband.		xˢ	
Item for the probat of the will wᵗʰ the writing and ingrossing thereof & of the Inventoryes the bond & other charges thereunto incident.		xvˢ	iiijᵈ

Sum	xxijˡⁱ	xiiˢ	xᵈ

Inprimis to the poore of Binsted		x^s
. . . . (*rotted away*) . . . Chichester ...		[vj^d]
Item to Richard & Gregory Hayne the sonnes of this Accomptant for their several legacies of xx^s a pece.		xl^s
Item to Alice Annis Elizabeth & Margaret Gruggen her Grandchildren their like legacies of xx^s a peece.	iiij^li	
Item to the two overseers of her will		x^s
Sum	vij^li	vj^d

The " ordinary charges of passing the account " are practically the same as in the previous account and amount to ...   xxxix^s
And the total shewn and to be shewn is... xxxj^li   xii^s iiij^d
Leaving in the Accomptant's hands ...   £269 14 9.

Richard Haines in his will[1] is called yeoman, and describes himself as " sick in body, but of perfect mind and memory." He desires his body to be buried in the churchyard of Binsted at the Chancel end. With the exception of 6d. to the High Church of Chichester and 5s. to the poor of Binsted,[2] he left all the rest of his property, besides the legacies mentioned in Gregory's account, " moveable & unmoveable, chattels & cattels," to his wife, whom he made sole executrix, his son Gregory and brother Thomas being overseers. The will was marked, sealed, and delivered in the presence of Robert Johnson, Timothy Johnson, and Gregory Heines, and proved *about* 1 March, 1638-9, by Gregory.

Agnes Hayne made her will 24 February, 1638-9,[3] describing herself as " weak in body but whole in mind and memory." Besides the above-mentioned legacies she gives her husband's apprentice Robert Cull one ewe and lamb, leaving all the rest of her goods to her son Gregory and her five daughters, with Gregory as sole executor, and Thomas Haines of Wiggenholt and William Chambers of Pulboro' overseers. She marked her will in the presence of Thomas James and Timothy Johnson. It was proved about 19 March by Gregory.

Of this Gregory we know but little. He apparently changed the spelling of his name (being perhaps the first of his race

---

[1] Chichester C.C. XX 130, 9 February, 1638-9.
[2] This does not tally with the above account.   [3] Chichester C.C. XX 128.

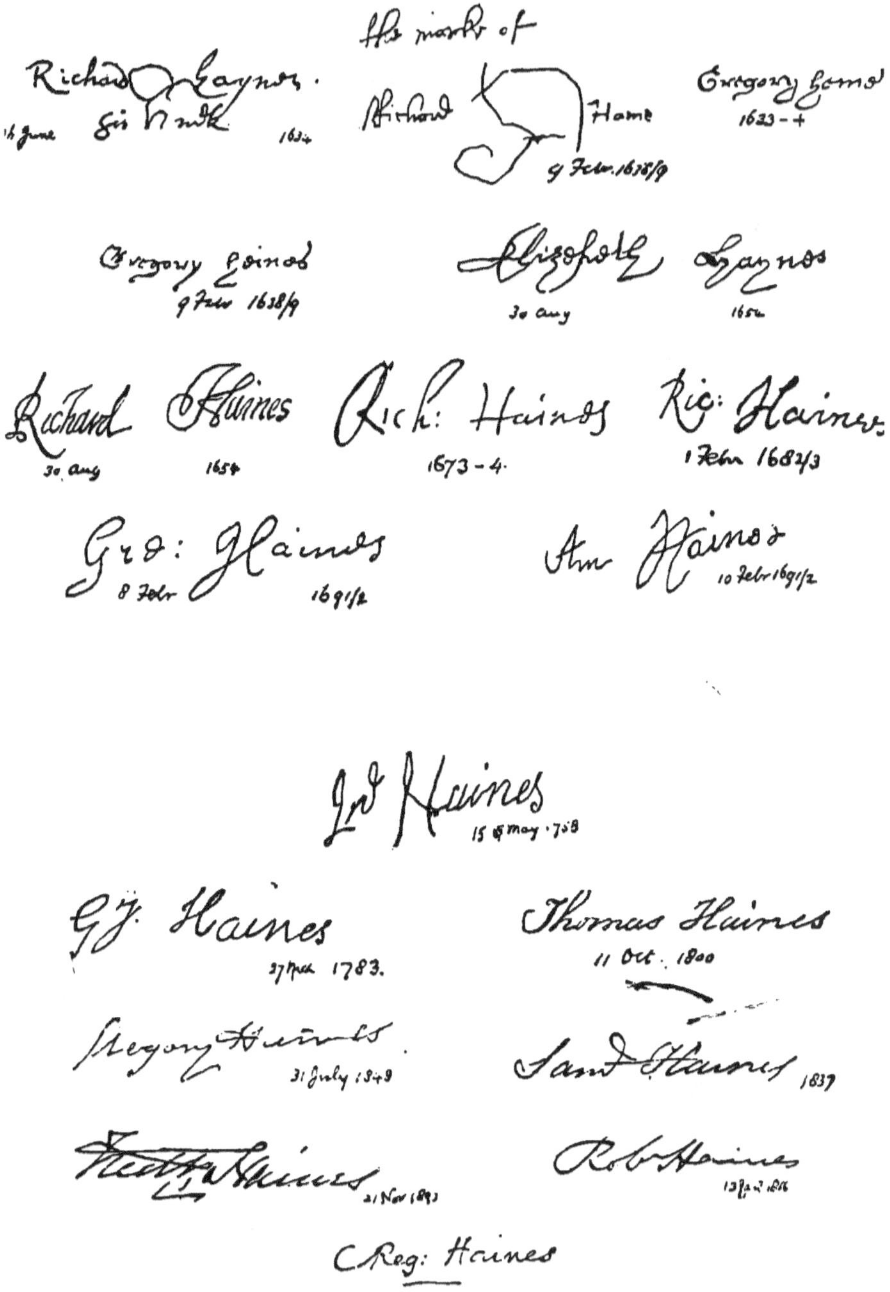

Richard Gaynor.
16 June Sis mark 1634

The mark of
Richard ⟨mark⟩ Hame
9 Feb. 1618/9

Gregory Gaines
1623 - 4

Gregory Gaines
9 Feb 1638/9

Elizabeth Gaynos
30 aug

1654

Richard Haines
30 aug 1654

Rich: Hainos
1673 - 4.

Ric: Haines
1 Febr 1682/3

Gro: Haines
8 Febr 1691/2

Ann Haines
10 Febr 1691/2

Jnº Haines
15 & May 758

GJ. Haines
27 Mch 1783.

Thomas Haines
11 Oct. 1800

Gregory Haines.
31 July 1848

Saml Haines 1837

⟨illegible⟩ Haines 21 Nov 1893

Robt Haines 13 Jan 1816

C. Reg: Haines

N.B.---The dates under the above autographs are added.

that could write) from Heine[1] in 1633 to Heines[2] in 1638. If there is any truth in a tradition heard through my father, that an ancestor of ours fought as a roundhead at Naseby (14 June, 1645). Gregory must have been the man. He must have been born about 1601 at Binsted, and he bought Sladeland, as above mentioned, with his father and mother in 1619. He seems to have settled at Sullington, where he was churchwarden in 1633. Soon after he removed to Shere in Surrey, where his son Gregory was baptized 24 May, 1636, and a second son William, 24 February, 1638–9. A kinsman (through the Hursts), Gregory Wright, also had a child baptized at Shere, 19 January, 1631–2.

In 1640–1 Gregory purchased for £670 the estate of West Wantley in Sullington parish of Richard Abbot, nephew of a late Archbishop of Canterbury. The estate derived its name from John de Wantele, who died 29 January, 1424–5, and lies buried in Amberley Church. The manor was granted in 1560 by the Crown to Robert Michell.[3] The Abbots had bought the property from Thomas Wickham, gent., in 1634. It is described as the manor, messuage, tenement, and farm of Wantley, al's West Wantley,[4] containing 100 acres and also five acres of pasture and a little cottage, some time a mill-house adjoining the farm, situate in Sullington and Storrington. It was charged with a rent to the Chief Lord of the feé, and a yearly rent of £12 to Holy Trinity Hospital, Guildford, and subject to a lease for 21 years (dated 21 June 15 Car. I) to Henry Stone at a yearly rent of £46. The entry in the "Feet of Fines" describes the property as "the manor of Wantley, al's West Wantley, with the appürts and 65 acres of arable, 20 of meadow, and 20 of pasture land."[5]

At the same Easter Term is entered a fine from which we learn that Gregory Hayne bought from Edward Lipscombe and Thomasine his wife 1 messuage, 1 barn, and 1 garden with appürts in Shere.

Later in the year his wife seems to have been at Binsted, as the baptism and burial of a son John is recorded there 18 December, 1641.

[1] So he signs the Bishop's Transcripts of Sullington Register, as church-warden.
[2] Signature to his mother's will.   [3] Dallaway's Sussex II, 122.
[4] Close Roll, 17 Car. I, pt. 16, No. 17, Hayne v. Abbot. Indenture 26 January, 1640–1. See also deed of mortgage 1st February, 1682–3. The farm of "Round-abouts," also owned by Richard Haines, son of Gregory, contained 35 acres.
[5] Pedes Finium, Easter Term, 17 Car. I, 4 June, 1641.

In 1645, 20 April,[1] he was taxed £1 15s. 9d. for Sladeland, as his share of a subsidy laid upon the Rotherbridge hundred of Sussex to maintain the army of Sir Thomas Fairfax and Lord Leven in Ireland. Gregory Hurst, son of Gregory's stepfather, was taxed £1 3s. for Crafold in the same parish of Kirdford, and was an assessor for collecting the subsidy.

Gregory[2] was buried at Sullington 1 March, 1645–6, in the very crisis of the Civil War. The inventory of his goods has been preserved at Chichester, and I will make no apology for transcribing it.

The list of possessions does not give evidence of striking luxury or wealth. The goods were appraised on 23 March, 1645–6, by William Chambers, Richard Greene, Richard Wolff at Sullington, and by John Founstaple and Richard Nunum at Kirdford.

Inprimis his waring aparell & mony in his purse   ...   iij^{li}

In the Kichen.

Itm̃ five brase pootes four brase Cittell 2 furnices 2 skillets and 3 old brase kittell 1 bruing tub 4 kiffers 1 cupberd 1 kneeding troe 1 bucking tub with other lumber.   x^{li}

In the halle.

Itm̃ 1 table and frame 1 forme 2 foulling peces 1 musket[3] 5 speetes 2 driping pans.   iij^{li}

In the barler.

Itm̃ 1 table and frame 1 forme 4 joyned stooles 1 cuperd 1 joyned chere.   xl^s

In the buttry.

Itm̃ 4 barrells 1 firking 1 tune ...   .   x^s

In the Milke house.

Itm̃ 1 dussen of Truges 2 charnes 1 rening tube 1 powdering troe 4 hoges of baken.   xl^s

In the Lofte over the Kichen.

Itm̃ 1 flocke bed 4 playne Chestes with other lumber...

In the Lofte over the halle.

Itm̃ 2 feether beeds 2 joyned Chestes 4 teke bollsteres 4 blankets 2 Coverlets 2 phillibers with pillers 1 set of curtayns 1 warning pan.   x^{li}

[1] The original taxing paper is in the possession of H. F. Napper, Esq., of Laker's Lodge, near Billingshurst. On 10 July, 18 Car. I, Gregory paid 15s. towards a loan for Charles I.

[2] He died intestate.

[3] Perhaps he used this at Naseby.

In the Littell Chamber.

Itm̃ 1 Cuberd 1 fether bed [and] all belonging to him 1 chest. — xl⁸

In the Lofte over the Littell Rome.

Itm̃ 2 fetherbeeds and 4 bollsterste 4 blankets 2 Coverlets [rotted away] Chest. — iij⁰

In the Loft over the parler.

Itm̃ one fether bed 1 flocke beed and joyned bedstedel 2 bollsteres 2 pilles 2 blankets 1 Coverlet 2 joyned Chests. — v⁰

Itm̃ 10 pare of Tier shetes 1 holland sheet 20 pare of flaxen sheets 2 dossen of dieper napkins 2 dieper towells 3 dieper table Clothes 1 flaxen dapell Cloth 2 dussen of flaxen napkins 6 pilli Cothes. — x⁰

Itm̃ 3 dossen of puter Disshes 3 brase Candell stickes 1 puter Candellsticke 1 flagon 2 dussen of spones. — iij⁰

Itm̃ one sillver boolle¹	xxx⁸		
Itm̃ 4 oxen	xviiij⁰		
Itm̃ 3 steeres	x⁰		
Itm̃ 7 kine and Caves	xxi⁰		
Itm̃ 5 younge Beastes	x⁰		
Itm̃ 2 horses 2 Colltes	xiij⁰	x⁸	
Itm̃ 15 Copells of Sheep and Lames and 1 baren Sheep.	vij⁰	x⁸	
Itm̃ 2 open hoges 5 biges	xxxv⁸		
Itm̃ all belonging to husbandrie as Weenes Wheeles plowes harroes Chaynes and other imbellments.	viij⁰		
Itm̃ one passell of heaye	xxx⁸		
Itm̃ wheate upon the ground	xvi⁰		
Itm̃ Teares sowen upon the ground	xl⁸		

Sum̃a ... ... clxxxv⁰ v⁸

On the same day was taken an inventory of his goods at Kirdford :—

Inprimis 10 akers of wheat upon the ground ...	xx⁰		
Itm̃ 5 Wenners 1 hefer and Calfe and 1 stere ...	x⁰	v⁸	
Itm̃ 14 Coppells of Sheep	iiij⁰	xiij⁸	iiij⁰
Itm̃ 2 hoges and 7 piges...	xliiij⁸		
Itm̃ 1 kill of stone	xx⁸		
Itm̃ 7 hundred of brome fagets	xx⁸		

¹ This heirloom should still exist somewhere in the family.

Itm woats Redy thresed   ...   .   jˢ
Itm one lease of a Messuage or tenemᵗ & 80 ⎱
   acres of land in Kerdford for 10000 yeares. ⎰   ccˡˡ

                         Suma   ...   ...   ccxliˡˡ   xijˢ

The sum total was £416 17s.

Admōn of his goods, since his widow renounced her claim to administer, was granted to Gregory Wright and Gregory Hurst, kinsmen of the deceased, the children being minors.

We know little besides about Gregory Heines. He married Elizabeth Pollard 10 July, 1632, at Sullington.[1] After her husband's death she was fined 1s. at Court Leets of the manor of Storrington, 4 March, 1649–50, 14 October, 1650, for non-appearance. On the 30 August, 1654, when Richard her son had attained his majority she, with him, assigned Sladeland to her other son Gregory. She made her will[2] 15 March, 1655–6, and was buried 22 March following at Sullington. In her will she describes herself as sick of body, but of good and perfect remembrance, and desires to be buried in Sullington Churchyard, giving 20s. to the poor of that parish. To her second son Gregory she gives £100 and all the household goods at her house of Sladeland, and also " *my silver bowl,* and the feather beds in the parlour chamber, and the cupboard standing in the parlour, and also a third part of all my pewter." To Jane her daughter £200 in lieu of her right of the lands in Kirdford, left by her (Jane's) father, " being lease lands and settled by me and my eldest son Richard upon Gregory my second son by deeds of indenture," this sum to be left in hands of Jane's brother Richard till she should be eighteen, the interest of it to go to pay for her dress, schooling, and board. The great chest of linen standing in the parlour loft she gave to Gregory and Jane equally, Jane to have the great pewter flagon, the cupboard in the hall, and the bedsteads in the parlour loft, together with one-third of all the pewter. To Jane her kinswoman,[4] living in her house, she gave 20s. at twenty-one and all her woollen wearing apparel; and after mentioning a legacy to her servant Jane Pennell, she made Richard, her son, residuary legatee, and her loving friends and kinsmen, Gregory Wright and Gregory Hurst, overseers. She marked her will in the presence of Henry Hayne[5] and Mary Parram.

---

[1] Styled *widow* in the Bishop's Transcript of her marriage register, but not in the register itself. Her maiden name was Bennet.

[2] P. C. C. 326 Berkley.   [3] See pedigree.   [4] See pedigree.

[5] Her late husband's 1st cousin. She was apparently able to write, as her signature is appended to the deed 30 August, 1654, mentioned above.

CHAPTER IV.

LIFE OF RICHARD HAINES.

"Let us praise famous men, and the fathers that begat us."—Eccl. xliv. 1.

THE eldest son of Gregory and Elizabeth was the Richard Haines whose memoir I have taken upon myself to write. He first, as farmer, Baptist, patentee, projector, social and economic reformer, and philanthropist, raised his family above the rank of yeoman.

England was entering upon troublous times when he was born. Charles, with Laud and his "High Churchmen," was just organizing his attack on the Puritans, and the first writ for Ship-money was issued the next year. Gregory Heine, as churchwarden for that year, endorses in the Bishop's Transcripts the baptism of his eldest child, Richard, on 4 May, 1633[1] thus: "Richard Hayne ye sonne of Griggory Hayne was baptized." Matters in England were going from bad to worse. On 3 November, 1640, the Long Parliament assembled, and on 22 August, 1642, the Royal Standard was unfurled at Nottingham.

It was when the royal cause was practically lost, and the King was on the point of surrendering to the Scots that Gregory died. In 1654, the year after the dissolution of the Long Parliament, and the proclaiming of Cromwell as Lord Protector, Richard came of age. In assigning Sladeland to his brother in this year, as always subsequently, he signs his name Haines. On 24th November of the same year a deed was drawn up "between Richard Haines of the one part, Mary Greene, Thomas Duppa[2] of Storrington, gent., and Richard Greene of Sullington, yeoman, of the other part, by which Richard Haines, in consideration of a marriage intended between him and Mary Greene, and of a marriage portion paid to him, agreed that Thomas Duppa and Richard Greene should stand seized of the following premises;[3] that is of all the rooms called the parlour, the hall, the chamber

---

[1] The Register itself gives 14 May.

[2] Married Joan Greene, probably first cousin to Mary Greene, 20 October, 1637, at Storrington.

[3] These must be rooms in his new house which was finished 1656. See the photograph.

over the parlour, the little cellar, and the room over the said
cellar, parcels of one messuage and tenement of Richard Haine
in Sullington, and also of one barn, known as North Barn, and
also of the moiety of all the gardens, orchards, and backsides
adjoining, and of all those 7 acres of land adjoining the Common,
called Bine Common, and also of all the close of land known as
Pittfield, and also of the piece of land, estimated to contain
5 acres, adjoining the Pittfield, and of the parcell of land,
containing about 11 acres, adjoining the old Field Lane, and of
the close called Culverfield, and of the six acres adjoining, and of
the parcell of land, known as West Broadfield, adjoining the land,
called Eastwrith Hill, all said premises situate, lying, and being in
the parishes, fields, villages and hamlets of Sullington, Storrington,
and Washington, being of the yearly value of £30."[1]   These
premises were thus secured under the above-named trustees for
the use of Richard Haines in his life and after his decease for
the use of his wife Mary, and then to his and her heirs male, and
failing them to the right heirs of Richard.

On 14 December of the same year the Sullington register
records that "*Richard Haines* and *Mary Geene* (sic) were married."

West Wantley is at the present day transformed into a modern
dwelling house.   It has two sitting rooms on the ground floor,
the large one to the right as you enter by the porch (which faces
south) is oak-timbered, and has a splendid chimney corner and
ingle nook, with deep recesses in the chimney for curing hams,
and a cupboard let into the left hand recess (see photograph, p. 88).
There are seven bedrooms, with uneven timber floors and slanting
roofs.   Behind the front door used to run a long beam of oak
to bar the door, and the recess into which it fitted is still there.
The door handle is formed by the knocker, which lifts the latch.
In the room over the kitchen is a cupboard let into the wall
over the mantelpiece for· holding tobacco.   Over the porch can
still be seen the initials and date,

H.

R.   M.

1656.

[1] See Record Office, Chancery Suits B. and A. before 1714; Reynardson, No.
19; answer of Gregory Haines to bill of complaint of Charles Weston, 15
October, 1686.

West Wantley House—Front door with inscription above it.

On 18 September of this year he proved his mother's will in London. On 12 April previously had been born to him, perhaps in the new house, his first child, Mary, who was baptized and buried 12 June following.

We may conclude from the baptism of the child that the father had not yet joined the Baptists. However, a son, born to him on 30 September, 1657, was buried unbaptized on 29 October following.

On 9 February, 1656-7[1], "Richard and Mary sold to Thomas Longe one messuage one barn one garden one orchard 20 acres of land 6 acres of meadow 12 acres of pasture and common of pasture for 80 sheep eight bullocks two horses eight hoggs one gander and two geese with appūrts in North Stoke for £41." The property was no doubt Mary Haines's, and is mentioned in her father's will as "my lands at North Stoke." Later in the same year at the Trinity Term is recorded a fine, showing that Richard and Mary Haines sold to Richard Feilder and his wife Mary "one messuage, one barn, one garden, ... (*MS. injured*) . . . . and common of pasture for all manner of cattle in Storrington." This property also probably came from the Greene side.

On 1 March, 1658-9, was born[2] the second son Gregory (second of that name in the direct line). He was not baptized till 28 March, 1702, at Storrington.[3] The next son Richard was born 17 June, 1661, and a son John on 19 August, 1663. Little is known concerning these two sons or their possible descendants. Richard *may* possibly be identical with a Richard Haynes who, like the Richard Haines of this memoir, was "buried in the Upper Church," Christ Church, Newgate Street, 5 August, 1685, but there is no evidence to prove this. As to John we may, with much probability, identify him with the John Haines who married Sarah Seale of Nuthurst on 22 January, 1684-5, at Sullington.[4] No children can with certainty be ascribed to this couple, as there were two other John Haineses living at the time in the immediate neighbourhood. But I am inclined to think that an entry in Washington parish register under the year 1700 (with no day)

---

[1] See Record Office: Feet of Fines, Sussex, Hil. Term, 1656-7.

[2] Sullington Register.

[3] This we learn from the Bishop's Transcript. It does not appear in the Register.

[4] Admōn. of her goods was granted to her husband 4 October, 1701, and an Inventory of her goods mentions the single fact that she was entitled to a legacy of £5 under the will of her father Richard Seale, late of Nuthurst.

may refer to children of John and Sarah. The entry runs in a fragmentary and unusual way :—

Haine, Richard and Sarah filij [of][1] bapt[d-2]

From Richard or John must have descended the mysterious "William Haines of Devonshire" (thus curiously described in the will of Mary Greenfield,[3] née Haines), whose son Gregory received a legacy under her will, and dying in 1770, aged 48, lies buried at Kirdford.

On 21 August, 1662, Richard was overseer to the will of Richard Browne of Sullington, yeoman, probably the same who witnessed the assignment of Sladeland 30 August, 1654.

On 20 April, 1666, a second daughter Mary was born, who may have married John Penfold ;[4] and a son Stephen on December 16, 1668, who was buried 17 January, 1669–70.

The Hearth Tax returns for 1665[5] show that Richard paid 5s. for five hearths in Sullington parish, the largest householder being George Goble with seven hearths. On 8 June, 1668, Richard was surety for a marriage between Richard Langley, joiner, and Jane Rogers, widow, of Sullington.[6]

In the will of Gregory Haines of Blakehurst in the parish of Warningcamp, co. Sussex, yeoman, he is mentioned as "loving brother and executor." Gregory probably died at Sullington, as he was buried there 28 February, 1670–1, only four days after the dating of his will.[7] His will was proved by the executor on the following 11 November at Chichester. In the will the testator speaks of Sladelands as then in his tenure or occupation for the term of 9000 years and upwards, and as containing 100 acres of land. This he leaves to his son Gregory, and failing him to his daughter Mary, but only when they come of age. Till then the executor was to enjoy the profits of the lands, wherewith to maintain the children. To Mary his daughter he left £100 "in lieu of" her share in the lands to be paid her at the age of 20 out of the said

[1] In another hand.

[2] The Washington Register under date 28 September, 1699, records the birth of Philippa, daughter of John and Sarah Haine.

[3] 9 August, 1755. The son Gregory is described as "kinsman." The only other possible ancestor for this William Haines of Devonshire is the William son of Gregory born at Shere in 1638–9. [4] See pedigree.

[5] See Record Office, Addit. Subsidies, 17 Car. II.

[6] On 24 March, 1682-3, he witnessed the will of Thomas Mellersh, Gent., of Thakeham (P. C. C. Drax, 128), and on 28 December, 1683, he witnessed with John Haine the will of Thomas Steele of Storrington, miller.

[7] Chichester C. C., XXV, 32b.

lands. To his wife Margaret he left £4 per annum, also to be paid out of said lands. To Elizabeth Pratt 10s. at 21. His brothers (in law), Richard Everenden of Horsham, gent., and Richard Carpenter of Sompting, yeoman, were named overseers; and the will was signed and sealed in the presence of Jane Beeding and William Wheeler. A memorandum was added, leaving to such child as his wife went withal, if a son, £100, if a daughter, £60, out of the profits of said lands, at the age of 21.

His wife Margaret (née Lidbetter), whom he married 13 October, 1660, at Sullington, married again after his death (some time before 1678) John Jelly of Kirdford, as we learn from the rolls of Pallingham Manor[1] which Lord Leconfield kindly allowed me to inspect. In spite of this she is described in the marriage licence of her daughter Mary (9 June, 1692)[2] as Mrs. Margaret Haines, widow. She was buried at Sullington 14 April, 1694, as Margaret Jelly. Her second husband perhaps survived her.

VISIT TO THE NETHERLANDS.—Between the date of Gregory's death and 1677 Richard Haines paid a visit to the Netherlands. The object of the visit we do not know. It may have been for commercial purposes, or from reasons connected with the Baptist church. The earliest Anabaptist Churches were formed in the Netherlands, and Richard may have desired to inspect their working. The exact date of the visit we do not know, but as he does not mention it in the two books published in 1674, we may conclude that it had not yet taken place. We know that there was war between England and Holland from 1664 till July, 1667, and again from 1672 till February, 1674. Most probably the visit was made about 1676, and may have been made with the express object of examining the Dutch administration of their Poor Laws, upon which Richard bases his own scheme.

The following are the passages in his books which prove that this visit took place. Writing in 1677 (the earliest allusion we find) he says, " I have been informed beyond the Seas . . . . ."[3] and again in 1679 :—

> "At Leiden I saw a fellow most severely whipt upon a Scaffold, erected for that very purpose before the Spin-house, in view of many thousands, and after Committed to the Rasp-house for that he under

[1] 22 May, 30 Car. II (1678) John Jelly in right of his wife, late the wife of Gregory Haines, held Sladeland—fined 1s. for default.

[2] Office of Vicar-General.

[3] Postscript to *Proposals for Building Almshouses*, p. iii.

pretence of being zealous to serve the States, inrich himself by abusing and oppressing the Poor."[1]

and again in the same year :—

> "I cannot but maintain, that what is Proposed is undoubtedly practicable, for that it is no new Project, but with Great Success practised at this day by our Neighbours, being satisfied by what I have seen that this very thing viz. the Industry of the Poor accomplish't by these very Expedients, is that whereby the Wealth of the Netherlands is raised and maintained."[2]

One other passage there is, in an earlier book (1674), which seems to refer to this visit, viz.: "Such an one as I never heard of before, either here or beyond the Seas,"[3] but this, I am almost sure, does not imply personal observation beyond the sea, for speaking again of the Roman Church, to which also he is here alluding, he says, in another passage, "his sentence of Excommunication is no more, than as though his Triple-Crowned Brother beyond the Seas, with his Bell, Book, and Candle had done it."

FRIENDS AND SOCIAL POSITION.—Before entering upon a history of the controversy in which Richard Haines became engaged with his whilome pastor and friend, Matthew Caffyn, it will not be amiss to gather together the few scattered hints, in his own and Caffyn's published works, that give us any insight into his private life during the dozen or so years that lay between his adhesion to the Baptist community and his quarrel with Caffyn.

It is quite clear that he was the most important member of the little Baptist congregation which met at Southwater, near Horsham, and of which Matthew Caffyn, who lived at Broadbridge in an outlying corner of Sullington parish, was Minister, or "Messenger." In 1664, the "Conventicle Act," followed by a second Act of the same sort in 1670, made "any meetings for more than five persons for any religious worship but that of Common Prayer" liable to be punished by fine, imprisonment and transportation. The Baptist community of Southwater, under so notorious a Nonconformist as Caffyn, was peculiarly liable to be raided, and Richard Haines boasts that his presence alone saved it from molestation more than once :—

> "Have I not been careful," he says,[4] "to make good my Place at the Meeting to which I usually went, insomuch that some in time of Persecution said, If they could but persuade me not to come, or were it not for me, they

---

[1] *Method of Government*, pp. 7, 8.
[2] *Breviat of Proposals*, postscript, p. 6.
[3] *New Lords*, p. 24.   [4] *Ibid.*, p. 56.

would not spare you? but by means of my constant being there, your Meeting was never yet disturbed, whilst all those round were visited."

This shows us that he was a man of some mark in his native county, and we have further proof of this in the accusation, brought against him by Caffyn, of consorting with "great persons." Caffyn, he remarks, "sharply rebuked[1] me, because sometimes, although but upon occasion, I kept company with Great Persons, notwithstanding that he knew that those persons of quality are both sober, honest,[2] and of good report, and well deserving their places of Authority, and the love of all honest men, for that they are favourites to that which is good, and punishers of those that do evill."

Who were these "Great Persons"? Among them, no doubt, were several members of the Royal Society, with whom we find him corresponding with some intimacy a few years later, such as John Beale, D.D.,[3] one of His Majesty's chaplains, the Right Hon. Viscount Brouncker,[4] President of the Royal Society, who "was pleased to peruse my proposals, and express his sentiments very favourably thereupon." Among his acquaintances, if not among his friends, was Thomas Firmin,[5] citizen of London, well known for his philanthropic labours in connexion with the employment of the poor. But the persons meant may have been those whom he speaks of in his book on Cider as partners in the patent for making Cider royal—"such," he says, "as I have made choise of, as being Persons of Esteem for Quality, Estate, Loyalty, and other Considerations, namely, Henry Goreing,[6] Esq.; one of His Majesties Deputy Lieutenants and Justices of Peace for the County of Sussex, eldest son of Henry Goreing, Baronet; Herbert Stapley, Esq., eldest son of Sir John Stapley, Baronet; Thomas Peckham, gent., and others." Perhaps his partner, in the Spinning Engine patent, Richard Dereham, Esq., was another "great person," but I know nothing of him.[7]

---

[1] *New Lords*, p. 8. *Protest against Usurpation*, p. 18, quoted by Caffyn (*Raging Wave*, p. 16).

[2] *Ibid.*, p. 42. On p. 28 we are told that Caffyn boasted how he had rebuked great persons and cast them out of the Church.

[3] *Proposals for Building*, etc. (1677), postscript, p. xvi, where from Dr. Beale he says he has "received by letter some considerable and pressing incitements to proceed." [4] *Ibid.*

[5] *Ibid.*, p. ix. See also Thomas Firmin's *Proposals for the Employment of the Poor.*

[6] *Aphorisms upon Cyder*, *Supplement*, where also he mentions sending samples of his cider to "persons of quality."

[7] Patent Office, Patent No. 202, 18 April, 1678.

Richard Haines seems to have had interviews on the subject of his proposals with some of the highest persons in the realm. His tract on *England's Weal* (1681) was dedicated to Sir Patience Ward,[1] Knt., Lord Mayor of London, and M.P., " humbly intreating, that . . . your Honour would be pleased to recommend these reasons and the matter proposed, to that Honourable House and to improve your interest to have the same read before them." It may be that Sir Patience played him false.[2]

Prince Rupert, whom our author eulogizes for his princely clemency, prudence, generosity, courage, and patriotism,[3] and again as " that eminent promoter of the prosperity of our Kingdome,"[4] himself read and approved the proposals for restoring the woollen manufacture,[5] and " was pleas'd to honour" their author " with his approvement, advice, and encouragement therein."[6] Moreover (he adds) " judging it necessary that I should first offer the same to His Majesties consideration, in order thereunto did introduce me to His Royal presence." Charles the Second, as we know from John Evelyn, was always ready to encourage promoters of new projects, and he referred Richard Haines to Mr. Secretary Coventry, who " gave his approbation (of the proposals) to His Majesty at the Council Table, where it passed without any obstruction."[7]

Elsewhere,[8] the author speaks of the king as having given him " a signal instance of his Royal approbation and encouragement," and again in 1681 he says[9] of the king—" who hath been graciously pleas'd to declare, that he would be ready in his Station, to encourage it all he could."

In his attempt to get a patent for cleansing hop clover, Richard was also brought into contact with the notorious Earl of Shaftesbury, Lord High Chancellor of England,[10] and therefore Keeper of the Great Seal. Speaking of the second hearing of his case, he says: " I went to the Right Honourable the Earl of Shaftesbury, then Lord High Chancellor of England, and without petition, bribe, or

---

[1] His portrait is in the Hall of the Merchant Tailors' Company.

[2] See below, p. 71, *Aphorisms on Cyder*, p. 3 (1684).

[3] *Prevention of Poverty* (1674), p. 1. This tract is addressed to him as " The Most Illustrious Prince, Duke of Cumberland, Earle of Holdernesse, Knight of the Garter," etc. 　　　　　　　　　　　[4] *Model of Government* (1678), p. 8.

Breviat of Proposals (1679), title page.

Proposals for Building, etc., postscript, p. 1.

[7] *Ibid.* 　　　　　　　　　　　　　　　[8] *Model of Government*, p. 8 (1678).

[9] *England's Weal*, p. 13. 　　　　　　　　[10] 1672.

fee, was admitted to treat with his Honour, who after several times discussing the matter, was pleased to confirm what His Majesty had graciously granted unto me, under the Great Seal of England."[1]

The persons named by the House of Commons on 17 December, 1680, to draw up a bill "for restraining vagrants and promoting the woollen manufacture," in pursuance of Richard Haines's proposals, were Mr. Pilkington, Sir Trevor Williams, Sir Richard Cust, Sir Robert Clayton, Mr. Duboys, Mr. Love, Sir Patience Ward, and Sir John Knight,[2] some of whom may well have been the author's friends. Sir Robert Clayton, like Thomas Firmin above-mentioned, was connected with Christ's Hospital.

Among members of his own persuasion, Richard was undoubtedly acquainted with such leading Baptists as W. Kiffin, T. Plant, T. Hicks, whom he mentions in his *Appeal to the General Assembly of Baptists* (1680) as Independent Anabaptists, not concerned in the action of the Caffinites. There were also Mr. G., Mr. W., Mr. P., Mr. C., Mr. T., mentioned as "church officers[3] of known integrity, the most eminent in London," who sided with Richard against Caffyn. They belonged to a branch of the Baptist Church, not in full communion with the General Dependent Baptists.[4] A letter from Richard Haines to Mr. G. is alluded to in Caffyn's first book.

With Caffyn himself Richard lived for many years on terms of great intimacy. "I have received," says the former, "more profit and kindness of him than of any other person whatever, and therefore none may believe I can hate him, but Love him above all others."[5] Again says R. H.: "His confidence in me was such, that he did believe I would submit to his own terms."[6] And R. H., on his part, expresses the greatest confidence in Matthew Caffyn as a faithful friend,[7] to whom in consequence he naturally disclosed his project of taking out a patent. Much no doubt to his surprise Caffyn "would not by any means allow of Letters Patents."

[1] *New Lords*, p. 52. The Earl is again mentioned in the title page to the *Breviat of Proposals*, 1679, as having perused and approved his proposals.

[2] Journals of the House of Commons, ix, 682.

[3] *New Lords*, p. 11. *Protestation against Usurpation*, p. 12 (quoted in Caffyn's *Raging Ware*, p. 23).

[4] Caffyn's *Envy's Bitterness*, pp. 2, 4. *New Lords*, Pref. p. iv, and p 42. See also Caffyn's *Raging Ware*, p. 23, where a Mr. J. is added as mentioned by R. H. in his *Protestation*, etc., p. 12.

[5] *New Lords*, p. 33, quoted from Caffyn's words.

[6] *Ibid.*, p. 35.

[7] *Ibid.*, pp. 2, 35.

This was the rift within the lute of their friendship, which caused such subsequent discord.[1]

No doubt Caffyn was becoming jealous of Richard Haines and his growing reputation. To consort with great persons was in Caffyn's jaundiced eyes subversive of Baptist principles.[2] He objected to a member of his congregation occupying himself in matters of public interest, and tells us himself that he did "cautionally" remind him that "while his understanding was deeply exercised about civil controversies he might forget his Christian obligations."[3] We have a sneering reference to R. H.'s first book, *The Prevention of Poverty*, in the words " a man that pretends to such ingenuity as to teach the whole nation how they should become rich."[4]

HIS PRIVATE CHARACTER.—Though accused of haughtiness and perverseness[5] by Caffyn, our author's general tone, except when his ire is specially aroused, is modest and humble, and the peroration of his earliest work is couched in an unselfish and patriotic vein : " Oh how glad should I be," he says, " if I might in any wise be an Instrument to promote the future Honour, Safety, and Well-being of the and of my Nativity, Land its Inhabitants ! Yet if my desires therein should be answered, let God have the Glory ; and those who are under him in Authority, that shall approve of the Means, and prosecute the same, receive the *whole Praise and Honour* ; for to myself Nothing is to be ascribed, since I have done but what is my Duty, as I am a Subject enjoying Christian Liberty, and Civil Rights and Priviledges."[6] In another place he disclaims the idea that he has any "itch of fame,"[7] adding, " I can justly assure the world, I am so far from any such contemptible Vanity, that I am rather a beggar for the Poor and Distressed."

In connection with the Baptist body he has nothing to reproach himself with. "Did I come amongst you," he asks,[8] "for any sinister or selfish ends ? Did I ever gain so much as one penny thereby ? But suppose I had received profit by you, have you not received of me for every penny some pounds[9] ? and that not

---

[1] But R. H.'s real crime was the refusal to "adore" Caffyn. *New Lords*, p. 21.
[2] Caffyn's *Raging Wave*, p. 16.
[3] *Ibid.*, p. 15.   [4] *Ibid.*, p. 24.
[5] *Ibid.*, p. 13.   [6] *Prevention of Poverty*, p. 21.
[7] *Proposals*, postscript, xv.   [8] *New Lords*, p. 34.
[9] *New Lords*, pp. 35, 53. " Whether he thought himself beholding to me for any contributions of mine I know not, but this I know that he never gave me thanks for it, nor did I desire any. But possibly he might not know what my

by Constraint, but willingly? Sure I am that of late years, I have
been very Careful, not to come short of any of you all, in what I
might serve you in; so that against the Church, I know not that
I have transgressed in any case, although to my grief in many things
I have transgressed against my Lord and Saviour, of whom through
Grace, I comfortably do hope to find Mercy."[1]　Again in another
place: "Have I been such a one as to have to your discredit, and
the dishonour of the Truth, which I have professed, lived in
any notorious Sins? or have I through infirmities transgressed
against my God, and refused to be reformed? . . . Have I carried
myself loftily to the meanest. . . . Or can you think that I
now neglect my Business, and spend my Time and Labour, hereby
to make a Party, or for any self-ends to engage you to myself?"[2]

In making his second appeal to the Assembly of Baptists he
challenges any one to show that he had wilfully or knowingly
done wrong either to man, woman, or child, or in any case been
"unfaithful to any that relyed on him or despised Admonition for
sin committed against the Most High God, or ever designed or
practised anything of revenge against any person."[3]

The only charge even the malice of enemies could rake up against
him was, that he had taken money of a neighbour in compensation
of damage done to his corn and pasture by the said neighbour's
cattle lying in it, and R. H., even so, had only taken action when
that neighbour dealt dishonourably with his own brothers in a case
which was injurious to Richard also.[4]　But in three passages Caffyn
hints at "many transgressions committed somewhere in the family,
and not voluntarily confessed, but through care and diligence
discovered."[5]

With regard to the family and home life of Richard Haines we
unfortunately find in these books but few particulars.　Caffyn,
indeed, quoting from R. H.'s last work,[6] speaks of "his seeming

contributions were, because I never gave him anything that I remember, but
always delivered it to one of his Deacons to be disposed of according to their
discretion." Caffyn in *Envy's Bitterness*, p. 31, says the Deacons S. L. and D. P.
distributed the alms partly to the poor and partly to Caffyn himself.

[1] *New Lords*, pp. 36, 37. "I was not conscious of any known sin by me
committed; but what through Grace was repented, of, so that with a good
conscience I through mercy do, and then did to my great comfort believe, that I
whom you have unmercifully condemned, my Lord and Saviour doth and will
justifie."

[2] *Ibid.*, pp. 56, 57.　　　　　[3] *Ibid.*, p. 7.

[4] *Ibid.*, p. 14.　　　　　[5] Caffyn's *Raging Wave*, pp. 1, 11.

[6] *Protestation against Usurpation*, p. 18.　See Caffyn's *Raging Wave*, p. 11.

willingness that the reader should make observation of the good
disposition and frame of his spirit on his performance of family
duties and the government of his family, so as in many years he
hath not known anything committed by them worthy of public
blame."

It is clear—to me at least—that, in spite of this quarrel,
Richard was not of a contentious disposition. He claims to have
often acted as peacemaker "between neighbour and neighbour
when in the way to ruine one another."[1] He was evidently affable in
his manners and persuasive in his speech; for one of his former
friends, who finally sided with Caffyn, says that "he was made to
doubt by reason of Richard Haines's smooth words."[2] No other
allusions to personal traits of character appear, unless it be when
Caffyn speaks of his opponent scoffingly as a "dreamer."[3]

His Two Dreams.—In reference to these R. H. says: "Though
I am far from Practising or Justifying any Superstitious Observation
of Dreams, as knowing that they are oft times caused by Natural
means, and prove only Delusive motions of the ever-busie Fancy,
retained by the waking memory, whilst the Judgment and dis-
tinguishing Faculties, to-gether with the external Senses, lie fast
lock'd up in the Charms of Sleep; yet since we have both examples,
and positive Texts, showing that in Dreams was one way whereby
the Lord was pleased heretofore to communicate himself to his
Servants, I dare not censure all Representations of that kind as
vain. . . . Nay, some Reasons I have, considering the Time and
several Circumstances, to apprehend, that a certain Dream of mine
(the Relation whereof might occasion such his Lordship's scoffs) may
prove no less certain in the event, than the Dreams of him, who
for his Dreams was envied by his Brethren, and for the satisfying
your curiosity, who have not heard it, I shall here faithfully
relate it, as it happened, thus.

"On the day on which you were pleased to deal with me as an
Offendor of the weak Brethren, I arose early in the morning,
resolving, as at other times, not to omit the performance of any
thing that might be my duty towards God; in order whereunto I
prepared by fasting and prayer,[4] to rely on him only for his

---

[1] *New Lords*, pp. 8, 42.
[2] Caffyn's *Raging Wave*, p. 26; *Envy's Bitterness*, p. 26. [3] *New Lords*, p. 49.
[4] See also *New Lords*, p. 52. "Whereupon I did apply myself to the Lord by
fasting and Prayer several Days, Desiring that he would assist me in the work
(*i.e.*, of publishing his Defence), or otherwise withhold me from it, by what means
best pleased him; yea I did desire the Lord to bring upon me those Evills which

guidance and assistance without the least premeditation what to Answer. And with Sincerity I can say it, as I went out; so did I come home, with a gracious confidence of his Mercy and Favour; But it being then somewhat late in the Evening, so soon as I had refreshed myself, and performed my Duty as at other times, I went to Bed; and in my Sleep I had a Dream, That I was standing a little distant from that House wherein this unhappy and ill-managed meeting was; and as I stood still, observing the House to be full of People, and myself at a distance, as a Person not regarded; Behold a great Fire did on a sudden appear in the House; at which I stood amazed, crying out, Your house is on Fire; but immediately it seemed to me to Blaze through the Windows on the South-Side of it; whereupon with a loud voice I cried to them within to depart the House, telling them what danger they were in, and often saying The House is on Fire: But all the Care and pains I could take to persuade them was in vain, and wholly contemned; But whilst I was busie thus warning them to escape, behold all the House seemed to be in a Flame, the Fire breaking violently forth, even through the Roof of it. Then did I observe every Person suddenly to be in motion, and every hand set to work, whereby the Fire began to abate, and in short time after was quenched. This being done, I then came into the House, where I found all the People in a little disorder, some walking about and others sitting still (in that room where they had compassed their unhappy Act of unmerciful Tyranny) but at the upper end of the Table where the unjust Judg or false Apostle used to stand and perform his Devotion, I beheld the perfect form of a Pulpit with the door open, and on the outside of the Pulpit door there was a little woodden-pin, on which there hung a very bright key (of which I did often take notice) but this Pulpit being empty I inquired for the person that should be in it, but none made an answer, till at last it was observed by all that the Party belonging to the said place was lost, and could nowhere be found, also that my Company was Acceptable."

He says he told this dream the next day to his servant, who was one of their company, and knew more of his mind than any other. He then relates his other dream.

"Another dream[1] somewhat remarkable I had some days before there was a stop put to my obtaining the great Seal of England,

that false Apostle did predict should befal me, rather than that I by this means should dishonour his Glorious-name."

[1] *New Lords*, p. 51.

D

for the Confirmation of his Majesties grant before the late Lord
Keeper,[1] by reason of the untrue Information of two Conspirators,
who suggested, That I was not the first Inventer, and that I designed
to prohibite all persons from Cleansing of Clover, All which was
utterly false ; Some few days I say before this stop was made I
being at London, in my sleep had this dream.   That as I was going
about my business, in Order to have his Majesties grant Confirmed
under the great Seal, behold there stood in my way a Church as it
were quite Cross the street, so that I could not pass by it, whereupon I stood still to Consider, whether there was no other way by
which I might Go whither my business lay, but whilst I was thus
Considering methoughts a strange thing came into my mind, viz.
That I must go over the Church which seemed to be of a considerable Height, and on the middle of it stood a very High and
Stately Steeple, which seemed to overtop all the Churches in
London, at the sight whereof I was somewhat afraid of Climbing
so High as to get over the Church, but so it was, over it I must
and up I got to the Top of the Church, and being there, the lofty
Steeple standing in my way, over that I must go also, which I did,
and went down again to the ground on the other side, where looking up to the top of the Steeple I returned thanks that I came
over so dangerous a place without hurt, but passing towards my
business, methoughts I was discouraged, and given to doubt, that
at that time I should be frustrated of my intent."

QUARTERS IN LONDON.—It is clear from several indications
that Richard was "much in London."[2]   During his many rides
backwards and forwards along the Sussex roads, which were
proverbial for their mire,[3] he must have had much occasion to
rue their badness.

In one passage of his first book against Caffyn he mentions
coming to his " Quarters in London."   " Being hungry," he says,
" I asked the Maid for such Victuals as the house did afford . . .
and went upstairs into my Chamber, and there at one Table, and
a very little one too, we three could eat and drink together."[4]

We do not know whereabouts in London these quarters were,
but we may conjecture that they were near Christ Church, Newgate

---

[1] Lord Shaftesbury was dismissed November, 1673.

[2] Caffyr *A Raging Wave*, p. 25 (1675).

[3] See De Quincey, Essay on Travelling, xiv, 295. "An Italian of rank, who
has left a record of his perilous adventure, visited, or attempted to visit Petworth
. . . about the year 1685. I forget how many times he was overturned within
one particular stretch of five miles," etc,   [4] *New Lords*, p. 11.

Street, as he is described, at his death, as being of that parish.[1]
He also had some connection with Southwark and his nephew
Gregory was, in his marriage licence in 1692, described as of
Southwark, draper.

His Books.—His books were printed, published, and sold, as
follows:

> 1674. *The Prevention of Poverty*, printed for Nathaniel
> Brooke at the Sign of the Angel in Cornhill.[2]
>
> 1677. *Proposals for Building in Every County a Working
> Almshouse or Hospital*, printed by W. G. for R. Harford,
> at the same. Sold also by Mrs. Walton at the foot of
> Parliament Stairs.[3]
>
> 1678. *Provision for the Poor*, a single sheet,[4] with allowance.
> Printed for D. M. and sold by Mrs. Walton at the foot of
> Parliament Stairs.[4]
>
> 1678 *A Model of Government*, with allowance, Roger
> L'Estrange. Printed for D. M. and sold as above.[5]
>
> 1679. *A Method of Government for Publick Working Alms-
> houses.* With allowance. Printed for Langley Curtis on
> Ludgate Hill.[6]
>
> 1679. *A Breviat of Proposals* for restoring the woollen
> manufacture. Printed, as preceding.[7]
>
> 1681. *England's Weal and Prosperity proposed.* Printed for
> Langley Curtis in Goat Court on Ludgate Hill.[8]
>
> 1684. 2 April. *Aphorisms upon making Cyder Royal.* Printed
> by George Larkin, and to be had at the Marine and
> Carolina Coffee House, Birchin Lane, price 6d.[9]

[1] In his advertisement in *London Gazette*, 22 December, 1684, he mentions
Dr. Morton's Buildings in Grey Friers in Newgate Street as the place where his
cider was kept in vaults; and also Three Crown Court in Southwark.

[2] Copies are in Brit. Mus. (104, g. 20; 1027, l. 16); Trinity College, Dublin,
R.R.N. 61, No. 9; Pat. Office, No. 4838; Library of Faculty of Advocates.

[3] See *Provision for the Poor*, p. viii. Copies of this are in Brit. Mus. (104, m.
54; 1027, 1, 16, Harl. Misc., iv, p. 489), Trinity Coll. Libr., Dublin; and I have
a copy which I purchased for 10s. 6d.

[4] See *Model of Government*, p. 2. There is a copy in the Bodleian (Pamphlets,
141). See also Bodl. Wood, D. 27.

[5] Brit. Mus., 1027, 1. 16.

[6] Brit. Mus., 1027, 1. 16. Bodleian: Wood, D. 27. 9. See also Record Office,
State Papers Dom. Ser. Car. II, 281, a. 248. This is wrongly dated 1670.

[7] Brit. Mus., 1027, 1. 16.

[8] Bodleian: Wood, D. 27; Brit. Mus., 104, m. 55; 104, n. 15; 1027, 1. 16.

[9] Brit. Mus., 113, K. 57. Also in Bodleian Library, Guildhall Library.
Library of Patent Office, and of Faculty of Advocates.

1684, 1 May. *Supplement to same,* at same, gratis. Printed by Thomas James for the author.[1]

Licences for right to make the cider were to be had at the Coffee house above mentioned, and at another in Three Crown Court, Southwark, while the cider itself was sold at a Mr. Woodward's, Distiller, in the Old Bailey.

We do not know where R. H.'s other books were published, viz., the two against Caffyn,[2] *New Lords, New Laws,* in 1674[3] ; *A Protestation against Usurpation,* in 1675 ; and the *Appeal to the General Assembly of Dependent Baptists,* 3 June, 1680,[4] with postscript, 7 June of same year.

PRISONS, THE SOCIAL PROBLEM, AND TEMPERANCE.—No doubt Richard Haines was familiar enough with the London of his day. Unfortunately he has left no reference either to the plague or the fire which both occurred in his time, though probably he had not established himself in town before then. In one passage he makes an eloquent protest against the management of prisons.[5] " I have observ'd such dogged Cruelties in some of our Prisons, where many poor famishing persons have been crowded up in one little Room, without any thing to lie on, save Straw, and that so seldom changed, that 'twas become muck, and onely fit to breed Vermine[6]; and to aggravate their misery, the Jaylor fastned broad thin Plates of iron pent-house-wise[7] across the Gates of the Prison to prevent those who were charitably disposed, that they should not give them Beer through the Grates but that they might be forced to drink his, and pay two pence for little more than a pint." In the same passage he speaks of the "Debtors in Prison having but three halfpence a day and what they can beg to live on."

As a moral and religious man, he is vehement against " all

[1] The only copy is in the Guildhall Library.

[2] Caffyn's two books were *Envy's Bitterness corrected with a Rod of Shame,* 1674, and *A Raging Wave Foaming out his own Shame,* 1675.

[3] This seems to be a proverb. Thomas Hardy, in his *Far from the Madding Crowd,* says, " New Lords, new Laws, as the saying is." The only copy of the pamphlet is in the Bodleian, 133; where also are the only copies of Caffyn's books.

[4] The only copy is in the British Museum.

[5] *Model of Government,* p. 6.

[6] A correspondent to *Notes and Queries* (8th Ser., 1, May 14, 1892) mentions a petition to the House of Lords in 1673 which states " that many thousand miserable creatures (insolvent debtors) are languishing and perishing in prisons and holes, being almost starved and eaten up with vermin."

[7] A Shaksperian compound.

Impudent Night Walkers and Nurses of Debauchery . . which are a Destruction to the Estates, Bodies and Souls of many Hundreds,"[1] and he recommends the " pious wisdom of the City of London to find out a means for checking this social evil."

In the matter of liquor R. H. shows no teetotal leanings. The great invention of his later years, which he fondly hoped would make his fortune, was a new method of making cider to equal foreign wines in strength and flavour. In perfecting this he spent many years.[2] The normal consumption of cider per man he estimated at 1 quart a day, which seems a large amount, but it is clear from another passage that he considers drunkenness the vice and sin which it is.[3]

RELIGIOUS, POLITICAL, AND SOCIAL VIEWS.—There is abundant evidence throughout Richard Haines's writings to show that he was a thoroughly religious man. Soon after his marriage he must have embraced the doctrines of the Anabaptists,[4] professed by the Arminian, or General Dependent, Baptists, over one of whose churches Matthew Caffyn was head or Chief Apostle. For 15 years after this he lived at peace with all men, doing his duty towards his Baptist brethren, bringing up his family in the fear of God, winning the respect and esteem of many "persons of quality" in the county, and living a useful happy life as a yeoman farmer of considerable means, not without ambition to do good in his generation in a wider sphere than a little Sussex hamlet could afford him. All this time he kept his eyes open, and interested himself, if not in politics, yet in social economics. Which side he took in the Civil War is not known, but Sussex was Cromwellian, and probably Richard sympathized with the Protector. There is but a single reference in his works to " the past generation,"[5] and this is couched in studiously vague terms. His active brain was teeming with projects and methods for ameliorating the condition of the people, and advancing the power and wealth of the nation. But he did not on that account neglect his own business of farming. Two of his three patents were connected

---

[1] *Proposals*, etc., p. 8.
[2] *Aphorisms*, etc., p. 3.   [3] *Ibid.*, p. 10.
[4] " Baptists existed because there were those who could not conceive that anything short of the strong heart-felt conviction of the adult could make him a fit subject of an ordinance which was a sign of the Christian profession." Gardiner's *Civil War*, I, p. 313. It was from the Independent Church of Amsterdam that the English Baptists were an offshoot.
[5] *Model of Government*, p. 8.

with agriculture, and he was evidently a shrewd practical farmer, and has left us many useful hints (as will appear later on), on the conservation of forests, the cultivation of fruit trees, and the proper treatment of different soils.

KNOWLEDGE OF THE BIBLE.—All this could not have left much time for reading, but Richard knew at least one book well and that was the Bible. He is always ready to support an argument with a passage from the Scriptures. He quotes, in one place or another, from nearly half the books of the Canon. It is his firm conviction that a nation's happiness depends solely on the goodwill[1] and pleasure of God, and he does not shrink from saying (in 1681) that "the . . . Rod in the hand of the Almighty is now in an high manner lifted up against the whole land, the King, and the Church, yea, and against the Religion and Worship which God hath appointed ; so that Misery, Desolation, Death, and unmerciful Cruelties, do (as it were) stare in our Faces."[2] The saving of souls he reckons as worth a hundred thousand times more than the saving of lives.[3] In the spirit of the words, "I will have mercy and not sacrifice," he affirms that "God hath a greater regard to the Poor than to the External Religion and Worship which he himself commanded."[4]

If the Baptist discipline allowed of it, no doubt Richard at times preached to the congregation. We know he was a fluent speaker, and his books show that he could reason a question out. An incidental specimen of his scriptural exposition may be given. It is on that disputed point " Sin against the Holy Ghost," on which he sensibly says : " In my opinion it is that sin only which is committed under the highest degree of saving means (to wit) God by his Holy Spirit and Word opposing, and the person persevering in his intended wickedness, so that whether it be the Sin of Usurpation, Rebellion, Tyranny, Hypocrasie, Idolatry, etc., any of these may thus be committed against the Holy Ghost, and so become impardonable."[5] He had an abiding sense of the omnipotence of God, "the Most High, before whom the greatest Monarchs on Earth are but animated Shadows,"[6] and a deep faith in his Redeemer, " my Blessed Lord and Saviour whose favour is better than Life."[7] The Bible he looked upon as the one Guide of

---

[1] *Proposals*, etc., postscript, p. vi.
[2] *England's Weal*, pp. 10, 11.   [3] *Proposals*, etc., p. 11.
[4] *England's Weal*, p. 11.   [5] *New Lords*, p. 39.
[6] *Ibid.*, p. 30.   [7] *Ibid.*, p. 33.

Life, and he is never tired of speaking of it as "the alone infallible and unerring Rule,[1] the Pole Star of God's word,[2] the most infallible Directory to bring men to Heaven,[3] the Royal Road and King's Highway to Life and Glory,[4] the Touchstone to which all practices must be brought, and the Sacred Dyal with which all motions must be compared,[5] and, finally, that Sacred Boundary which as a River of Life divides the Church of Christ from that of Anti-Christ."[6]

ATTITUDE TOWARDS ROMANISM.—The Roman Church he naturally regards with a holy horror, and had evidently read a good deal about it. He holds Caffyn up to odium by calling him a little Pope, and comparing his doings to those of his "Triple-Crowned Brother beyond the Seas."[7] He is acquainted with the ceremonies at the election of Popes, and their pretended unwillingness to take the office. He speaks of their title "Servants of the Servants of Christ,"[8] and of kissing the Pope's toe.[9] He mentions Pope Clement (*the First*, he calls him) as selling pardons and indulgences, on the ground that "one drop of our Saviour's blood had been enough to have saved all mankind," and that, whereas all his blood had been spilt, the overflow had been given as a treasure to be disposed of by the Chief Officers of the Church."[10] Pope Innocent III's name naturally suggests the play upon it—"nothing seemingly more humble, nothing more Innocent."[11] He has a hit at an unnamed Cardinal, who declared "that an honest man ought not to be a slave to his word.[12] On the other hand he speaks of Luther as "that holy man."[13] In his argument against Caffyn he adduces the case of a certain religious fanatic or impostor named Hacket, who pretended to be sent from heaven as the destined Emperor of Europe. He was proclaimed in Cheapside by his followers as the Lord Jesus, and led astray many, among them persons named Arthington and Coppinger, the former a learned, sober, conscientious, and religious man.[14] Elsewhere another crazy fanatic, John the Taylor, the so-called "King of Leyden," is spoken of.[15]

---

[1] *New Lords*, pp. 7, 12, 39, 57. [2] *Ibid.*, p. 24.
[3] *Proposals*, etc., postscript, p. vii. [4] *New Lords*, Preface, p. iii.
[5] *Ibid.*, p. 55. [6] *Ibid.*, p. 43. [7] *Ibid.*, p. 37. [8] *Ibid.*, p. 25.
[9] *Ibid.*, pp. 25, 52. [10] *Ibid.*, p. 13. [11] *Ibid.*, p. 25.
[12] *Ibid.*, Preface, p. v. [13] *Ibid.*, p. 33.
[14] *Ibid.*, pp. 22, 55, where R. H. mentions the book, "Arthington's Seduction and Repentance," from which he got the above particulars. The affair took place in the reign of Elizabeth. [15] *Ibid.*, pp. 22, 47.

CHAPTER V.

THE QUARREL WITH MATTHEW CAFFYN.

EXCOMMUNICATION OF RICHARD HAINES.—Richard Haines, by observation and experiment, lasting over a number of years, and costing him " not less than thirty pound,"[1] had discovered something which he thought might be useful to all farmers. Wishing to turn an honest penny by it, he set about getting a patent for his invention, not dreaming that such an act, within the competence of any citizen of whatsoever religion, could be objected to on religious or other grounds. Making his application, therefore, in the proper quarter, he obtained the issue of a warrant[2] on 19 August, 1672, to the Attorney-General "for preparing Letters Patents to secure to Richard Haynes of Wantley, in the parish of Sullington, co. Sussex, for 14 years, advantage of his invention for severing and cleansing the seed called Nonsuch Trefoyle or Hop Clover from the huske."[3]

The terms of the patent, when Richard finally obtained it, were briefly as follows :—[4]

"Whereas by the humble petition of Richard Haines of Wantly in the psh of Sullington co. Sussex Gent as also by the certificate of diverse of our loving subjects living in the same county we are given to understand that the sd R. H. of his extraordinary care & study hath found out and discovered ' A way to sever divide and make clean the seed called nonsuch trefoyle or hop clover from its husk and also from the mixture of course grass or weed that naturally cleaves unto it a thing yet never attained unto by any person whatsoever by which means the seed becomes so pure and cleane that it brings forth much more grass than ever the other did' Know ye that we grant unto the sd R. H. especiall license that he during the terme of 14 years may use this innovation in this our Kingdom of England & Principality of Wales yielding and paying therefore yearly during the said tenure to this receipt of our exchequer at Westminster the sum of 20 shillings at the Feast of St. Michael."

[1] *New Lords*, p. 3.
[2] Hist. MSS. Commission, Report ix. p. 448*b*.
[3] *New Lords*, pp. 1, 2. It might be called yellow clover, as it bears a three-leaved grass and yellow flower.
[4] See Patent Roll, 24 Car. II, pt. 8, No. 21. Printed in Patent Office Library, No. 166, 3 February, 25 Car. II.

A provision was added that no one should be prevented by these Letters Patent from cleansing the seed in any other way.

But though, as was admitted by some of Richard's enemies,[1] the seed of yellow clover had been improved by the process, and though one of his chief opponents publicly declared[2] that he considered the patentee the real inventor of the process, and though no one's rights were thereby infringed, yet when the inventor disclosed his intention of applying for a patent to Caffyn, as to a dear friend, the latter most unexpectedly took umbrage[3] at the suggestion, and tried to dissuade him, and, when he persisted, asked him to discuss it in a meeting.[4] This Richard very properly declined to do, saying "they had nothing to do to meddle in such matters." Then ·Caffyn, thinking to coerce his dissentient follower, first worked up his congregation, who (we are repeatedly told) almost adored him, against the patent,[5] and then the public, falsely representing that the so-called invention was a thing previously known; that the inventor wished to prevent others from cleansing ordinary clover in the usual way; that the patent was not justified by great charge, long study, or more than common ingenuity.[6] These falsehoods, scattered broadcast, produced an effect among many honest people, and gave the enemies of the Baptist body a handle for reviling that sect in general and Richard Haines in particular.[7]

Meanwhile Caffyn put his religious machinery in motion and summoned Richard Haines to a Quarterly Meeting to debate the question, but being at a distance (in London probably) he could not be present.[8] However, Caffyn introduced the subject in a general way, without mentioning names, abusing patents and rashly exclaiming "What are the statutes of the realm to us?" Patentees he classed with idolaters and unclean persons, and finally threatened principal and abettors in this affair with excommunication.[9] The chief offender was moreover to be boycotted.[10]

---

[1] *New Lords*, p. 2.   [2] *Ibid.*   [3] *Ibid.*, p. 3.

[4] Caffyn's *Envy's Bitterness*, p. 12.   [5] *New Lords*, p. 3.

[6] Caffyn's *Envy's Bitterness*, p. 16.

[7] Caffyn's *Raging Wave*, p. 12; *Envy's Bitterness*, p. 17. See *New Lords*, p. 3.

[8] *Ibid.*, p. 3. *Envy's Bitterness*, pp. 9, 10.

[9] *New Lords*, pp. 4, 15.

[10] *Ibid.*, pp 19, 42. R. H. had a report of the proceedings from one who was present, but also "out of communion" with the body.

About the end of 1672, or beginning of 1673, a second meeting
was held for the consideration of the case.[1] At this Caffyn
condemned patents because they were of bad repute in the world
and a cause of offence to the weak brethren.[2] Richard Haines
then addressed the meeting, bound as arbiters to judge by the
Scriptures, and after pointing out that many things were un-
popular without being wrong, requested leave to reason with the
"weak brethren." But, says he, "this poor grace was denied me."
Caffyn, claiming a privilege (as he said) of twenty years' standing,[3]
repeatedly interrupted him in an insulting and upbraiding manner.
To the question, "Who is it that accuses me?" only Caffyn
answered, "I do." Further debate was useless, and Richard
Haines claimed to appeal according to Baptist usage.[4]

After further "prating against him with malicious words,"
and unfairly bringing in another accusation about a bargain of
clover, Caffyn then proceeded to excommunicate Richard Haines,[5]
threatening the same fate to one who "spoke but sparingly in
favour of his case." Asked for a definition of the offence, Caffyn
could only assert that "Patents were of the Devil."

After the meeting a paper "considerable large," drawn up by
Caffyn, and containing the grounds of the proceedings against him,
was sent to Richard Haines,[6] but it contained nothing new.[7] Nor
was the tension relieved by a private talk between the chief
parties, held at the house of one of Caffyn's chief adherents.[8]

The offender being excommunicated, one would have supposed
that his enemies would have let him get his patent in peace. Far
from it; they laid an information against it[9] by the mouth of two
emissaries before the Lord Keeper on the grounds above given.[10]

Some of those who were led astray by these misrepresenta-
tions[11] afterwards acknowledged their error, but in the first

---

[1] *New Lords*, p. 5. The first opportunity R. H. had of treating with the congregation on the subject.

[2] *Ibid.*, p. 4.

[3] *Ibid.*, pp. 5, 27; Caffyn's *Enry's Bitterness*, p. 13.

[4] This appeal was to (1) a neighbour Church; (2) Quarterly meeting of elders
and brethren from several congregations; (3) General Assembly in London.

[5] *New Lords*, p. 5. Caffyn's *Envy's Bitterness*, p. 13.

[6] *Ibid.*, p. 15, and Caffyn's *Raging Ware*, pp. 2, 12.

[7] Caffyn's *Enry's Bitterness*, p. 21. For Richard's own doings on that day see
above, p. 32.

[8] *New Lords*, p. 13.   [9] *Ibid.*, p. 51.

[10] See p. 41.

[11] *New Lords*, p. 18.

instance many persons, from several towns and parishes,[1] including several persons of quality, subscribed a petition against the patent.

Counsel was engaged on both sides, able counsel (unnamed) for the patentee, and for Caffyn's party Sir Edward Thurlow of Reigate,[2] and Sir Henry Peckham of Chichester. The case was argued before "Lord" Bridgeman,[3] Keeper of the Broad Seal. However, as Caffyn exultingly remarks, "they soon made judgement against the patent," and "it was threw out,"[4] Richard Haines's enemies boasting that any more interviews with high authorities on that subject would cost him £100 a time. So the patent, which had been granted, was not confirmed, and Richard went quietly home again, where he found his enemies jubilantly boasting that they were "justified on all hands, and glad they had done it."

But their victim was not the man to submit tamely to injustice. He drew up a statement of his case for publication, not forgetting with prayer and fasting to invoke a blessing on his work.[5] His reasons for publishing were, to purge the Baptist Church of errors, and to clear it in the eyes of the world, who were led by Caffyn's proceedings to credit it with "dangerous opinions."[6] To publish at all was against the grain, and would not have been thought of, had not Caffyn published the excommunication, and "that within three days, particularly to such as he had reason to believe hated" Richard Haines most.[7]

Pamphlet in hand Richard then (early in 1673 we may suppose) betook himself to London, intending to publish the same, when, to his surprise and delight, he found everything "smile upon him."[8]

A satisfactory interview with the new Lord Keeper, Lord Shaftesbury, resulted in the patent being confirmed.[9] So the book was laid aside, and negotiations for a settlement of the quarrel were opened up with one who pretended to be a common friend to Richard Haines and Matthew Caffyn. He wished the

---

[1] Caffyn's *Raging Ware*, p. 14; *Envy's Bitterness*, p. 16.
[2] Caffyn's *Enry's Bitterness*, p. 16; *A Raging Wave*, p. 14.
[3] Sir Orlando Bridgeman, Keeper from 1667–1672.
[4] *Enry's Bitterness*, pp. 7, 16; *Raging Ware*, p. 15; *New Lords*, p. 52.
[5] *New Lords*, p. 52.
[6] *Ibid.*, Pref. pp. ii and vii, and pp. 33, 35, 36, 47, 54.
[7] *Ibid.*, Pref. p. iii.   [8] *Ibid.*, p. 52.
[9] The patent was advertised in the *London Gazette* (No. 803), 28 July, 1673; (No. 872), Thursday, 26 March, 1674.

matter to be referred (as was usual) to a neighbouring congregation, but Richard refused this, knowing how great was Caffyn's influence in that part of England. Accordingly an informal[1] meeting of "London friends" was agreed to, and the friend engaged to bring Caffyn to it. Time and place were arranged by an "elder," only slightly known to R. H., and several church officers, equally strangers to him, were asked to be present. It took place at a Coffee house, and there Mr. G. and others "of the same differing persuasion from us"[2] (says Caffyn), spoke for R. H. The latter's account is that "in a full meeting of several church officers of known integrity, to wit, Mr. G., Mr. W., Mr. P., Mr. C. and Mr. T., . . . the most eminent in London,"[3] advice and admonition were publicly given to Caffyn, but by him wholly disregarded. Declaring their dislike of his illegal practices, they asked him "how he dared to do such a thing, having no Word of God for it,"[4] and finally bade him go home and reform the matter. When Richard returned to Sussex he found the congregation had hardened their hearts, and said of the "London friends," "We do not own them."

Loath as Richard was to publish his book, fearing to bring reproach on the congregation, yet, "after a long and weary waiting" without result, he again took his book in hand, but put it by again till the hearing of his appeal to the General Assembly in London, which he had now decided to make formally.[5] Caffyn was informed of this intention, and a letter sent to the congregation that they might be represented before the Assembly.[6] R. H. appeared in due course with his witnesses,[7] but Caffyn craftily came alone. He had, moreover, another quarrel on hand, and proceeded to make an attack upon a member named Monk,[8] against whom he had prepared a charge in writing. The sympathies of the meeting were with Monk, but much time

---

[1] *Envy's Bitterness*, p. 3.

[2] *Raging Ware*, pp. 19, 20. Caffyn says they were few, from no particular church, and not chosen delegates.

[3] *New Lords*, Pref. p. ii.   [4] *Ibid.*, p. 56; Pref. p. iv.

[5] *Ibid.*, p. 6; Pref. iv.

[6] *Ibid.*, p. v. Probably in June, 1673.

[7] Among them a certain H. S., asked by R. H. by letter to attend: see *Envy's Bitterness*, pp. 19, 20.

[8] He had written a book called *Cure for the Cankering Error of the New Eutychians*, published 1673, aimed at a heresy of Caffyn's that our Lord was not of the seed of David, and did not take His flesh of the Virgin Mary. *New Lords*, p. 6.

was taken up by this attack. But finally Caffyn did introduce
the question of excommunication, and R. H. asked definitely
whether the Court could and would decide the case. It does not
appear what answer they made to this. Caffyn then proposed
that six or more persons, chosen by the Assembly, should with
the Quarterly Meeting in the country, be the judges in the case,
Caffyn and his congregation only appearing as witnesses.[1] This
R. H. refused.[2] Then Mr. M(onk) suggested that a committee of
six or more members, R. H. apparently to have the choice of
persons, should settle the matter then and there.[3] The Caffinites now tried to adjourn the meeting on the ground of want
of time. That pretext set aside, Caffyn fell back upon the plea
that his congregation were not there, and appealed to the rule
of the General Assembly that an appeal could not be made to it
until the question had been brought before a neighbour congregation.[4] One of Caffyn's party seconded his objection, and
the matter stood adjourned.[5] After this fiasco Richard lodged
his appeal for the next General Assembly to be held in London
20 May (1674).[6]

On this occasion he appeared " with urgency not common for
a hearing of the matter,[7] before such persons as he had chosen
or esteemed," consisting of numerous elders, messengers, and
brethren from city and country. Caffyn " exclaimed open-
mouthed against him "[8] when R. H. likened him to the beast
in the Revelation, giving humorous reasons for the similitude.
The appeal was now accepted and a decision come to, though
R. H.'s witnesses were refused a hearing.[9] With this decision,
says Caffyn, Richard Haines expressed at the time open dis-
satisfaction, but in his book stated that he did not clearly
understand it, though, as far as he did understand it, it was for a
reversal of the sentence of excommunication.[10]

[1] *Raging Ware*, p. 18; *Envy's Bitterness*, p. 6.
[2] *New Lords*, p. 7. [3] *Ibid.*, Pref. v, and p. 7.
[4] Caffyn says (*Raging Ware*, pp. 20, 21) he told R. H. in the presence of
James Smith that an Assembly could not judge the case. But R. H. objected,
that when notice of appeal was given, Caffyn had not denied the possibility of its
being heard, nor intimated that his adherents would be away.
[5] *Envy's Bitterness*, p. 5.
[6] *New Lords*, p. 7.
[7] *A Raging Ware*, pp. 18, 19.
[8] *New Lords*, p. 32.
[9] *Raging Ware*, p. 22, quotes *Protestation*, p. 10.
[10] *Protestation*, pp. 10, 11, quoted by Caffyn, *Raging Ware*, p. 18.

Either now or again at a later meeting the matter was debated, and patents judged lawful on Caffyn's own showing, without a witness being heard on the other side, after which several members of the Court subscribed a paper requesting Caffyn to put away the evil of his doings.[1]

After this the question seems to have come up several times for discussion, and R. H. was repeatedly asked to *refer* it and not *appeal*, and on his refusal to merely refer it, he was told that he must keep their rule of an appeal to a country congregation first. This " unjust and crooked course "[2] he was obliged to take, and no good resulting therefrom, he again brought the matter before the High Court. The appeal was again opposed, but the opposers were outvoted. Then Caffyn's party slandered the witnesses and refused to allow them to use their papers, though years had passed since the events in dispute. Finally their evidence was disregarded. The names of the prominent Caffinites were George Hammon, Capt. Morcock, Uridge of Kent, Marner of St. Martin's-le-Grand, Thos. Croucher, Miller, Francis Stanley, and Amory, one of whom was chairman on this occasion. So fierce was the contention that the meeting broke up in confusion, the members saying that " God had withdrawn Himself from them."[3]

SENTENCE OF EXCOMMUNICATION REVERSED.—The final settlement did not come till seven years from the time the quarrel began. The last, and successful, appeal was made to the " General Assembly of Baptists convened in London from most Parts of the Nation " on 3 June, 1680. R. H. began by giving his reasons for originally making his appeal against Caffyn, one of the members of the High Court, immediately after the fact complained of had been committed—because theirs was the highest court, because the case was unique, and because Caffyn's action struck at the King's prerogative. From this Court, then, he expected justice—because, as several members of it had admitted, it had the power to redress grievances, because Caffyn's party had had full notice of the appeal, and had allowed it, and because the whole case was a scandal to the Baptist profession. Then his appeal had been opposed, and he had been obliged to go before a Quarterly Assembly in the country, on the promise that if justice were not done there, the High Court would accept the appeal and decide the question. But all this turned out to

---

[1] *Appeal to Assembly* (1680).
[2] *Ibid.*
[3] *Ibid,*

be a plan for wasting time, corrupting witnesses, and tiring out the appellant by expensive attendance with witnesses.

Therefore does Richard Haines proclaim to all whom it may concern, that unless they will now reverse Caffyn's acts, and admonish his abettors, thus showing that all this seven years' waiting is not mere hypocrisy and deceit; unless, that is, they will do him justice, he will himself indict Caffyn and his abettors in the Crown Office, if they think fit to take cognizance of such an offence.

A "Printed Paper,"[1] presented to the Court, summed up the charges against Caffyn as follows :—

> 1stly. That Matthew Caffyn, of Broadbridge near Horsham in Sussex, has contemned the Laws and Prerogative of the King, and threatens to excommunicate those who stand up for them.
>
> 2ndly. That he has excommunicated a "Protestant and Liege Subject of the Realm " for no transgression of any human law.
>
> 3rdly. That his Principles, Tenets, and Government are dangerous to the State, unjust and cruel to individuals.

Further the appellant impeached the above-mentioned members of the High Court, and demanded their removal from it as judges. Then he tore to shreds the pretext, urged by his enemies, that the Court could not redress grievances, concluding with this indignant outburst, "And now possibly with a pitiful Jugling Hypocrite (*sic*), you may exclaim against the thing, viz. : *Superintendency* and *Dependency*, which you owned when I entered my appeal, but now you really pretend the Churches of God are Independent : well, then, what are you a General Assembly for ? Are you nothing but Ropes of Sand, and are you not gross Hypocrites and Juglers not to tell me so before ? " Such a doctrine of Independency will, he points out, dissolve their General Council and set up a King-Pope in every parish.[2] If they declined to do him the promised justice, let them compensate him for all his expenses incurred in consequence of that promise. All the English Anabaptists,[3] he adds, are not to blame. Most of them are Independent, "they meddle not with State Affairs ; they assume not to excommunicate Persons, but upon the same terms as they baptize them, viz., plain text of Scripture for their warrant therein."

---

[1] This Paper has not survived.

[2] A danger not far from our own doors now, in this present year of grace.

[3] He mentions Mr. Plant, Mr. Hicks, Mr. Kiffin.

Magna est veritas et prevalebit! At last Richard Haines's perseverance in a good cause had its result, and the Court, blaming him only for his hard words used of Caffyn, reversed the excommunication, and ordered Caffyn to rescind it, which he promised to do. But R. H., partly in jest and partly in earnest, demands something further. As unjust imprisonment is punishable by a fine of 5s. an hour, so wrongful excommunication, a far worse crime, should be assessed much higher. But he will be merciful and accept 1s., nay even 6d, an hour for the seven years.

It was a great triumph, perhaps a unique one in the annals of Church Government, for a single individual, after so long a contest against so able and influential an opponent as the " Battle-axe of Sussex," supported by a strong party, to have succeeded in asserting his rights. That he did succeed at all must have been due to the justice of his cause, his own ability and determination, and to the fact that his character was one which attached to his side many influential friends and enabled their weight to poise the scale in his favour.

It seems probable that Richard remained a Baptist in spite of the quarrel. Early in the course of the dispute, he tells us his reasons for not deserting the Baptist Profession then, and these reasons were as strong in 1680 as in 1674. His reasons were[1]: " because I know not any other congregation of that persuasion corrupted with any of those errors . . . and forasmuch as I do upon safe and Scripture grounds believe that the way they profess is the way to Grace and Glory, I therefore dare not desert it, but desire to be found persevering therein with Heart and Affection. And that all good people may do the same, is the hearty prayer of him who is a lover of Truth, Righteousness and Peace, and of those who embrace the same."

As Richard filled the post of Churchwarden in Sullington parish in 1673 and in 1683, we may conclude that the sympathy of his fellow-parishioners was with him in his trial. The fact of his burial in Christ Church,[2] Newgate Street, does not prove that he had ceased to be a Baptist at the time of his death. His great opponent Caffyn was buried in the churchyard of Itchingfield, Sussex.

---

[1] *New Lords*, Pref. ad fin., pp. iii, vi.

[2] The Secretary of Christ's Hospital tells me he believes it was a mark of distinction to be buried in that church.

Sullington Church (exterior) with fine yew.

Sullington Church (interior).

Appended Note on Matthew Caffyn.

Caffyn was evidently a man of commanding personality, wielding extraordinary influence among the Baptist churches in the south of England.[1] We learn from other sources that he endured persecution in defence of his faith, and he hints at this when he says that he had always preached submission to authority, and had subscribed to a document in that sense.[2] In another passage he pretends to be afraid that Richard Haines wishes to incite the magistrates and judges of assize against him. His temperament was perfectly imperturbable, for Richard Haines says of him " I think all the World cannot put him into the least show of Passion,[3] and that Machiavel might have been his Pupil in the Arts of Dissimulation. He salutes you as Joab did Abner; with a kiss and all hail my Brother, but at the same time fails not to smite you under the fifth rib."[4]

Various are the misdemeanours attributed to Caffyn : that he acted as eavesdropper, to which Caffyn naïvely replies, that it was only against J. E., an abettor of R. H.[5]; that he told a deliberate lie[6]; that he favoured his friends, even so far as to let off with a mild rebuke a kinswoman who had committed fornication with another member of the congregation,[7] while he showed spite against a friend of Richard's for an old fault confessed and repented of, and received an accusation against Richard Haines from a non-Baptist.[8]

Reference is constantly made to Caffyn's polemics against the Roman Church, though he never attacks its Infallibility[9]; against Bishops, whom he calls usurpers[10]; and " with a high hand against Quakers, charging them with Pride and Self-conceitedness, that they despise Dominions and speak evil of Dignities, and that their look is more Stout than their Fellows."[11] Yet, in spite of all his pious hatred of the Pope and all his doings, Caffyn, by the illegality of

---

[1] *New Lords*, Pref. p. iv.

[2] *Ibid.*, p. 31 ; *A Raging Wave*, pp. 15, 16.

[3] Still his equanimity seems to have been disturbed on one occasion at least · see above, p. 45.

[4] *New Lords*, p. 21.

[5] *Ibid.*, pp. 9, 46.

[6] *Ibid.*, pp. 10, 12.

[7] *Ibid.*, pp. 11, 12.

[8] *Ibid.*, pp. 9, 42.

[9] *Ibid.*, pp. 45, 202. Pref. p. ii.

[10] *Ibid.*, p. 5.

[11] *Ibid.*, p. 26, quoted from Caffyn's book against the Quakers, p. 55.

E

his own acts, his usurpation and arbitrariness, was, with his congregation, within "less than a Sabbath day's journey of Rome."[1] We are not surprised, therefore, to learn that Caffyn approved of auricular confession, and made it essential for absolution before death.[2]

The theory upheld by Caffyn, that a congregation must submit to the pleasure of its "weak brethren" in all cases, lawful and unlawful, Richard Haines pleasantly calls the "Caffinian Error."[3]

Another doctrine of Caffyn's, in which Richard Haines seems disposed to agree with him, was that believers should not marry unbelievers, but Caffyn went further and said that those who did so should be excommunicated, and the union, so far as the believer was concerned, should be regarded as fornication.[4]

But Caffyn also fell into positive heresy.[5] For this and other errors respecting the Trinity and other Scriptural doctrines Caffyn's most intimate friend, Joseph Wright of Maidstone, convinced of the corrupt tendency of his principles, appealed to the Assembly against him.[6] It was a just nemesis on one who had turned against his own friend. "To Caffyn," says the author of the history just quoted, "is to be attributed the introduction of those errors respecting the doctrines of the Trinity and the Person of Christ which have destroyed the glory of the Baptist denomination."[7]

It must have been a bitter thing for Caffyn to reverse his sentence of excommunication. We have no knowledge of how this was done. But no real reconciliation was, we may imagine possible between the two men. An early death cut off Richard Haines in the midst of his work and powers, while Caffyn lived to be 86 years of age. Born in 1628 he died in 1714.

---

[1] *New Lords*, p. 43.　　　　　　　[2] *Ibid.*, p. 44.

[3] *Ibid.*, p. 24. In the present case the "weak brethren" were only offended because Caffyn told them to be so. See *ibid.*, pp. 14, 20, 27.

[4] *Ibid.*, p. 12.　　　　　　　[5] See above, p. 44.

[6] Ivimey's *Hist. of English Baptists*, II, 571.

[7] *Ibid.*, p. 569. The quarrel with R. H. is referred to on p. 572. Cf. also Crosby's *Hist. of English Baptists*, IV, pp. 338, 341.

CHAPTER VI

RICHARD HAINES'S LITERARY STYLE.

"Le style c'est l'homme."—Buffon.

THE LITERARY ASPECT OF RICHARD HAINES'S WORKS.—Our
author makes many apologies for himself as a writer, alleging his
want of skill and education ; more especially does he do this in
the "Epistle Dedicatory" to his first book against Caffyn.
"Since neither Náture nor Education have (*sic*) furnisht me with
those Arts and Accomplishments which I must acknowledge
necessary to all such as expose their writings to the Publick eye :
let me entreat . . . your favourable construction . . .
as often as you find me unskilfull in Language or Methodical
Order; for . . . I have never been exercised in such publick
endeavours."[1] In another place, writing during the same year, he
alludes to his "Unworthiness and Obscure Condition," and to his
treatise as "these mean lines" and " these unpolish'd Papers."[2]
"Though incapable, and not sufficiently qualified to do any considerable Service,"[3] and though he had met with little encouragement,[4] yet he boasted that he had " improved his small Genious
to the utmost."[5]

Caffyn does not hesitate to accuse him of disingenuousness
and mock humility in thus depreciating his works, in that he
employed "a transcriber, a man learned in the law "[6] who (by
R. H.'s own confession, says Caffyn) "supplied· with amendments
his matter when he had not made it true English."[7] Again in his
Introduction to *Enry's Bitterness,* Caffyn asserts that "another
person, whom both Nature and Education had furnish'd with
accomplishments necessary for such public concerns, did frame
his matter into that form and manner of language in which it
now appears." I cannot think there was much in this alleged

---

[1] *New Lords,* Pref. p. vii.
[2] *Prevention of Poverty,* Pref. i, ii, iii.
[3] *Ibid.,* p. 2.
[4] *Ibid.,* Pref. p. iii.
[5] *Proposals,* p. 4.
[6] *A Raging Wave,* p. 22.
[7] I cannot trace this admission in R. H.'s existing books.

assistance.[1] Richard Haines's later works, in which it is not likely
that he received any help, show the same characteristics of style as
his earlier ones. The language in all is racy and rather homely,
proverbs and proverbial expressions are common, and Scriptural
allusions incessant.

Here is a specimen of his homelier style :—" Thus my beloved
Brethren, But his weak Little Children, whilst he is as it were
Singing to you a pleasant Song of Rome's ruin being at hand and
Rocking you into the peaceable sleep of vain Confidence in his
Cradle of pretended Safety, Hath he not all on a Sudden Led you
over this Bridge of Infallibility quite Across Scripture Authority,
and Squat you down in the very Lap of the Great Whore of
Babylon."[2]

He speaks of Caffyn's " groundless, boundless quarrelsome
humour,"[3] his " tyrannick love, or love by antipathy,"[4] and again,
" as for his Wisdome is it not from beneath ? And his Love as
deep as Hell ? Oh rare Love ! "[5]   " In brief, he kills you with pure
kindness, and under pretence of the highest Love, makes you an
example of sober Revenge."[6]   " What an Innocent, a Turtle, to
turn Devouring Eagle ; or a Lamb couchant on a sudden to start
up into a Lion Rampant ! "[7]

Metaphor is frequently used. Prosperity is compared to a
refreshing stream,[8] poverty to the camp of a warlike king[9] ; " his
Proposals are as a Ship without Governour, running a drift among
the raging waves between the highest Rocks, and the shallow
Sands, attended with Storms, Calms, and Cross-winds ; yet laden
with Treasure sufficient to enrich the whole Kingdom."[10]   The
recent discovery of the circulation of the blood supplies a favourite
simile.[11]

The sentences occasionally have an epigrammatic form to point
the argument, e.g., " The Industry of one is gratified with the
Contempt of Others " ; " We talk of brave things if Words would

---

[1] At the end of *New Lords* (p. 58) the author says some errors are due to his
absence from the press.

[2] *New Lords*, p. 43.   [3] *Ibid.*, pp. 23, 28.

[4] *Ibid.*, p. 33.   [5] *Ibid.*, p. 34.

[6] *Ibid.*, p. 21.

[7] *Ibid.*, p. 24.   This is the only reference to heraldry.

[8] *Prevention of Poverty*, p. 17.

[9] *Ibid.*, p. 28.

[10] *Model of Government*, p. 7.

[11] *Prevention of Poverty*, p. 3 ; *Proposals*, postscript, p. iv ; *England's Weal*, p. 9.

do the Work "; and again, quoting the cynicism of his opponents—
" Let the Poor beg, starve, steal, and be hang'd and damn'd."[1]

There is a fair sprinkling of unusual words and expressions,
perhaps some that may serve to illustrate the *New English
Dictionary* or the *Dialect Dictionary*. Thus, directions are given
to prevent the " *huzzing* and *sputtering* of cider," or " its *fretting*, if
it be *prick't*," viz., become eager[2]; to teach the poor how to *swingle*
or *hitchel* hemp or flax[3]; to detect the *size, i.e.* the strength, or
proof, of spirit.[4] A statute is mentioned enacting that " on every
Fall of Underwoods so many *Standels, Tellows*, or young Trees
should be left to grow up for Timber."[5]   Ground is spoken of as
being " as warm and *Lue* from the wind as may be."[6]

We find many good, but now obsolete, words and expressions
as "Card" for " Chart," " Vapour" (subst.) for " Brag," "docible "
" outlandish,"[7] " stand in " for "cost"; also some quaint ones, as
" to levy an objection," "midland" for "inland" counties,
" scandle," for "scandalize,"[8] " expenditors," " otherways," " uneasi-
ness " (*i.e.* difficulty), "asquint," "natives of ships," "neighbour "
(adj.), " great belly,"[9] " deputation " (= "allowance ") "less plenty,"
" more plenty," "very plenty," "overture" (=preface), "companies"
(= committees), " arch " coupled with dexterous. A compound
not without merit is "self-ended," used of men whose thought
and wishes end in self. "Pent-house-wise," which also occurs, is
Shaksperian.

Some phrases of a more modern cast also appear, as " competent" distance, "substantial " yeoman, " at a pinch," " on that
very score," " hair-brain'd,"[10] " on a firmer basis."[11]

The grammar, though in the main correct, is not always above
suspicion, *e.g.* in the sentence " for the sake of she that he loveth
best."   A Quakerism appears in " What hast thee to say ? "

Worth noting perhaps are " certainest," " put case," " land kind
for corn,"[12] " wool kindest to be converted," "tollage," " consump-

---

[1] *England's Weal*, p. 9.
[2] *Aphorisms on Cyder*, p. 12.   [3] *Proposals*, p. 7.
[4] *Aphorisms*, p. 13, and Supplement to same.
[5] *Prevention of Poverty*, p. 9.   [6] *Aphorisms*, p. 16.
[7] See Nehemiah xiii, 26.
[8] Shakspere's *Julius Cæsar*.
[9] Shakspere's *Measure for Measure*, II, 1, 100. *New Lords*, p. 12.
[10] Shakspere has "hare-brained."
[11] The strong term "Devilish" is used once, and in one place a blank is left for
a "swear" word to be supplied. See *Appeal to General Assembly*.
[12] *Prevention of Poverty*, p. 7.

tive of," "high country wines," "vast sluce of treasure," and the
curious phrase "we may modestly, though at rovers, guess it."[1]
The expression "cross the great design" is found in Cowley.
Among names of liquors we get *Stum*, a sort of "must," *Mum*, a
decoction of wheat malt, *Frontimack*, old *Hockamore*, and also
Purl Royal, or wormwood. Proverbs and maxims abound such
as :

> One soweth, another reapeth[2] ;
> To make a mountain out of a molehill[3] ;
> Idleness in youth is the seed plot of the hangman's harvest[4] ;
> Much talking, little doing[5] ;
> Crush the cockatrice in its egg [6];
> Zeal without true knowledge is most dangerous[7] ;
> Kissing goes by favour[8] ;
> The case is as broad as long[9] ;
> Like rotten wood in the dark, of more show than substance[10] ;
> Let charity begin at home[11] ;
> Interest governs all people in the world, both good and bad[12] ;
> No good man can possibly be uncharitable[13] ;
> A whetstone, though blunt itself, sharpeneth other things[14] ;
> Most dangerous is it to play with thunderbolts ; and to jest
> with things that are sharp and burning.[15]

Two homely ones are—"to cry for a fairing[16]" and "if the cap
be made of wool, he shall pay the debt,"[17] which the writer calls
"the vulgar proverb." In this connection we may perhaps quote
the fable of the magpie and pigeon : "The Old Fable is significa-
tive of the Mag-Pye teaching the Wood Pigeon to build a Nest ;
to every Direction the other contemptuously cry'd—*This I can do*
and *this I can do*; which at last so incensed the Pye, that she left
her in the midst of her work with the Reprimand—Then do't,
then do't ; and ever since the simple Pigion for want of a little

---

[1] *Prevention of Poverty*, p. 2. Is it an archery term?
[2] *Aphorisms*, Supplement. [3] *New Lords*, p. 5.
[4] *Prevention of Poverty*, p. v. [5] *Ibid.*, vii.
[6] *New Lords*, p. 25. [7] *Ibid.*, p. 22.
[8] *Ibid.*, p. 12. [9] *Ibid.*, pp. 13, 44.
[10] *Ibid.*, p. 55. [11] *Proposals*, postscript, p. xi.
[12] *Model of Government*, p. 5.
[13] *Ibid.*, p. 8 ; *Proposals*, postscript, p. xv.
[14] *Prevention of Poverty*, p. 20. See Hor. Ars Poet., ll. 304, 305.
[15] *New Lords*, p. 53. [16] *Ibid.*, p. 58.
[17] *Ibid*, p. 72.

patience and gratitude is forc'd to be content with a sorry imperfect Lodging for her young ones."[1]

The spelling is throughout erratic. Consonants are frequently doubled, *e.g.* "leggs," "upp," "pattent," "pitty," though the reverse sometimes occurs, *c.g.* "jugler." The letter y is a common substitute for i, as in "joyn," "dayly." Incorrect plurals are found, as in "boyes," "girles," but "moneys" is spelt rightly. The letters i and e are constantly confused, *c.g.*, in "diserve," "destinguish," "devel," and "divel"; and we meet with the older t for c, in "physitian," "vitiousness," etc. We naturally find "thred" (but also "thread"), welth, neer (but meak) supream, enow, neighbor (but neighbour too), "pallet" for "palate," "oar" for "ore." "Allege" appears as "alleadge" and "allegdg," and we have "priviledg." Both "queries" and "quaeries," "permote" and "promote," "phlegmatic" and "flegmatic" are found, and all three forms "murther," "muther," "murder."

Perhaps the unknown transcriber is responsible for some of the variations. The spelling is on the whole respectable enough for the time, and seems to show that Richard had some grammar school education. He may have gone to Steyning Grammar School, but the records there do not go back so far. The only allusions to schools in our author are where he expresses a preference for Public Schools[2] and Universities over private schools and tutors, and where he alludes to the ill effects of long sitting on growing boys.[3]

KNOWLEDGE OF HISTORY.—He had, as we have seen, a considerable knowledge of Papal and Italian history, and he quotes one remark from Bacon, that " to make even wishes that are not absurd deserves commendation."[4] One reference there is to early English History, where he says that Edgar, King of England, took "greater delight in his shipping, than any Recreation whatsoever . . . and therefore once every year he would sail round his kingdom with a navy of stout ships, consisting of 4000 sail, which (saith the Historian) we find upon Record "; while of Henry VII he says "tho' justly numbered amongst the wisest Monarchs of that age, his Incredulity is reported by some Authors to have cost him the Immense loss of the West Indian Treasures . . . And even Ferdinand of Castile was beholding to the Importunities of

---

[1] *Aphorisms*, p. 2.
[2] *Provision for the Poor*, p. v.
[3] *Proposals*, postscript, p. xii.
[4] *Prevention of Poverty*, p. 21.
[5] *Ibid.*, p. 11.

the Lady Isabella, for accepting the Discovery of this New World from a despised Columbus."[1]

There is no evidence that Richard Haines had ever read Shakspere, or, what is more surprising, Milton, or what is most surprising of all, Bunyan, who was a Baptist like himself. There is no reference to Cromwell, but the words, "I love the word Reformation well, but the thing better,"[2] seems to me an echo of some expression in one of Cromwell's speeches.

[1] *Aphorisms,* Introduction.   [2] *Appeal to Assembly.*

CHAPTER VII.

RICHARD HAINES AS SOCIAL AND POLITICAL ECONOMIST.

THERE is no doubt that Richard Haines spent a great deal of time and money (in fact he seriously impoverished himself by it) in publishing his books, and perhaps in taking out his patents,[1] the most promising of which he did not live to exploit. As has been seen, he met with much opposition and discouragement. This is how he speaks of it, " I know whoever will attempt anything for publick Benefit, may expect these Three things (the first is necessary, the second Customary, and the third Diabolical), viz. To be the Object of wise mens Censure, other mens Laughter, and if advantagious to himself, Envies implacable displeasure; of which last, I have had share to the highest degree that Revenge could express; and this too from a pretended loving Brother, a person of an honest Profession, and of as debauched a Conscience ; yet I say, notwithstanding such discouragements, I have spent some time for Publick Advantage."[2]

THE PREVENTION OF POVERTY.—In the same year in which he was engaged on his book *New Lords, New Laws*, Richard brought out his first book on matters of public interest, entitled *The Prevention of Poverty*. His object was partly economical and partly social. He wished to deal with the question of the poor, and to improve trade. That his political economy was at fault in several particulars is not surprising, but no one who reads his pamphlets can doubt that he was actuated by the sincerest patriotism and religious feeling.[3] The title of this, his first book of the kind, was as follows :

The Prevention of Poverty : or, A Discourse of the *Causes* of the Decay of Trade, *Fall of Lands*, and *Want* of Money throughout the Nation ; with certain *Expedients* for remedying the same, and bringing this kingdom to an eminent degree of Riches and Prosperity : By Saving many Hundred Thousand Pounds yearly, Raising a full Trade, and Constant Imployment

[1] Caffyn says that his first patent did not bring him in anything to speak of.
[2] *Proposals*, etc., p. 4; *Aphorisms*, p. 2.
[3] See *Prevention of Poverty*, p. 21.

for all sorts of People, and increasing His Majesties *Revenue*, by a Method noway burthensome, but advantagious to the Subject.

This shows that Richard Haines's attention was first turned to the question of the balance of trade, the fall of lands in the country, and the want of money. He describes the general poverty (1674) thus: "A General Poverty seems to have invaded the whole Nation, *Leases being continually thrown up in the Countrey, and Tradesmen daily Breaking in the City.* In brief, all conditions of men seem to have chang'd their stations, and sunk below themselves; the Gentry, by reason of the *fall* of *their Lands* and *uncertainty* of *Rents*, being brought to live at the rate of a Yeoman; the Yeoman can scarce maintain himself so well as an ordinary Farmer heretofore; the Farmer is forced to live as hard as a poor Labourer anciently; and Labourers generally, if they have families, are ready to run a begging."[1]

He first deals with the causes of this poverty and their suggested remedies. The causes he takes to be the increase of imports and decrease of exports. Among the former are French wines, brandy, linen cloth, iron, timber, mum, coffee, chocolate, suet, and saltpetre,[2] all of them except the first and third being imported within the last forty years. The total value of these (at a guess) he puts at two or three millions. On the other hand English manufactures, especially woollen cloth and iron, had decreased. Much bullion was consequently lost to the nation by going beyond the seas, and a general impoverishment was the result. Some attributed this to the great taxes and imports levied at this time.[3] In combating this objection our author enunciates the economic fallacy, that the taxes paid to the King merely caused money to circulate, none being hoarded by the King, or sent beyond seas.[4] The real cause he says is our bad husbandry and bad economy. The only remedies are, to make new manufactures for English goods, which may employ the idle lands in other ways than for corn and cattle; and to prohibit imports that are superfluous as linen cloth, or injurious, as brandy. English ground can grow enough flax and hemp for the whole nation, and not only so but the result of their cultivation will be to raise the value of land from 20s. to 40s. or even 50s. an acre per annum.[5] All idle

[1] *Prevention of Poverty*, p. 1, 1674.
[2] *Ibid.*, p. 2. Mum was made of wheat malt.   [3] *Ibid.*, p. 3.
[4] What about Charles's subsidies to the French King?
[5] *Prevention of Poverty*, p. 5.

hands,[1] that now only find work in harvest time will be employed all the year round, while the tramps and vagrants that infest the country will disappear.[2]   The many hundred thousand pounds now paid for imported linen would be saved to the Kingdom. Sails and cordage, too, which we buy from abroad, we could make for ourselves of home-grown hemp. Nor would this restrict the area for corn on the whole, but rather secure an advantageous rotation of crops, beneficial alike to corn and cattle.

Other imports are described as absolutely pernicious, such as the "*growing trade* of that *outlandish, robbing,* and (by reason of its abuse) *Man-killing Liquor*, called BRANDY."[3]   If any such spirits are necessary ("for Seamen or the like"), they can be made at home.[4] Under this head the nation would save £300,000. Baysalt again could be procured from our own waste lands by the sea and this would result in a saving of £50,000 yearly.[5]

Again iron most certainly need not be imported, as it is to the amount of several hundred thousand pounds a year.[6]   Here Richard Haines forgets not to quote the objection of the political economist, that it is true husbandry to buy in the cheapest market. Yes, says our author, but though it would cost us more at first to make our own cloth, it would soon be otherwise, and besides it is better to give £20 for something of one's own growth[7] than £15 for the same sort of article from beyond the sea, because, in the first place, our idle hands are employed in the manufacture, and in the second place there is more money in the country. The second argument is unsound; and the political economist

---

[1] Estimated at 580,000 in the whole country. Writing in 1678 he puts the number of *beggars* at 100,000 or 200,000, and in another place mentions 30,000 or 40,000 as yearly bred up to beggary. *Provision for the Poor*, p. v ; *Breviat of Proposals*, p. 1 ; *England's Weal*, p. 2.

[2] He complains that the laws against them were not put into force, owing to remissness of officers, a fear of retaliation by arson, etc.; and he mentions a scene at Chichester Assizes (at which he was present), where they filled the court while Lord Twisden was giving his charge and elicited some severe remarks from that judge (1673). *Prevention of Poverty*, p. 6.

[3] *Ibid.*, p. 8.   [4] He is thinking of his cyder-royal.

[5] *Ibid.*, p. 22. He includes saltpetre in this estimate.   [6] *Ibid.*, £400,000.

[7] This is not recognised sufficiently by the Freetrader. There is an amusing and instructive story of a Spanish Deputation to the Spanish Home Secretary, or Chancellor of Exchequer, praying him to lay a heavier tax on foreign cloth. The official in question, enslaved to the fetish of Free Trade, pointed out that they could get the cloth so much cheaper and better made from abroad. The answer was complete and crushing. "So could we get a cheaper and better Minister from abroad."

rightly objects that it is goods not money which pays for commodities,[1] that consequently a large import trade implies a good export trade.[2] In answer to this Richard Haines can only say that forty or fifty years ago, when imports were much less, we had more to export and trade was better. Our chief imports then were silver and gold, commodities we cannot produce at home. Now it is essential for us to produce more commodities for export, or we shall be drained more and more of our money. By prohibiting the above-mentioned imports, therefore, we shall benefit ourselves every way.

But, on the other hand, certain things should be prohibited from being exported, e.g., fuller's earth and wool,[3] the conversion of which latter into cloth would employ great numbers of people. Here we hold an impregnable position, for woollen cloth cannot be made without fuller's earth, and this is only found in England.

Then French wines should be more heavily taxed. If necessary, wine can be produced in England,[4] and even if not, our own home liquors can take their place,[5] and the nation will save £1,000,000 at least. The diminution in customs would soon be made up by the general improvement of trade, due to these measures.

Then follows a complete fallacy. By debasing the coinage one-quarter of its value, the country, says Richard Haines, might gain four millions. But, as we see from another passage, he holds that money is principally intended for the convenience of traffic between persons of the same nation only.[6] He fails to see, therefore, that by his own showing money is not wealth at all, but a means of barter. One great advantage in debasing the coinage, he believes, will be that we shall keep our money at home, as foreigners will not take it at our valuation. Hitherto, and some considered it an honour to the country, they had preferred English

---

[1] Our author in another place recognizes that industry, not money, is the life of a trade. *England's Weal*, p. 6.

[2] *Prevention of Poverty*, p. 12.

[3] *Ibid.*, p. 13.

[4] The Marquess of Bute makes a large sum by his Welsh vineyards in favourable years at this day: in spite of a Mr. Lynn, who, in *Notes and Queries*, makes the absurd statement that wine cannot be now made in England because the Summer is one or two days shorter than it was thousands of years ago.

[5] *Prevention of Poverty*, pp. 14, 18.

[6] *Ibid.*, p. 19.

gold to their own, as being heavier in weight.[1] Our money being refused, our commodities would get a sale, as foreign nations would have to take them in exchange for their own. If France refuse to give her wines in return for our beer and our leathern shoes, then we must fall back on our home-brewed liquors. By making all the fiscal changes suggested England would save yearly two and a quarter millions sterling.

The book was shortly, but favourably, noticed in the *Philosophical Transactions of the Royal Society.*[2]

THE SCHEME FOR BUILDING ALMSHOUSES.—There is no mention, so far, of any scheme for building almshouses. We may, therefore, presume that Richard Haines had not yet gone abroad and seen the system of working these in Holland. Though he has perceived the necessity of encouraging home manufactures, he had not yet formulated any scheme for effecting this, nor immediately connected it with the relief of poverty and the abolition of vagrancy.

His next tract, three years later, entitled, *Proposals for Building in every County a Working Alms-House or Hospital as the best Expedient to perfect the Trade and Manufactory of Linnen-Cloth,* takes up the question in a more systematic way. This new scheme was no visionary one. It had been, and was being, successfully worked in Holland, and Richard had evidently been impressed by what he had seen there.

EXAMPLE OF THE NETHERLANDS.—More than thirty years before this John Evelyn[3] in his *Diary* had spoken in the highest terms of the Spin-houses, Rasp-houses,[4] and Hospitals of Amsterdam. He says the Spin-house "was a kind of Bridewell, where incorrigible and lewd women were kept in discipline and labour, but all neat."[5] The Rasp-house was where the "lusty knaves were compelled to work, and the rasping of brasil and logwood for the dyers is very hard labour."[6] The hospital was for lame and decrepit soldiers, and, Evelyn adds, for State order and accommodation it was one of the worthiest things that the world could show of that nature.

---

[1] *Prevention of Poverty*, p. 18. So it is still. *Ibid.*, p. 16, we are told that "Guinny Gold" was light, and that an old groat hadn't 2*d.* worth of silver in it.

[2] IX, 252, 22 February, 1674-5.

[3] Richard Haines must, we would think, have had some acquaintanceship with the author of *Sylva.*

[4] Only in Amsterdam. The Spin-houses were in every city. See *Provision for Poor*, p. viii.

[5] *Diary,* I, p. 22 (1641).　　　　　[6] *Ibid.*, p. 23.

" Indeed it is most remarkable what provision has been made and maintained for publick and charitable purposes and to protect the poor from misery and the Country from beggars."[1]

Richard Haines was therefore justified in saying that his proposal was " undoubtedly practicable,—for that it is no New Project, but with great success practised at this day by our Neighbours."[2] " To say that the English are less trusty is too gross an affront to put upon our Country."[3]   Why should these houses fail ?[4]   In Holland none of them fail.   Not a beggar is suffered or bred up in those countries where such houses are erected and well governed.[5] " It is judged," he says in another place, " that to one Pickpocket, Cutpurse, etc., in Amsterdam, there are 100 in London ; and to one sturdy Beggar in Holland (in time of peace) there are 400 in England."[6]

TRADE COMPETITION.—In the present importance to this country of the question of trade competition it will not be without interest to hear what our author had to say on the subject 200 years ago : " But were it so, that we were upon equal terms with the Dutch in respect of Industry, it is easie to be demonstrated that England would excell all Nations in the World in that Trade, which is the only Mother and Nurse to bring forth, and encrease Riches, Seamen, and Navies of Ships, etc., as appears, if we consider that the United Netherlands, notwithstanding their Provisions for Bread, Beer, Flesh, Clothing, Timber, Iron, materials for Manufactures, etc., together with their vast expence to maintain their Land against the Water, etc.   All which costs them (as 'tis adjudged) at least ten times more than the Natural Product of their Land is worth ; yet we know that for Trade, Fulness of People, Moneys, Treasure, Seamen and Shipping, they are more famous than any Nation in Europe."[7]

OBJECTS OF HIS SCHEME.—The objects which Richard Haines had in view were : to maintain the poor ; promote the linen manufacture[8] ; reform beggars, vagrants, etc.   But he anticipated the subsidiary advantages of keeping our money at home, and an improvement in value of land and in trade.   He claims, as his

---

[1] Evelyn, *Diary*, I, 401. Addenda.

[2] *Breviat of Proposals*, pp. 5, 6.

[3] *England's Weal*, p. 9.   [4] *Method of Government*, p. 8.

[5] *England's Weal*, p. 1.   [6] *Provision for Poor*, p. viii.

[7] *England's Weal*, pp. 5, 6.   Holland was the Common " Spicery " of the Northern nations.   *Prevention of Poverty*, p. 14.

[8] This matter was under debate in Parliament (1677).

only motive in making his proposals, a patriotic desire to serve the King and his country.[1]

The above-mentioned desirable results[2] were to be obtained by building in every county public working almshouses for the housing, feeding and education of (a) Children from five or six years old, at present supported by the parish; (b) partial cripples; (c) all unmarried chargeable persons and vagrants, who were to be educated " in all good manners towards God and man," and kept there till they could earn their own living.   Among prospective inmates were afterwards included debtors and even such felons as were convicted of perjury and forgery.

MANUFACTURE OF LINEN CLOTH.—The work in these houses was to be the manufacture of linen cloth.[3] It is estimated that sufficient linen cloth (except of the finest sort) could be made in them to supply the whole nation to the value of £1,350,000 yearly.[4] There being 52 counties, if one working almshouse were established in each with 2,000 spinners apiece on an average, the cloth daily spun would be worth £5,200.[5]

With a view to facilitating the process of spinning, Richard Haines invented an engine, whereby one person could turn 50 wheels for 100 spinners, leaving the hands free to draw the tire from the distaff.

The inventor describes his contrivance as " an Expedient both for ease and quick Dispatch, so as that the weak may do as much as the strong, and the strong much more than before."[6]   The engine did not prevent one spinner stopping while the others went on.[7]

PATENT FOR SPINNING ENGINE.—The patent for this invention was taken out 18 April, 1678, in the names of Richard Dereham and Richard Haines, Esqrs., as the inventors of "a new spinning engine never used in England, whereby from 6 to 100 Spinners and upwards may be employed by one or two persons to spin linen and worsted thread with such ease and advantage that a child of

---

[1] *Prevention of Poverty*, p. 20.

[2] *Proposals*, p. 1; *Prevention of Poverty*, p. iii, etc.

[3] *Proposals*, p. 1. This was the first suggestion. Wool was afterwards substituted for linen.

[4] For ¾ lb. of thread at 12d. per lb., makes 1 ell of cloth at 2s. per ell, and 2 spinners can spin ¼ lb. of thread in one day. Thus 2,000 spinners will spin in one day 1,000 ells of cloth = £100.

[5] *Proposals*, p. 3.

[6] *Ibid.*, p. 4, postscript, p. xi.   See also *Bread for the Poor*, by Philo-Anglicus, p. 5. Brit. Mus., 1027, l. 16.

[7] *Proposals*, p. 6.

five or foure yeares of age may doe as much as a child of seaven or eight yeares old, and others as much in two dayes as without this their invention they can in three dayes."[1]

The inventor, though naturally hoping that he may receive some benefit from his idea, yet wishes it in any case to be reserved for use in the public Almshouses only. Besides the spinning engine he mentions a hemp-mill invented by himself, "by which 50 men without striking a stroke may beat as much hemp in one day as 100 shall do in two days."[2] He computes that his inventions will save the country £164,000 in spinning alone.[3]

COST OF ALMSHOUSES.—The cost of the Houses would have to be met by a county rate, which would be very soon covered by the improved value of land.[4] Besides, the poor rate, which averaged 12d. in the pound, would be much lessened.

In the 52 counties there are reckoned to be 9,725 parishes. Taking each parish to be worth £1,500, the poor rate brings in £14,000 or so in each county. This will amply provide for the building of the houses, which in size will be proportionate to the wealth and numbers of the parish.

Big houses will succeed better than small ones because they can be governed better, and the education of the inmates can be better organised. The hard work of turning wheels, fitting tire to the distaff, reeling yarn, swingling and hitchling hemp, could be done by convicts—better so than transport them—but they would have to be separated by a grating from the others.

It is easy to pick holes in this scheme, but we must remember that a very similar system was being most successfully worked in Holland. Had the idea been taken up enthusiastically, it might well have proved a satisfactory settlement of the Poor Question, and been an incalculable boon for England.

In a supplement, or postscript, to the above proposals, Richard Haines brings forward some additional arguments for the scheme. Even if the engines fail to answer expectations, and money for the

---

[1] Patent Office, No. 202.

[2] *Proposals*, pp. 4, 10, 11.   [3] *Ibid.*, p. 5.

[4] *Ibid.*, postscript, p. ii. Hemp could be grown on any indifferent good land, *e.g.* in Sussex, between the downs and the sea, while many thousands of acres in the Weald (spelt Wild) would suit flax. The crop would be worth in either case £4 to £6 an acre. *Ibid.*, p. 9. A crop of flax from one acre spun into good cloth is valued at £50. Land will rise from £100 to £122 10s. in value. *Ibid.*, postscript, pp. vi, vii.

maintenance of the Houses has to be found, every £100 in each county could easily contribute 26s. a year, which is little to take out of the increased profit of lands.

English flax is as good as East Country flax, though perhaps inferior to Dutch flax, but the market for ordinary and coarse cloth is much greater than for the fine ; and English workmen are surely as good as foreigners.   Mr. Thomas Firmin,[1] citizen of London, has afforded a practical proof of this in his weaving and spinning establishments, where a child of five or six years old, in good health and of a moderate intelligence, can be taught in six weeks to earn its living by spinning.   "This judicious person," says Richard Haines, " shew'd me more than £500 worth of very good substantial cloth of his own working."

ADVANTAGES OF THIS SCHEME.—The author thus sums up the advantages of his project: "What with the Decrease of Poor People, The happy Reformation, and total Restriction of Beggars, Vagrants, Nurses of Debauchery, etc., The Yearly increase of Ten or Twelve Hundred Thousand Pounds, which now will be kept at home, that before went beyond the Seas for Linnen ; the great Improvement of Lands ; the Exportation of Linnen of our own growth, etc., The Worth and Advantage of the whole cannot amount to less than Two or Three Millions Sterling per annum to the Nation : and over and above many lives preserved and (with God's blessing on the means) many souls saved ; which if so, certainly it will be the best Bargain and happiest that ever the Nation made, all circumstances considered."[2]

Soon after[3] the "*Proposals*," came out a single sheet on the same subject, entitled, *Provision for the Poor, or Reasons for The Erecting of a Working Hospital for every County As the most necessary and onely Effectual Expedient to promote the Linnen Manufactory with Comfortable Maintainance for all Poor and Distressed people in Citie and Country.   By which all Beggars, Vagrants, etc., throughout the Nation may speedily be Restrained, and for ever Prevented In*

---

[1] Spelt Virmin. *Proposals*, postscript, p. ix.   He employed 600 spinners abroad. A book by Thomas Firmin, called *Some Proposals for the Employment of the Poor*, mentions a Work-House set up in Little Britain for the employment of the poor in linen manufacture (1676–1682).   His nephew, Mr. James, was his partner, and their business was conducted at Garraway's Coffee House.   At his native city. Ipswich, he established a linen manufactory for French refugees.   He was a Unitarian.   He died in 1697, aged 66.

[2] *Proposals*, postscript, p. xvi.

[3] *I.e.*, in 1678.

F

Pursuance to Certain Proposals to the King and Parliament—with allowance.

He sums up the great design again, thus : " The ends aimed at are :—1. The more speedy and profitable promoting the Linen Manufactory.   2. The easing all oppressed Parishes of the Charge of the Poor.[1]   3. The most effectual Expedient to Restrain, Reform, and employ all Beggars, Vagrants, etc., and render them serviceable to the Publick.   4. The good Education of Poor Children and others in religious and virtuous Principles, planting in them Habits of Industry, Labour, etc."

The Houses, he adds, will take no longer than two years at most to erect.[2]

FURTHER EXPLANATION OF SCHEME.—Later in the same year was brought out *A Model of Government for the good of the Poor and The Wealth of the Nation with such a Method and Inspection That Frauds, Corruptions in Officers, Abuses to the Poor, Ill Administration of Materials, etc., therein may be prevented.   The Stock raised and preserved, All poor People and their Children for ever comfortably Provided for, all Idle hands Employed, all Oppressed Parishes eased, all Beggars and Vagrants for the future restrain'd, poor Prisoners for Debt relieved, and Malefactors Reclaimed ; to their own Comfort, God's Glory and the Kingdom's Wealth and Honour.   Humbly offered to the Consideration of the Great Wisdom of the Nation, viz., His most excellent Majesty and both Houses of Parliament.*   This tract was written to reassure those who required a guarantee that the money would be well spent, the poor properly looked after, suitable persons put in authority, and justice administered.   The method of government suggested, which was in the self-interest of all concerned, was to be as follows :

All contributing parishioners, meeting quarterly, were to elect[3] representatives or delegates to inspect the Houses, who were to receive while on business 2s. 6d. an hour if on horseback, 1s. an hour if on foot, for a week at a time.   The delegates to be of equal authority and plenary power, sworn, and accountable to the parish, with new chairmen chosen daily ; drunkards, gamesters, swearers, and persons guilty of bribery to be ineligible ; some of

---

[1] *Provision for Poor*, p. iv, where he deplores the unthriftiness of the poor.

[2] *Ibid.*, p. viii, *ad fin.*   During building the contributions of each parish would be paid fortnightly or monthly.   Overseers from each parish would watch the building.   *Model of Government*, pp. 4, 5.

[3] A neglect of this to be fined £5.   *Method of Government*, p. 3.

the inferior offices to be reserved for deserving inmates; in case of
disputes between parishes and overseers,[1] or between overseers
and the trustees of each House, an appeal to lie to the Justices,
and a regular account of moneys to be rendered to them at the
Easter sitting, to whom also the poor generally should have
right of appeal.

Over each House was to be set a " Godly Minister of a good
kind disposition and exemplary conversation,"[2] and all children
in each House were to be taught English one hour a day.

The workers in the Houses could earn 18*d.* a day for every
man and 9*d.* for every woman, while cripples and children, instead
of costing the parish 1*s.* 6*d.* to 2*s.* a week, will earn up to 9*d.* a day.

In 1679 a fresh presentment of the same case was offered to
the public under the slightly different title of "*A Method of
Government for such Publick Working Alms-Houses as may be
Erected in every County for bringing all idle hands to Industry
as The best known Expedient for restoring and advancing the Woollen
Manufacture. Humbly Offered to the King's Most Excellent Majesty
and both Houses of Parliament, with allowance.*"

Here there is a suggestive change; "Wool" is substituted for
"Linen," as the material to be worked up in the Houses.

In the same year a further statement of the same arguments
appeared under the title of *A Breviat of Some Proposals Prepared
to be Offered to the Great Wisdom of the Nation, The* KING'S MOST
EXCELLENT MAJESTY *and Both Houses of* PARLIAMENT, *For the speedy
Reforming the Woollen Manufacture, By a Method practised in other
Nations. Already Perused and Approved by those known Promoters
of England's Weal and Safety, The Most Illustrious* PRINCE RUPERT,
and the Right Honourable, the EARL OF SHAFTESBURY, *And since
Heard and Encouraged by divers Members of the House of Commons, who upon Perusal was* (sic) *pleased to Declare, That the
same would be of great Advantage to the Nation. Desiring the
Author to give his Attendance to the House when they are at
leisure; and in the mean time to Publish this Brief Account
thereof, for General Information.*

Thus all the wool produced in the United Kingdom would be
worked up by ourselves, and £4,000,000 worth of cloth might
be made by the 200,000 persons engaged in the manufacture.[3]

---

[1] *Method of Government*, p. 5.   [2] *Ibid.*, p. 6.
[3] Wool at 12*d.* per lb. = £12 per pack, and cloth = 4 times unwrought wool in
value.

England enjoys two great advantages in this matter.   First, English wool is necessary for mixing with other wools to make cloth, and secondly, no good cloth can be made without fuller's earth, of which England has a monopoly.[1]   Why not, as the Swedes with their iron, first undersell competitors, and then, when they have given up their manufactories, raise the price of the commodity to a profitable price ?[2]

The clothiers should be forced to set themselves up near the Houses and put themselves into touch with them by threatening them, if they demur, with a repeal of the embargo on the wool export.

Eighteen months or two years later, Richard Haines made a fresh effort to get his scheme carried in Parliament.   He recapitulated his arguments in a last tract called ENGLAND'S WEAL AND PROS-PERITY PROPOSED AS REASONS for Erecting PUBLICK WORK-HOUSES in every County. . . . Humbly offered to the Consideration of the Great Wisdom of the Nation, and presented to the Honourable HOUSE of COMMONS. . . . To which is added *A Model of Govern-ment for such Work Houses prepared by the same Author and Printed in the year* (79) *intended to have presented to the last Parliament.   Pursuant to a Breviat of Proposals for the promoting of Industry, and speedy restoring the Woollen Manufactory, by him formerly published.*

RECEPTION OF THE SCHEME.—From the above analysis of his pamphlets it will be seen that Richard Haines, not from "any itch of fame," but "from philanthropy," was persistent in his efforts to procure for his proposals the acceptance of Parliament and the nation.   His first tract was dedicated to Prince Rupert, who, after reading it, honoured the "author with his Approvement Advice and Encouragement therein,"[3] and introduced him to the King, who desired him to hand over his proposals to one of his Secretaries.   Mr. Secretary Coventry spoke in its favour at the Council Table, and it passed there without obstruction.[4]   The author then printed his proposals, and they issued from the

---

[1] *Breviat*, p. 2.

[2] *Ibid* , p. 4.   The Swedes not only " forced us to quit our foreign markets, where before we vended very much, but also to desist from making enough for our own use; and then when we had . . . let fall our iron works, they raised their Iron to as high a rate as before."

[3] *Proposals*, postscript, p. i.

[4] *Ibid.*, pp. i, ii; *Model of Government*, p. 8, *ad fin*; *England's Weal*, p. 13.

press immediately after the adjournment of Parliament at Whit-suntide.[1]

They met with the approval of Archbishops, Bishops, and Divines,[2] of M.P.'s,[3] several noble peers, and public-spirited, honourable, and worthy persons.[4] Among these he specially mentions Viscount Brouncker, President of the Royal Society, and the Rev. Dr. Beale, one of His Majesty's chaplains.

Among contemporary writings, the only references to Richard Haines and his proposals, that I have found, are these.

Thomas Firmin, at the end of his tract *Some Proposals for the Employment of the Poor* (*about* 1678–1680), says : " If any desire a further account, of the benefit that will accrue by setting up the Linen Manufacture, there is lately printed by a very worthy gentleman, some proposals concerning this matter, which are worth the perusing, and may be had at the Angel in Cornhill."

In another tract entitled *Bread for the Poor* (or *Observations on certain proposals lately offered to the King's Majesty and both Houses of Parliament*) *by Philo-Anglicus Gent.*, London, 1678, we find (p. 4): " We cannot but observe and applaud a very profitable proposal lately made by one Mr. Richard Hains, a person though to us unknown further than by his worthy labours and that we are informed he is a Sussex gentleman, yet certainly his zeal for promoting things tending to the public good and his industrious genius in the happy dis-covery of them, no less than the pains he takes to divulge them, that being reduced by authority into practise they may accomplish the good ends desired, deserve both public notice and thanks, wherefore, though he has lately printed the same, yet the book not being so generally dispersed as might be wished, we shall recite some parts of it here, for *Omne bonum quo communius eo melius.*"

But there is another tract in the British Museum[5] which bears generous testimony to the worth of Richard Haines's work. It is called " *Proposals for Promoting the Woollen Manufactory Promoted, Further making it appear that the nation will thereby increase in Wealth, at least £5,000 per day for every day in the year on which it is lawful to labour. And that the strength and safety of the king and kingdom, together with a most happy reformation will be*

[1] June, 1677.   [2] *Model of Government*, p. 8.
[3] *Ibid.* and *Breviat*, title page.
[4] *Ibid.* and *Method of Government*, p. 2.
[5] 712, g. 16.

accomplished therein. All which is most plainly demonstrated, By several wellwishers thereunto, inhabitants and citizens of London. Licensed Ap. 29, 1679." On p. 2 we find: "The last Parliament hath almost every session made it a great part of their business to hear and encourage those who had anything to offer for the recovery of this trade; and yet till the late *Breviat of Proposals* published by one Mr. Richard Haines came out, it must be acknowledged That neither the Exporter of Wool, nor opposer of the same, or any others, have offered any certain expedients for bringing all idle hands to industry, whereby the wool may be converted as it grows and arises, on such terms, that the Cloth we have to spare may be exported as fast as 'tis made. . . . Wherefore we cannot think it unreasonable to joyn our suffrages with him and stir up all active spirits to promote and encourage that which will best accomplish this good design." And again on p. 4: "It is the greatest thing of such a kind and easiest to be accomplished that hath been offered to the King and Parliament to promote the Wealth Strength and Safety of the Kingdom since in it the Woollen Manufacture hath been encouraged."[1]

My hopes ran high when I discovered in the additional catalogue of MSS. at the Bodleian Library a MS. labelled "Richard Haines," but it turned out to be an essay *On some Considerations to be proposed to the wisdom of Parliament for an Act to abate the growth of Popery and for the more effectual relief of the poore of the Kingdom, by a native of Stafford.* On p. 3 the author says, mentioning the *Proposals, etc.,* of Richard Haines (1677): "Let him have his spinning engines and devices to breake hempe which are not contemptible for his good meaning and well-timed Contrivance." The only reference to Richard Haines in any modern work that I am acquainted with is in Dr. Cunningham's *English Industry and Commerce.*[2]

Needless to say Richard Haines's proposals met with opposition, some of it from factious, cantankerous people, such as will always oppose new suggestions by others, but some from serious and worthy objectors[3] who urged that neither the quantity of wool to be worked, nor the number of poor to work it, had been ascertained, or denied that English flax was as good as foreign flax, or English artificers as skilful, but this "affront on the English nation" has been

---

[1] Sir Mat. Hale, in a pamphlet, "A discourse touching provision for the poor" (1683), shows signs of having read Richard Haines's tract. *Ashm.,* 1142, 143.

[2] Bk. vii, The Stuarts; Ch. vi, The Poor, p. 202.

[3] *Breviat,* p. 5.

dealt with before.   Others said they must be satisfied that the
Houses would be well governed; others still, less easy to deal with,
were content to reiterate that " the old way was the best,"[1] that the
work would be done better at home, that parents ought to bring
up their own children, that the new scheme would part husband
and wife, and make slaves of the inmates of the Houses.   It was
no idea of personal advancement that induced Richard Haines to
press his proposals.   " The desired End," he says,[2] was the "glory
of God and the Prosperity of the Nation."   His proposals were
intended to be presented to the last Parliament[3] (1679), but for
some reason they were not so presented.   Entrusted to Sir
Patience Ward, Lord Mayor of London, to bring before the
Commons, the question was not brought forward till the very end
of the year 1680.   Our author himself says[4]: "The thing was so
readily approved of that an Order was made for bringing in a Bill
Pursuant to the effect of my proposals, *Nemine Contra-dicente;* which
Bill I at my further Charge, procured to be drawn and prepared ;
And had not the Person whom I first intrusted, and who promised
to read my Petition in the House of Commons, from time to time
delayed so to do, till within a week before the Dissolution of the
Parliament, there is no reason to doubt but it had past into an
Act, and at this day[5] been practised to the Inestimable benefit of
the Nation."   The journals of the House of Commons, 17 December,
1680, have an entry that the petition was read, and leave granted
to bring in a Bill, the matter being referred to a Committee.[6]   The
entry is endorsed, " Ordered not presented."   This Parliament was
prorogued 10 January, 1680–81, and dissolved the 18th of the same
month.

So by bad luck more than anything else failed a scheme which
was well conceived, practicable, ably presented, and received with
favour.   Had it become law, as it so nearly did, it would have
revolutionised our methods of treating the poor.[7]

[1] *Model of Government*, p. 7.
[2] *Proposals*, postscript, p. xvi, ad fin.
[3] See above, p. 28.
[4] *Aphorisms*, p. 3.
[5] Ap. 1684.
[6] See above, p. 29.
[7] Richard Haines points out that these Houses would ensure that no descendant
of those who built them could ever be reduced to absolute beggary.   *Proposals*,
postscript, p. xvi; *Model of Government*, p. 8; *England's Weal*, p. 9.   I am not
aware that any of Richard Haines's numerous descendants have ever begged their
bread.

CHAPTER VIII.

CURRENT AFFAIRS IN CHARLES II's REIGN.

IT may be of interest to students of this period. if we collect here the few references there are in Richard Haines's works to current affairs. Some have been already incidentally dealt with, such as the condition of prisons, in connection with which we are further told of the convict system, that in 1677 "Foreign Plantations had so little occasions for Convicts that Merchants refused to take them off the Sheriffes hands, without being paid for their Passage, so that above 80 convicts in Newgate lately obtained a general Pardon, on that very score, because they knew not what to do with them."[1]

Commenting on the recent failure of Clerkenwell Workhouse, which remained a "gazing stock to discourage all publick spirits,"[2] he gives the true reasons for its miscarriage. Bridewell, again, he affirms must fail because "the Labour there is only a punishment."[3] But Christ's Hospital he holds up as a model to imitate.[4]

Turning now to the Vagrancy Laws, we have an allusion to the custom of passing tramps on from parish to parish by passes,[5] such as are to be found in many parish chests.[6] In this way vagrants pleasantly and profitably made the "grand tour" of the whole country. This system led to law suits between parishes,[7] as to which parish was chargeable for any particular tramp. Richard Haines is quite abreast of our times in strongly depre-cating almsgiving to beggars, and suggests a fine of £5 for the offence. He has no Malthusian heresies, and looks with satisfaction on an increase of the population,[8] if his scheme. for housing and feeding the poor be adopted.

Good servants being difficult to get then, as now, one of the advantages of his Houses would be the training up of good ones.

---

[1] *Proposals*, p 8.
[2] *Method of Government*, p. 7.
[3] *Proposals*, p. 8.
[4] *Model of Government*, p 6.
[5] *Provision for Poor*, p. v.
[6] *E.g.* that of Storrington, Sussex.
[7] *Provision for Poor*, p. v.
[8] *Proposals*, p. 11, postscript, p. x.

A dark picture is given of the poverty of the country in 1674 and the distressful state of England in 1681 is described (in rather vague terms),[1] the allusion being possibly to the persecution of certain religious sects,[2] and partly to a conspiracy against the King. As to Charles II, his want of morality could not but have been distasteful to the strict (though for a time excommunicated) Baptist, still the latter is ready to acknowledge,[3] as also was John Evelyn, the King's readiness to welcome inventors and patronize improvements of all kinds.

As an Englishman[4] and patriot, Richard Haines took a great interest in the Navy. We have seen his allusion to King Edgar, his plea for the planting of hemp to supply cordage for our ships, his emphatic assertion that the safety of the kingdom depends on ships and seamen, and that being dependent on others for timber and iron was a " matter of very pernicious consequence."[5] If the " Houses " prosper shipping will increase ; those who oppose the " Houses," oppose the increase of our navy, and so are enemies to the true wealth, safety and interest of the English nation.[6]

Appendix on the Woollen Trade.

From these pamphlets we glean some interesting facts about this trade in the 7th decade of the 17th century. In his earliest effort (1674) Richard speaks of it as " that Ancient Staple Trade of this Nation, the Making and Exporting of Woollen Cloth,"[7] and mentions in another place that the Englishman had the reputation of being the only excellent artificer for woollen cloth.[8] The woollen manufacture comprised ten-thirteenths of the total manufactures of the kingdom. Though it had greatly decreased[9] during the last forty years[10] (*i.e.*, from 1633), yet in 1681 our author can

[1] *England's Weal*, pp. 10, 11.
[2] From *England's Weal*, pp. 10 f., we see that the question of religion was a burning question in 1681.
[3] *Aphorisms*, p. 3.
[4] One of those Southern English of whom Gladstone spoke so scornfully.
[5] *Prevention of Poverty*, p. 11.
[6] *Method of Government*, p. 8; *Brevial*, p. 4 ; *England's Weal*, p. 5.
[7] *Prevention of Poverty*, p. 15.   [8] *Proposals*, postscript, p. viii.
[9] *Prevention of Poverty*, p. 13; *Proposals*, postscript, p. xiii. He fears that it may be irrecoverable.
[10] *Prevention of Poverty*, p. 3.

still call it the "main support of that Trade which maintains and encreases the Wealth, Strength and Glory of the English Nation."[1]

Statutes were passed for encouraging the home consumption of wool, and the celebrated one for burial in woollen is glanced at by our author, quaintly enough, when he speaks of the "dismal low markets in Golgotha, from whence there are no returns."[2] Wool, which had been 12*d.* a lb., had fallen in 1681 to 8*d.* or even 6*d.*;[3] export of unwrought wool was illegal, and consequently as it could not be converted into cloth fast enough,[4] there was a glut in the market. Yet it seems, from one passage, that during nine months, 1680–1681, so much wool had been exported that the foreign markets for English cloth had been destroyed.[5] Some time previously wool had been made a monopoly in the hands of the clothiers, export being prohibited under the severest penalties.[6]

England, therefore, producing more wool than any other nation,[7] and half this being unconverted by our own clothiers,[8] the rest was either wasted or smuggled abroad, every £100 worth of wool so exported being a loss (in cloth) of £1,000 to us. Wherefore, says Richard, since England alone has fuller's earth and since French and Spanish wool require a mixture of English wool, the French being so short and fine, the Spanish so short and coarse, that they will neither "work together nor yet apart,"[9] let us prohibit altogether the export of fuller's earth and wool, and to get all our wool converted at home, set up these Alms-Houses, where all our English, Scotch[10] and Irish[11] wool can be made into cloth. Thus we shall conquer the competition of France and Flanders[12] and control the supply throughout the world.

---

[1] *England's Weal*, pp. 1, 5. The authors of the tract *Proposals for promoting the Woollen Manufacture Promoted* call it "the golden manufactory," and state that an Act of Parliament has made the exportation of wool a capital offence.

[2] *Ibid.*, pp. 7, 8.   [3] *Ibid.*, pp. 2, 6.

[4] Little more than half was converted. See *Breviat*, p. 5; *England's Weal*, p. 7. Yet in 1631 ten millions worth of woollen draperies was exported. *Ibid.*, p. 3.

[5] *England's Weal*, p. 6. The export was by smuggling.

[6] *Ibid.*, pp. 3, 4.   [7] *Breviat*, p. 4.

[8] Amounting to 100,000 packs worth £12 per pack, when wool was at 12*d.* per lb. *Breviat*, pp. 3, 5; *England's Weal*, p. 6.

[9] *Ibid.*, p. 3, as affirmed by the clothiers before Parliament.

[10] *Method of Government*, p. 2.

[11] *Ibid.* and *England's Weal*, pp. 2, 7.

[12] *England's Weal*, p. 3.

CHAPTER IX.

RICHARD HAINES AS YEOMAN FARMER.

Τὸ τεχνίον, ὃ ἔμαθες, φίλει. M. Aurelius, iv, 31.

FARMING.—Though he busied himself in matters of public interest, and tried to raise himself above his position of yeoman, yet Richard Haines was by birth and training a plain Sussex farmer. He evidently knew his business well, and probably made much more by his farming than by his philanthropic, or inventive, efforts. Caffyn indeed sneered at the small results of his first patent, saying they would not amount to 30d.,[1] and no doubt through the factious opposition made to it the legal expenses he incurred were considerable. We know by Richard Haines's own admission that he had spent divers hundreds of pounds on his public enterprises,[2] no inconsiderable sacrifice from one who confesses that " Money, beneath Grace and Glory and what is conducting thereunto, is most to be desired."[3]

" Painful Husbandry, that ancient Employment,"[4] was what occupied most of Richard Haines's time, and in this connection we must put first his enthusiastic tribute to the fruitfulness of the soil of England, " which by the Industry of its . . . Inhabitants, might so easily become the Garden of Europe."[5] From his practical experience as a farmer we learn many hints, such as, " Clover and Trefoil prepares (sic) the Ground for Wheat, as much as a good crop of Tares or French-Wheat, otherwise called Buck-Wheat, can do."[6] His own familiar chalk lands, and the Weald of Sussex, are spoken of with commendation as suitable for hemp and flax, and interesting statistics are given of the value of such land so sown.[7]

TIMBER.—In these days, when the conservation of existing forests, and the planting of new ones, are matters that engage the attention of Governments, and, as in the case of " Arbor Day " in America, excite the enthusiasm of multitudes, it is not

---

[1] *A Raging Wave*, p. 5.
[2] *Aphorisms*, p. 3.
[3] *Prevention of Poverty*, p. 4.
[4] *Proposals*, p. 10.
[5] *Ibid.*, postscript, p. xvi.
[6] *Prevention of Poverty*, p. 7.
[7] See above, p. 64. *Proposals*, p. 8, and postscript, p. ii.

uninstructive to hear what Richard Haines has to say about the
cultivation of timber.　His remarks are judicious, and again
display his practical common sense and his patriotism.　He
laments the imminent destruction of our supplies of oak timber,
" deservedly accounted the best in the world, and a great Strength
and Ornament to the Kingdom," giving this as the reason,[1]
" because the *only nurse* that maketh the Oak, and other Timber
to flourish is *Under-woods*, and where *Under-woods are not*, there
cannot [be] (or very rarely is) any good timber."　He then
recites the " wholsom Statute," still on the Statute Book but
evaded,[2] " That on Every Fall of Underwoods they should leave
so many Standels, Tellows, or young Trees to grow for Timber ;
which indeed they will do, but then at the next Fall of the same
Wood, *viz.* about nine or ten years after, they will cut those very
Standels . . . left before, (so that they never become Timber) and
then they leave new ones, and this successively whereby the
Intention of the Statute is unworthily defeated."

He denies that ironworks destroy the forests, or on the other
hand cause arable and pasture to be turned into forest land.　The
woodlands in the country, which are still considerable, would, if
properly husbanded and managed, be sufficient for all purposes.[3]

CIDER.—But it is in Richard Haines's treatise on the making of
cider,[4] etc., that we find the most useful hints on the cultivation
of lands.　The treatise was written to explain and set forth his
invention for the making of cider-royal (as he called it) according
to a patent he had taken out.　As early as 1674 his attention[5]
had been turned to the making of home-grown spirits as good and
as strong as foreign wines and brandy.　He quite recognises that
such spirits and wines are beneficial, and even necessary articles,
of human consumption.　They cause appetite and help digestion.
Sack, the praises of which were sung by Falstaff, comes in for due

---

[1] *Prevention of Porerty*, p. 9.

[2] Mr. J. B. Morris, writing to *Notes and Queries* (8th S., 11, 5 November, 1892),
mentions a Statute of Henry VIII (1543) which says " there shall be left standing
and unfelled, for every acre, twelve standels or storers of oak, or in default of so
many, then of elm, ash, asp, or beech."　He also quotes from John Norden, *Surveyor's
Dialogue*, London, 1607, p. 213, a complaint so similar to that of Richard Haines in
the text that I think it possible the latter had Norden's book in his possession.

[3] *Prevention of Poverty*, p. 10.

[4] There is an attempt being made to restore the cider industry to its ancient
prosperity, and Mr. C. W. Radcliffe Cooke, M.P., recently delivered an address on
the subject to the Farmers' Club.

[5] See above, p. 59.

commendation.[1]   Ordinary French wines sold at 12*d.* per quart, canary and champagne at 2*s.*   Beer is little mentioned; the prison price (an extravagant one) is given above as 2*d.* for a little more than a pint.   It is stated that an acre of land will yield half as much again of cider as of beer.[2]

PRICE OF CIDER.—The price of cider varied from 20*s.* per hogshead in some years to 30*s.*, which latter sum represents 1½*d.* a quart[3]; but in 1682 good cider sold in the West of England at 10*s.* per hogshead, or ¼*d.* per quart, and in 1683 it stood at 20*s.* a hogshead.   A quart per diem is considered an average consumption for each person.   If his new cider-royal cost 2*d.* a quart, this would mean £2 a year, or a little more per man.

Richard Haines's last book, though not on such public and important subjects as his others, was evidently written *con amore*, and is perhaps of the most permanent value to us now. This is how he introduces it to the public: *Aphorisms upon The New Way of Improving Cyder, or Making Cyder-Royal lately discovered For the Good of those Kingdoms and Nations That are Beholden to Others, and Pay Dear for Wine Shewing That Simple Cyder, frequently Sold for Thirty Shillings per Hogshead (viz. Three-half-pence a Quart) may be made as Strong, Wholsom, and Pleasing as French wine usually sold for Twelve-pence a Quart; Without Adding anything to it, but what is of the Juice of Apples; and for One Penny or Three-half-pence a Quart more Charge, may be made as good as Canary commonly sold for two Shillings.   As also, how one Acre of Land worth now Twenty Shillings, may be made worth Eight or Ten Pound per Annum To which are Added, Certain Expedients concerning Raising and Planting of Apple-trees, Gooseberry-trees, etc.   With Respect to Cheapness, Expedition, certain growing and Fruitfulness, beyond what hath hitherto been yet made known."*

It is dedicated to " All Kings Princes and States, who have No wines of their own Production," including the " Kings of the two Northern Crowns " and the States General of the United Provinces.   The author's efforts to transmit his suggestions to Poland were frustrated by the "remote distance and small Entercourse from hence thither."[4]

Though wine, our author remarks, *can* be successfully grown in England,[5] yet practically our nearest substitute for wine is the

[1] *Prevention of Poverty*, p. 18.   [2] *Aphorisms*, p. 14.
[3] *Ibid.*, Introduction.   [4] *Ibid.*
[5] See above, p. 60 n., and *Prevention of Poverty*, p. 14.

juice of apples, wildings and pears,[1] and other fruits. But few persons have cultivated the art of making cider, and what is made is crude and unwholesome, compared with wine. This treatise is written to explain a method of making a cider-spirit or cider-wine which shall supersede wine.

PATENT FOR CIDER-ROYAL.—This was taken out 6 February, 1684, in the following terms, that, whereas Richard Haines, of Sullington, co. Sussex, Gent., and partners with considerable charge and pains have found out "an art or method of preparing, improving, and meliorating cyder, perry, and the juice or liquors of wildings, crabbs, cherrys, goosberrys, currants and mulberrys so as to put the strength or goodness of two or three hogsheads of any of the said liquors into one and render the same much more wholsome and delightful . . . being a new invention . . . we having a more especial and favourable regard unto the art and invention aforesaid . . . grante unto the said Richard Haines and partners during the term of 14 years . . . license to practise this art exclusively."

On 22 December, 1684, the *London Gazette* contained an advertisement informing the public that the above patent had been granted to Mr. Richard Haines and partners, and giving notice that the cider could be had at the vaults under Dr. Morton's buildings in Grey Friars in Newgate Street and in Three Crown Court in Southwark, and licences could be taken out at the office in the Marine Coffee House in Birchin Lane, and at the Coffee house in Three Crown Court.

METHOD OF MAKING THE NEW CIDER.—This, which can hardly be called a "mystery," as the patent expresses it, was as follows: "Put the strength of two hogsheads into one; which for to do, put one Hogshead of cyder, and some part of the other, into a Copper-Still, and then put the same into your other Hogs-Head and fill it up, stir it about well, and keep it close-stopt, except one day in Ten or Twenty let it lie open five or six hours."[2] Within three months this will be as strong as the best French wines and as pleasing though different in taste. Additional spirit and more sugar according to pleasure will make this cider like canary, and one pint of good spirit added to a gallon of the cider will make it equal to Spanish wines. So the juice of pears, cherries, mul-

---

[1] *Aphorisms*, p. 5.
[2] *Ibid.*

berries, currants, and especially gooseberries, by the addition of their own spirits[1] can be made equal to canary

WHAT AND HOW TO PLANT.—One acre of land planted with apple trees may bring in £8 worth of cider-royal, though its price be but 2d. a quart. Plant thus: Eight score Red-strakes and Golden Pippins per acre 16 feet apart, which at only 1 bushel per tree will bear 160 bushels per acre. Each hogshead of cider requires 20 bushels of apples, and 8 hogsheads of ordinary cider will make 4 of cider-royal. This at 2d. per quart will make £2 per hogshead.[2]

By planting the trees 20 feet one way and 12 the other you can plough between and plant grass or corn. But gooseberries and currants so planted will be better, and will yield 4 hogsheads of wine-royal, which again at 2d. per quart will give £8 more per acre.

PROFIT ON FRUIT-GROWING.—But apple trees usually bear from 4 to 20 bushels a tree, and so, taking the lower number, we may get 16 hogsheads instead of 4, and this if sold at 3d. (instead of 2d.)[3] a quart will produce £48.

Again, gooseberries and currant trees, as experience teaches,[4] well husbanded one with another, may yield a gallon apiece. As 16 trees will stand on one rod of land, 4 feet apart, one rod will thus produce 2 bushels of fruit. There being 160 rods in an acre, the total yield will be 320 bushels, i.e., 8 hogsheads of wine. This at 3d. per quart is £24, which with the £48 above makes £72 for each acre of land, at present not worth more than 20s. per annum.[5]

QUALITIES OF THE NEW CIDER.—Not only is it stronger and more palatable, but also more wholesome, no longer being cold, sickly, and apt to generate wind. Being the product of our own soil, it must needs suit our constitutions better than outlandish liquors. It can be recommended as an appetizer and tonic, and even excessive indulgence has no harmful effects.[6] A home-brewed article, consumed at home, it will save us half a million pounds yearly.

WINE-ROYAL.—A bushel of good ripe currants[7] makes 6 or 7

---

[1] Brandy and spirits of wine and grain will do, if drawn fine, but not so well. The least suitable are spirits of ale and beer.

[2] Aphorisms, p. 6.

[3] Being as good as wine at 12d. per quart, it must sell for 3d. a quart at least.

[4] Aphorisms, p. 7.   [5] Grain crops brought in £8 per acre.

[6] Aphorisms, pp. 7, 10.

[7] Twenty bushels of currants will make 2 hogsheads of wine. Ibid., p. 11.

gallons of wine. To every bushel of currants add 12 quarts of water. After 12 to 16 hours press and strain and put in a cask till the liquor begins to clear. Then rack off from the gross lee. To each gallon add 1 pint of good spirit, and sugar *ad lib.* Stir well for ¼ hour, and stop close for 3 months. So with other fruits, but gooseberries make the best wine.

COST OF LABOUR.—This may be defrayed by saving the spirits drawn from the apples after they have been pressed for cider.

BEST FRUIT FOR THE PURPOSE.—The Red-Strake, a kind of wilding, is suitable, but the best apple for the table and for cider too is the Golden Pippin, a quick grower and good bearer, yielding the most liquor and the best. The very husks of the latter, even when cider has been made from the fruit, will yield more spirit than others. Nor is it any more difficult to raise good fruit than bad.

It is certain that good wildings and good crabs are better for cider than the most delicious summer or winter table fruit or sweet apples (the Golden Pippin alone excepted). The bitter sharp crab is much better than a bitter sweet apple, because its juice will give twice as much spirit. The sweet and sour tastes are left behind in the earthy phlegmatic part of the cider. The spirit of sour cider will not be sweetened by any amount of sugar. If you fill the still with metheglin (new sweet mead, made of honey, etc.)[1] neither spirits nor sweets will result, but only water, unless you allow it to ferment. So with the juice of fruits, fermentation only will produce spirit, and the sourer the juice, the more spirit will result. Nevertheless, apples of bitter taste make bitter cider.

THE ADDING OF SPIRITS TO CIDER.—The staler the cider, the longer is the time required for the spirits to be incorporated. If added before fermentation, they will evaporate[2] and be cast out. The best time is about a month after the cider has been made and racked two or three times off the lee. Then add the spirits, either with sweets or without, but well beaten together with some cider. When put into the cask, stir well and bung up close. The cider-royal will be ready in 2 or 3 months,[3] but the longer it lies, till quite meliorated, the better. If the season be warm, open the cask occasionally.

STRENGTH OF SPIRIT NECESSARY.—This should be one-third

---

[1] *Aphorisms*, p. 11.   [2] *Ibid.*, p. 12.
[3] Other wines will take 4 or 5 months.

stronger than proof, costing 4s. per gallon, and should be well drawn.[1]

BOTTLING.—Let the cider be very fine, then choose a clear day, wind N. or E. Make sure that the bottles are dry, and don't quite fill them by a wineglassful. Lay the bottles on their sides.[2]

FAULTS OF COMMON CIDER.—Mustiness and "fretting" till the spirits are spent are common faults. Cider will be musty if apples are gathered into the house wet, or if a musty vessel is used. Musty cider will produce musty spirit. Cider will fret if the fruit is gathered before it is ripe, or the cider is made before the apples have lain long enough. The apples must lie in a heap, and sweat, and get dry again, before they are fit for the press. If in spite of care the cider frets, draw it off into another vessel once in a week or ten days, taking the lee from it when rackt. Don't have the vessel full by a gallon, nor stopt close, until it ceases to huzz and sputter. When the cider becomes quiet, fill up and stop close, but open again in 2 or 3 days, and, if the cider is not yet quiet, let the vessel lie open an hour or less at a time. Before putting the cider into the cask, burn a match of brimstone, dipt in coriander seed, in the empty cask.[3]

HOW TO ADD THE SUGAR.—Make it into a syrup by dissolving it in water, one cwt. being sufficient to make 16 gallons, and so proportionately. Boil the water down to a syrup,[4] and when cold add it to the cider. A little coriander seed bruised (in a bag) and put into the mixture while boiling will give it a good scent. Of these sweets put in 2 or 3 gallons per hogshead, but not until the cider has been finally rackt and is past fermenting. Before adding the sweets mix them with the spirits you intend to add and with a like amount of cider. Then stir all with a strong staff in the bunghole for 7 or 8 minutes. Brown sugar raises the colour of the cider, but it is as sweetening as the white and cheaper, being 5d. a quart.

NO WASTE.—Steep the husky part of the apples, which have been pressed for cider, in water for 2 or 3 days, draw the liquor off and allow it to ferment. This with the lees of the cider will give enough spirit, when added to the cider, to make it as strong as French wine.

---

[1] *Aphorisms*, Appendix.   [2] *Ibid. ad fin.*

[3] *Ibid.*, p. 12.

[4] *Ibid.*, p. 13. Directions are given for purifying the sugar by boiling with the whites of eggs, which carry off the scum.

STORAGE.—Put the cider and spirits into a wooden cask; a vessel of 6 gallons requires 2 quarts of sweets, and 3 of spirits of cider. It will keep 2 or 3 years, and be the better for it, but keep the cask full. In 2 months' time the liquor will have wasted a quart or so, which loss must be made good with liquor as strong or stronger.[1]

STALE CIDER REVIVIFIED.—Take a hogshead of tart new cider, before it is quite clear, and mix it with a hogshead of the old in two other vessels, adding sweets and spirits in proportion to your new cider. Do this in October or November, and before Christmas the cider will be as good as any other.

This cider-royal will be cheaper than beer and as good as wine, but the nobility and gentry can still go on drinking their Champagne, Burgundy, and Frontinnack, and their Greek and Florence wines.

PLANTING OF NURSERIES AND ORCHARDS.[2]—Appended to the treatise on the making of cider is a series of practical rules for raising nurseries for orchards. These are as efficacious now as they were then, and as fruit trees vary much in their growth and productiveness, many growers may find these hints useful.

PLANT SHALLOW.—The upper root must not be more than 1 or 2 inches under ground, the deepest not more than 8 or 10 inches. Clear away all suckers and superfluous branches near the root. *No downright root must be left.*

STOCK OR KERNEL.[3]—Select these from thriving crabs with clear body and great spreading boughs. As the head is full of branches and twigs, so proportionally does the stem abound with roots and fibres; and as the tree, so will be the product. Trees so raised are worth 1s. each, while others not so chosen are not worth 1d. From such kernels can be raised trees that, in 10 or 12 years after the kernel is put into the ground, will produce a bushel a tree.

PLANTING OF KERNELS.—As soon as these are taken out of the crabs, put them (in autumn or, if frost prevents, as soon as possible) in the ground. If they have to be kept through the winter without planting them, put them in a mixture of dry sand within doors. As soon after January as the season permits, plant them about 1 inch deep in ordinary good ground with a warm aspect, and keep them weeded.

---

[1] *Aphorisms*, p. 14.   [2] *Ibid.*, p. 15.
[3] *Ibid.*, p. 16.

TRANSPLANTING.—In 12 months draw out the most thriving, and transplant into a well-dug and dunged nursery, in rows 2 feet apart and 9 inches from one another. *Cut off all downright roots*, spread out the small roots, and close up the ground round them. Next spring repeat the process with the next most thriving plants, and so on.

THE NURSERY.—Next autumn dig round the plants (before the leaf is off), and let the roots spread; but this digging between them must be done only this once a year. By digging when the leaf is on, you ensure the shooting again of any root accidentally cut off.

TWO YEAR OLD PLANTS.—After two summers' growth, the next winter, near spring, cut off the tops of the plants a foot above ground, and, the next March or April after, the biggest will be fit for grafting.

PLANTING OUT.—Then transplant into orchards. Don't set too deep. Dig holes 4 feet square, 1 spit deep, which is as deep as the roots should lie. Away with all trees that have a down-right root like a parsnip. They are only fit to burn. These come from apple kernels, and such as have not been transplanted, of which scarce one in a hundred is otherwise, but from crab kernels treated as above, scarce one in 400 is bad.

LABOUR.—One man's labour upon one acre of land, may, after 3 or 4 years, raise 10,000 trees a year, which at 3*d.* a tree comes to £125. Each acre will contain 120 trees, costing 30*s.* The planting will take 1*s.* 6*d.* per score, and so the whole cost per acre is less than 40*s.*

ORCHARDS.—Keep these weeded and the trees free from suckers. Protect from coneys, cattle, etc. At the corners of each four-foot hole for the tree, you may plant 4 currant or gooseberry bushes; but these require more dung than the apple trees. Mix the earth and dung before planting the trees.

SOIL.—All ordinary good land suits apple trees, but not hot and dry sand, nor wet and cold land. Gooseberries like a sunnier situation than currants.

LAYERING GOOSEBERRY AND CURRANT BUSHES.—About the end of February, or beginning of March, lay down every limb flat with the ground and cover every twig with good earth, turning out the tops so as to be above ground. Every twig will root and shoot out. Keep the uncovered stock free from branches.

Such are the main directions contained in the above treatise.

The book brought the author numerous letters of inquiry " from many persons of this kingdom purporting several questions" relative to the making of cider.   To these Richard Haines gives answers in the Appendix to the work, published shortly after the book itself.   Somebody had asked about the strength of the spirit required, and we have the following test given.

PROOF SPIRIT.—" There is a certain degree of size or strength which is called Proof, being the Standard between the Distiller of Spirits and those they sell them unto, which Proof is this: Put 8 or 10 spoonfulls into a glass viol (not above half full) and give it a sudden jogg ; then observe, if upon that sudden jogg a cap of bubbles arise and stand upon it for a competent space, viz., whilst you can tell ten or twenty ; this is that size of Spirits which they call Proof.   But in case such a Mantling or Cap does not stand upon the Surface of your Spirits . . . the same is either strong above Proof, or too weak, and will not come up to it ; now to know which of these is the cause is easie, for if it be above Proof it will look bright and clear ; if beneath, pale and wheyish."[1]

TESTIMONIES TO THE NEW CIDER.—All who had tasted this new liquor had drunk freely of it, and they too for the most part persons of quality, critical judgments, and nice palates, while one peer of the realm preferred it before any wine.   Many eminent doctors of physic gave it as their opinion that cider-royal must needs be a very sound and wholesome drink.

---

[1] Appendix to *Aphorisms*.   An addition of a little water will soon show whether the spirit is above proof, or weak.

CHAPTER X.

RICHARD HAINES'S DEATH AND BURIAL.

RICHARD HAINES'S DEATH AND BURIAL.—Death overtook Richard Haines before he could effectually utilize his invention. His wife Mary had died in November, 1684, and was buried on the 21st of that month at Sullington. Six months later Richard himself died. We do not know the cause of his death, but death lurked in many a corner of old picturesque insanitary London. We know that Richard Haines's health was not always good, for he speaks[1] of a time when he was not well, but implies that he had recovered. As the burial was on the next day but one to the death, we may perhaps infer that the illness of which he died was of an infectious nature.

The original warrant for the administration of Richard's goods runs as follows[2]: "30 May 1685. On which day appeared in person Gregory[3] Haines and affirmed that a certain Richard Haines, lately of the parish of Christ Church London, widower, died intestate on the day last past, and that he was the natural and legitimate son of the said deceased, and as some of the goods of the said deceased were perishable, he prayed that Administration might be granted him before the 14 days which usually elapsed." The register of Christ Church, Newgate Street, records the burial of "Richarde Haynes in ye upper Church on 31 May, 1685." The old church had been burnt down in the great fire and was not yet rebuilt.[4] Richard Baxter of the "Saints' Rest" tells us that his wife was buried there (1681) "in the ruines." Interments went on, and even divine service was held in a sort of tabernacle amid the ruins. The old Franciscan church, known as "Grey Friars," was more than 300 feet long, and one of the largest and most conspicuous churches in London. The new edifice covered only the choir of the old one. Richard Haines rests with royal dead,

---

[1] *New Lords*, p. 53.   [2] P.C.C. 1685 (No. 315), in Latin.

[3] George crossed out.

[4] It was rebuilt between 1686 and 1704 from designs of Sir Christopher Wren.

as four queens lie buried in the same church, Margaret, Isabella, Joan of Scotland, and Isabella, Queen of the Isle of Man.[1]

INVENTORY OF GOODS.—The inventory of the goods of Richard Haines, which his son Gregory had to put in at Somerset House, as his administrator, no longer exists there, but the late Mr. C. E. Gildersome-Dickinson, while engaged upon other genealogical work, came across a Chancery suit "Weston v. Haines,"[2] in which one Charles Weston, of St. Saviour's, Southwark, glass-seller, sued Gregory Haines for £70, being the value of glass bottles and corks supplied to his father the late Richard Haines. This suit has annexed to it a copy of the inventory of Richard Haines's goods, and supplies us with some interesting particulars which deserve to be given at some length.

According to this document " Richard Haynes late of Sullington in the County of Sussex Gentleman was . . . at the time of his Death possessed of . . . a very considerable personal Estate consisting of (amongst other things) in ready money Leases Plate Jewels Rings Debts oweing on Security and Debts oweing in his Shop Booke and otherwise Great Store of Glasse-bottles and other Earthen and Glasse ware, and Syder wherein he traded And alsoe consisting of . . . great quantities of Linnen Brasse Pewther Bedding Furniture and Household Stuffe of all sorts and divers horses cowes sheep and other Cattell and great quantities of Corne Graine and Hay and Diverse other Goods and Chattels to a very considerable value And was alsoe . . . or some in trust for him were seized in Fee of several messuages Lands Tenements . . . in s^d county of Sussex or elsewhere of the yearely value of sixty pounds and upwards which reall Estate as is given out by the Defend^t . . . was mortgaged for seaven hundred pounds or there-abouts." The plaintiff then goes on to complain that Gregory Haines had applied the personal estate to pay off the mortgage, and now asserted that he had no assets left with which to pay the plaintiff's debt, or any others "due on Book or simple Contract." Whereas, says the complainant, the mortgaged estate was sufficient to satisfy the mortgage and all other debts owed by the deceased on real securities. But the son refused to pay, and pleaded " plene administravit," concealing, as the plaintiff asserts, great part of the personal estate, and exhibiting no inventory,

---

[1] *City Churches*, by Daniell, p. 150.

[2] B. and A. before 1714: 83 Reynardson, No. 93, dated 26 June, 1686; with the "Answer" of Gregory Haines to same: 15 October, 1686.

or an imperfect one, "many of the goods Debts and other things part of the s^d personall estate being omitted . . . and such goods and things as are sett down therein are much undervalued and were or might have been sold for more then they are therein apprised at." In fact Gregory is accused of fraudulent manipulation of the estate in the way of putting down in his account as bonds paid off what were only collateral securities for the mortgage, compounding for debts and entering them as paid to the full, and other such things. Finally the complainant prays that Gregory may be forced to give an account of his administration of the estate.

In his answer the defendant admits that his father died possessed of a considerable personal estate, and also seised in fee of lands and messuages in Sussex called "West Wantley" and "Roundabouts," of the yearly value of £60 or thereabouts. He also affirms that an inventory was put in at the P.C.C., in which the deceased's goods were appraised at full value or even more. For instance, the cider did not fetch within £30 of the appraised value; while the lands above-named were mortgaged to Thomas Fogden of Fittleworth in Sussex for £900. This with interest due amounted to £1,000, being charged beside with a yearly rent of £12 10s. payable to the hospital of the Holy Trinity at Guildford. All this money was still owing.

Moreover a part of the mortgaged premises was by deed dated 20 November, 1654,[1] settled on Richard Haines for life, and in case of his decease on his wife Mary, and after her on the heirs male of said Richard and Mary. This part of the premises, consequently (worth £30 yearly), being the son's under the deed, could not be charged with the father's debts; while the rest was not worth the mortgage money and the yearly rent charge of £12 10s. Further Gregory denied that he had fraudulently concealed anything, or paid bogus debts. The whole estate was appraised at £569 6s., and £672 13s. 9d. had been paid away by the executor, some £20 or £30 of bad debts being crossed off. Moreover the real value of the estate was less than the appraised value.

THE INVENTORY.—A true and perfect Inventory of all and singuler the goods Chattels and Creditts of Richard Haines late of Wantley in the parish of Sullington co. Sussex, gentleman, but in the parish of Christ Church London deceased taken valued and appraised the fifth day of June in the yeare of our Lord one

---

[1] See above, p. 21.

thousand six hundred eighty and five by William Cavell and Richard Harraden as followeth vizt being only to the goods in and about the Estate and house in the said County of Sussex.

In the Parlor.

	£	s.	d.
Imprimis one Table and Carpet foure joyned Stooles thirteene Chaires one side board Table and Cloth a paire of brass Andirons a fire pann and tongues	2	18	0

In the parlor Chamber.

Item Two feather beds two bolsters one Blanket one Counterpaine one bedstead Curtains Vallens and Rodds two pillowes one Wicker Chaire one presse one table one side board table two Chests foure Chaires and one stoole...	5	0	0

In the hall Chamber.

Item One Bedstead one feather bed and Truckle bed and bed steddle two Counter paines one blocke and other Lumber ...	6	0	0

In the Porch Chamber.

Item One bedstead one feather bed and Boulster one Blanket and one Coverled	2	0	0

In the Pantry Chamber.

Item One bedstead one feather bed and Boulster one Blanket and one Coverled	1	10	0

In the two Garretts.

Item Two Bedsteads two feather beds two boulsters two blancketts ten bushell of none such in the huske one truncke and other Lumber	2	0	0

In the hall.

Item One table and one forme one Setle one Stoole five Chaires one Jack five Spitts one fowling peice one paire of Andirons tongues and Shovell two pothookes one fender one Cleaver one Cupboard one warming pann one Iron way beame twelve pewter dishes one flaggon and two Candlestickes two porrengers one Salt twelve wooden plates one box Iron one paire of Bellowes and other Lumber	4	0	0

In the Pantry.

Item five brass potts one Skillett two Iron potts five pewter dishes one Sawcer foure trayes two brasse Candlestickes one dripping pann and other Lumber	2	0	0

Interior of Dining Room, West Wantley.

(From a photograph by C. R. Helm s.)

In the Milke house.

	£	s.	d.
Item Five pewther dishes one brasse ketle foure trayes one Churne one frying pann one Buckett three milke vessells one poundering tubb two dressers and other Lumber	1	0	0

In the Kitchen.

	£	s.	d.
Item One Furnace one Limbeck five brewing tubbs and mault mill one Bushell two Cheese presses foure beere vessells one three leg tubb and other Lumber	3	0	0

In the Kitchen Chamber.

	£	s.	d.
Item Two Bushells of wheate eight beere vessells three lynnen wheelds one woolen wheele fifteen old Sacks and other Lumber	1	0	0
Item household Lynnen in all value	5	0	0
Item three grosse of glasse bottles value	4	0	0
Item In Hay	2	0	0
Item Two —— and a hogg-hutch		10	0
Item Eight Flitches of Bacon valued at	6	0	0
Item five hogsheads of Syder valued at	10	0	0
Item several bookes in the house valued at	2	0	0
Item foure Stalls of beere valued at		12	0
Item An old leade pump valued at...		12	0
Item A paire of pockett pistolls and a sword valued at		10	0
Item Wood and faggott upon the Ground...	1	0	0
Item Tenn Oxen and a Bulstag valued at...	55	0	0
Item Six two yearling Steares one Heyfer and one two yearling	15	0	0
Item Thirteene yearlings valued at	20	0	0
Item Three horses and one Mare and Colt valued at	21	0	0
Item foure Cowes and a Bull valued at	15	0	0
Item nine hoggs and Seaven piggs valued at	6	10	0
Item Tenn Acres of Oates valued at	8	0	0
Item Twenty Acres of Wheat valued at	50	0	0
Item Thirty six acres of Barley valued at...	40	0	0
Item Nine Acres of Bucke wheate valued at	1	0	0
Item Seaven Acres of tares	1	0	0
Item thirty six Acres of Mowing Grasse		15	0
Item Two waggons	5	0	0
Item Two dung cartes	1	15	0
Item Three plowes		16	0
Item Three horse harrowes and an Ox harrow	1	0	0
Item Six Yoakes		12	0
Item Six Iron Chaines valued at		15	0
Item two paire of Iron harnesses		8	0
Item two paire of Harrowing harnesses		1	0
Item one Rowler		1	0
Summe totall of the value of the deceased goods in and about his home in Sussex	321	10	0[1]

[1] N.B.—The sum total of sums as above given only amounts to £306 5s.

A true and perfect Inventory of all and Singuler the Goods Chattells and Creditts of the above mencõned Mr. Richard Haines which were in and about the Citty of London and County of Middlesex taken and valued and appraised the third day of June in the yeare of our Lord God one thousand six hundred and eighty five by Andrew Weston and Richard Hargreaves as followeth vizt. :—

	£	s.	d.
Impris In the first Celler under Doctor Morton's house in Grey Fryers neere Newgate Streete London Eleaven hogsheads of Cyder...	22	0	0
Item In the Inner Cellar forty hogsheads of Cyder and for want of being full we allow two hogsheads to make them up ...	80	0	0
Item In the other Cellar eleaven pipes and three flutts and an ullidge which is in all thirty and three hogsheads	[66	0	0][1]
Item In the three Cellars above mencõned is five hogesheads of Bottoms and Lees and fatt of ordinary Cyder conteyning two hogesheads and a half which we doe value at	3	0	0
Item There are alsoe twenty dozen of full bottles of Cyder and twenty dozen empty valued at	8	0	0
Item at the Marine Coffee house in Burchin Lane two hogesheades and a halfe and one hogeshead of Cyder and Bottles...	7	0	0
The Sume totall of both the aforesaid Inventories amounts to five hundred and Seaven pounds tenn Shillings	507	10	0

An Addiconall Inventory of all and Singuler the Goods Chattels and Creditts of the said Richard Haines late of Wantley in the parish of Sullington in the County of Sussex but in the parish of Christ Church London Gentl') deceased taken valued and appraised by William Cavell and Richard Harraden as followeth viz. :—

	£.	s.	d.
Impris One hundred Taggs	25	0	0
Item Three Coltes and one old mare ...	4	0	0
Item due to the deceased upon booke ...	32	16	0
	61	16	0

Besides the above, Gregory Haines in his answer to Charles Weston's Bill of Complaint admits having received £15 for glass bottles that were out in customer's hands when the Inventory was taken, and consents to being charged with them. This being so, and other glass bottles figuring in the Inventory itself, one cannot quite understand why Gregory declined to pay at least some of Weston's debt for these bottles.

¹ Sum not given in Mr. Dickinson's copy of original.

The total assets of the deceased amounted, therefore, to £584 6s. 0d., which at the present value of money would represent several thousands of pounds.

Now follows A Schedule of money paid for the Debts of the said Richard Haines.

Discharged :—

	£	s.	d.
Impris paid Thomas Duppa.a bond...	244	0	0
Item paid Mr. Stephen Evans and Mr. Peter Percivall goldsmith on bond	36	0	0
Item paid Mr. Samnell Short on bond	106	0	0
Item paid Mr. Richard Haines of Pulborough on bond	14	16	0
Item paid Mr. Edward Anderson on bond	23	10	0
Item paid John Butcher on bond	29	5	0
Item paid Robert Yeildall on bond...	10	0	0
Item paid William Holl on bond	22	8	0
Item paid . . . . Exec^r of Geo Eede on bond	16	0	0
Item paid Mr. Tho Ellis for two yeares rent of Barnes farme due at Michas one thousand six hundred eighty five	70	0	0
Item paid Sr Geo: Walker & Henry Peckham Esqs for one yeares rent due for a farme called Mooches	10	0	0
Item paid Mr. John Kettleby under-sheriffe of Sussex for a debt due to the late king	4	0	0
Item paid a bill under Mr. R. Haines hand to John Bard ...	9	18	0
Item paid to the master and bretheren of the Hospital at Guildford at Michas one thousand six hundred eighty foure ...	12	10	0
Item paid Apsley Newton Esq for a Herryott	4	5	0
Item paid Mr. Henry Shelley for foure Herryotts	16	0	0
Item paid Mr Abell for manageing of the Cyder in London ...	10	16	0
Item paid funerall Charges	8	0	1
Item paid for Lres of Admcon and the Inventory...	3	5	8
Item paid the duty of Excise	7	10	0
Item paid servants their wages	14	0	0
	672	13	9[1]

APPENDIX ON THE WANTLEY PROPERTY.

This was mortgaged as follows. On 9 May, 1677 (29 Car. II), for £300 to Robert Leeves of Rowdell, Washington, Clerk, at a peppercorn rent. The mortgage covered "Roundabouts Farm," containing 35 acres, and included also 60 acres of warren land occupied by Richard Haines and Robert Yeikloe. To release the property a payment of £336 was necessary by 10 May, 1679. Besides this £212 was borrowed from the same Robert Leeves on other security given by Richard Hayne.

[1] This total is 10s. too much.

These debts had reached the total of £688, when on 1 February, 1682–3, a fresh mortgage was made, by which Thomas Fogden of Fittleworth agreed to pay off the £688 due, and also to lend Richard Haines £212 besides, Richard Haines covenanting to pay Thomas Fogden, at the house of Richard Kelly the elder, gentleman, of Petworth, the sum of £990 in instalments by 2 February, 1684–5.[1] The money was not paid, and on 25 October, 1686 (2 Jac. II), a transference of the mortgage seems to have taken place, Mary Shelley of Champneys in the parish of Thakeham, paying Thomas Fogden £400,[2] and receiving the lands in mortgage on condition that Gregory Haines paid to Mary Shelley £440 at some time unspecified in the house of William Wheeler of Storrington. In this transaction Mary Shelley was trustee for Edward Shelley of Warnham.

This money was not paid, and yet on 23 July, 1687 (3 Jac. II), upon John Mitchell of Feildplace, parish of Warnham, husband of said Mary (Shelley), paying Gregory Haines £100, the same lands seem again to have been mortgaged to John and Mary Mitchell, on condition that, if Gregory Haines paid £105 at a certain specified time, he should recover the lands.

This money was not paid, but on 24 March, 1689–90 (2 William and Mary), the same lands were granted to John Cheale of Findon Esq., on payment to Gregory Haines, yeoman, of £200, on condition that if the said Gregory Haines paid the said John Cheale £210 by a specified date, the mortgage should be released.[3]

But this was not paid, and on 8 February, 1691–2 (3 William and Mary), the mortgage was transferred from John Cheale, trustee for Edward Shelley, to Richard Bankes of Storrington, gentleman, as trustee in his place, and on the same day Gregory Haines and Ann his wife sold all the above lands to Edward Shelley for £1,400, £528 18s. 4d. being paid in cash and £871 1s. 8d. being due for principal and interest on mortgage.

The West Wantley property is now in the hands of R. M. King, Esq. of Fryern, Storrington, who has most kindly allowed me to extract the above information from deeds in his possession.

---

[1] This deed was signed in presence of Richard Kelly and James and William Smith.

[2] Gregory presumably satisfied Thomas Fogden for the £590 further due to him.

[3] Witnessed by Will. Wheeler, Eliz. Wheeler, Joh. Wheeler.

CHAPTER XI.

THE DESCENDANTS OF RICHARD HAINES.

"Judge none blessed before his death : for a man shall be known in his children."—Eccl. xi, 28.

THIS is the obscurest part of the family history. Neither Richard nor his son Gregory, nor his grandson Gregory left a will, at least the first and third died intestate, and of the second neither will nor administration is to be found.

On 12 October, 1682, Gregory Haines witnessed the will of John Lee, mercer, of Thakeham.[1] About the time of his father's death, that is, most probably, between May, 1685, and March, 1686,[2] he married Ann ———; but neither marriage bond, nor licence, nor register of marriage has come to light.[3] All we know of Ann Haines, besides the date of her burial, is that she could write.

Gregory lived at Sullington after his father's death, and was churchwarden of the church 1687–1688.[4] In 1686 (Trinity Term) Gregory and Ann sold to George Barnard 1 messuage, 1 barn, 1 stable, 1 garden, 1 orchard, 40 acres of arable, 4 acres of meadow, 10 acres of pasture, 60 of furze and gorse and common of pasture for all manner of cattle with appurtenances in Sullington and Storrington.

On 8 February, 1691–2, as above stated, they sold the West Wantley property. In the Feet of Fines, relating to this, Gregory is called "gentleman," and the property sold is described as 1 messuage, 2 barns, 1 stable, 2 gardens, 3 orchards, 110 acres arable, 20 meadow, 30 pasture, 10 wood, 20 furze and gorse with appurtenances in Sullington and Storrington.

On 8 September, 1691, Gregory witnessed the will of Richard Harraden of Sullington, yeoman, the same person no doubt as had been appraiser of his father's goods.

---

[1] Chichester C. C., Vol. XXVII.
[2] She appears as his wife, Trinity Term, 1686 (Feet of Fines).
[3] The marriage most likely took place in Sussex or in London.
[4] See Visitation of Diocese, amongst the original wills at Chichester.

In 1693 (Trinity Term) Gregory Haines and Richard Baldwin bought from John Scutt and Mary his wife, and from Thomas Cole and Jane his wife, 3 messuages, 3 barns, 3 gardens, 3 orchards, 30 acres of arable land 5 of meadow, 10 of pasture, 10 of brush-wood, and common of pasture for one cow in Storrington and Cootham.

In 1700-1 (Hilary Term) Gregory and Ann, and William Wheeler, gentleman, and Elizabeth his wife, sold to William Blaker 60 acres of arable, 10 of meadow, 20 of pasture, and 80 of brush-wood in Storrington.

On 11 June, 1702, Gregory Haines of Storrington, yeoman, and Ann his wife, in consideration of £111 paid to them, and of £168 15s. paid to William Blaker of Buckingham, in Old Shoreham parish, and Mabel his wife, and of 5s. paid to William Wheeler of Storrington, gentleman, and his wife Elizabeth, sold to John Edsaw of Bognor in parish of Fittleworth, yeoman, several panels of land viz., 20 acres, formerly held by copy court roll of the manor of Storrington, known as Boxalls copyhold and land called Clarke's and 9 acres in Cootham called Cootham Mershes, and land called Court Garden and the Coggine Crofts, that Warren or Coney ground with all and every of the rabbits and coneys now in or belonging to the same, commonly called the West Commons, etc. The Foot of Fines gives the amount sold as 60 acres of arable, 10 of meadow, 20 of pasture, 80 of briar and thorn with appurtenances in Storrington.

On 9 October, 1702, Gregory was bondsman to the marriage licence of Charles Haynes of Petworth, gentleman, and Mary Penfold of Storrington, widow, with William Castell of Chichester, innholder (perhaps Mary Penfold was Gregory's sister). He also appraised the goods of said Charles Haynes 22 July, 1709.

In 1703 (Michaelmas Term) Gregory and Ann sold to John Edsaw, 2 messuages, 2 barns, 1 garden, 16 acres of arable, 5 of pasture, and common of pasture for a cow, with appurtenances in Coodham al's Cootham.[1]

And lastly in 1705-6 (Easter), Gregory Haines bought of John Penfold and Margaret his wife, 1 messuage, 1 barn, 1 stable, 1 garden, 1 orchard, 12 acres of arable, 4 of meadow, and 8 of pasture in Ashington and Washington.

By the above it appears that Gregory and Ann sold at one

---

[1] This property was called "Winters." See will of Robert Edsaw (Chichester Consistory Court, XXXI, p. 159).

time or another between 1686 and 1703, over 500 acres of land,[1] situated in Sullington, Storrington, and Cootham, buying on the other hand 55 acres in Storrington and Cootham in 1693 and in 1705, 24 acres in Ashington and Washington.

Gregory's children up to 1690–1 were baptized at Sullington, and then at Storrington, where his last child was baptized in 1697. On 28 March, 1702, he was himself baptized as an adult at Storrington Church,[2] when he is described as of Cootham. He was buried at Storrington on 8 February, 1727–8, as the register tells us.

His elder son Richard has left no traces, nor could he have had any descendants alive in 1755, as he or they would have been the nearest heir to the Sladeland property.

Gregory, the second son, was baptized on Sunday 4 July, 1697, at Storrington, and from him are descended all the certainly known descendants of Richard Haines. Ann Haines was buried at Storrington 9 March, 1735–6, but neither will nor administration of hers is extant. Meanwhile Gregory had gone to South Carolina as an Indian trader. He probably returned to England before his mother's death. Unfortunately none of the letters he must have written to his relations in England have been preserved. In the Record Office[3] in London, however, there is a copy of an official letter of his—the only document of the kind for the family previous to 1800.

LETTER OF GREGORY HAINES FROM SOUTH CAROLINA.

" May it please your Excellency,   "Sept. 7, 1723.

" Being bound for the Pallachocolas in January last, and our Belliargo[4] meeting with bad weather the traders got the start of me and seeing so many of them bound that way [I] thought they would be oversupplied. I altered my resolution and sat forward for the Charekees where I arrived in February and found those People extraordinary kind [and] courteous and continued trading there until the latter end of April and then sat forward for the Savana town leaving some good skins to be disposed of by John Millburne and arrived there about the 10 of May. In the beginning of July I sat out again for to see if my goods were disposed of and found that the best part of them was. I Packt my skins and made the best of my way to Savanah Town and from thence to Charles City to renew my Lycence I heard no news among those people but believe they are very hearty to the English only of an Engagement they had with some French Indians. The upper Cherrikees was going down a river in Canoes in order to make a Hunt and met with

---

[1] The sales in 1700–1 and 1702 refer to the same property.

[2] We learn this from the Bishop's transcript, not from the register.

[3] Board of Trade, South Carolina papers.

[4] A sort of vessel called Perriango in another part of the Correspondence.

some of the French Indians coming up and engaged with them for the space of 4 hours [and routed them ?] killed four of them and took most of their baggage amongst which was a small paper Book covered with Parchment with black lines ruled in it and every seventh line distinguished thus ——; which in my opinion was given to some Indians they had made a Christian of (*sic*) to know the Sabbath Day and to keep an account how many days they was in their journey every line being marked to the number of sixty four or five which I suppose was the time they was a coming I have no more news to insert at present but am your Excellency's most obedient Humble Servant to command.

GREGORY HAINES.

To His Excellency Francis Nicholson Esqre Capt. Gen. and
    Gov. in chief of His Majesty's Province of S. Carolina."[1]

In March, 1729–30, Gregory Haines was at a place called Keo(k)wee in the Cherokee country about 300 miles from Charleston. The Indians in that part were in a troubled and dangerous state, and threatening to join the French. Sir Alexander Cumming took the bold step of inviting the headmen of the Cherokees to meet him in the Town House of Necquassee, and there induced them to acknowledge, or coerced them into acknowledging, the sovereignty of England. The interpreter declared that, if he had known beforehand what Sir Alexander would have ordered him to say, he would not have dared to interpret it, nor would the Indian traders have ventured to be spectators of the scene, "believing that none of them could have gone out of the Town House alive, considering how jealous that people had always been of their liberties." However Sir Alexander Cumming, with his three cases of pistols and his gun and sword, carried his way with the 300 Indians. Still, fearing that he might not live to tell the tale, he drew up a report of the proceedings and made the witnesses sign a declaration of what they had seen and heard, as a testimony of His Majesty's Sovereignty over the Cherokees.[2] The following signatures were appended:—

Sir Alexander Cumming.	Daniel Jenkinson.
Joseph Cooper (interpreter).	Thomas Goodall.
Ludovic Grant.[3]	William Cooper.
Joseph Barker.	(Guide) William Hatton.
Gregory Haines.	John Biles.
	23 March, 1729–30, Keowee.[4]

[1] In another letter from John Barnwell of the same date, an Indian trader, Gregory Sissom, or Sisson, is mentioned.

[2] See Hist. Reg. Boston and Massachusetts, U.S.A., pp. 8, 9. The present whereabouts of the MS. cannot be traced.

[3] See below, p. 133.   [4] Keowee was on the Savana River.

Some of these Indian chiefs went to England on the *Fox*. Leaving Charleston on 7 May they reached Dover 5 June, and were presented to the King 22 June.[1] It is possible that Gregory Haines went home with them.

There had always been a tradition in my own branch of the family, handed down through Jane Haines, who died in 1870, that we were descended from an American ancestress. I had almost despaired of tracing her when I learnt from Mr. Edwin Haines of Beltring, Paddock Wood, Tunbridge Wells, that he had in his possession a certificate of marriage between Gregory Haines and Alice Hooke. They were married, it appears, on 4 June, 1719, at St. Philip's Church, Charleston, South Carolina. The certificate is dated 2 July, 1730 (4 Geo. II), and was attested by John Croft of Charlestown, sole Notary Public for the province of South Carolina, on the sworn evidence of Mr. Stephen Bedon of Charlestown, and Mary his wife, who deposed that on the 4th day of June, 1719, the Reverend Mr. William Wye, the then rector of the parish of St. Philip's, Charlestown, did (in their presence and in the presence of several other persons) join together in holy matrimony Mr. Gregory Haines and Mrs. Alice Hooke,[2] spinster, according to the rights and ceremonies of the Church of England. The church registers of this parish do not record the marriage, but the baptism of one son, Gregory Moore Haines on 27 February, 1727–8, and the burial of him and three other sons in 1728 and 1729, are found there. A Mark Haines, who married Elizabeth Porter at the same church, 8 March, 1744, *may*, as far as dates are concerned, have been a son of Gregory, but I do not think it likely. Gregory was living on 10 February, 1728, in a house near what is now the south-west corner of Church and Chalmers Streets.[3]

But the son, in whom we are most interested, and apparently the only one who survived, was John. We know the date of his birth, 4 December, 1723, but not the place, from the entry in his family Bible, written doubtless by himself.

Nothing more is known of Gregory except[4] that he was church-warden of Kirdford in 1735, until 6 March, 1751, under which

[1] See Rolls Series, Calendar of Treasury Papers, 1729–30.

[2] I can find no trace of the family in the Charleston records. There were Hookes at Ewhurst (1664), Surrey, and at Petworth, Sussex (George Hooke married Ann Gatford, 20 November, 1692), and at Wisborough Green. The Hookes of Bramshott, Hants, were entitled to arms.

[3] From some record in Charleston (unnamed by informant).

[4] See, however, note on next page.

date there is a reference to him in the Manor Rolls of Pallingham,
now at Petworth; "Death of Gregory Haines" (son of Richard
Haines's brother Gregory). "Mary Greenfield, widow, only sister
and next of kin, and administrator; who had assigned [Sladeland]
to Gregory Haines her kinsman, who being present acknowledged
ye same." Gregory died 29 November, 1752, and was buried in
Kirdford churchyard six days later. In the register he is called
Esquire,[1] while Mary Greenfield's brother Gregory is called
gentleman. On Gregory's tomb is the inscription:—"The late
Gregory Haines of Sladeland, Gent., aged 56."

He no doubt lived at Sladeland, but we find from an entry in
the above-cited Manor Rolls under date 14 October, 1755, that
Sladeland was not his. The entry runs: " Presented that the
information given the homage last General Court was wrong, for
that Mary Greenfield had not assigned as Gregory Haines had
alleged, but said Mary Greenfield died possessed thereof (*i.e.* of
Sladeland), who in and by her will had not particularly disposed
of the same, but the same then belonged to Mr. John Haines as
residuary and universal legatee, who being present in court acknowledged ye same." Gregory Haines unfortunately died intestate,
and on 4 January, 1753, administration of his goods, which are
described as "above value," was granted to his son John, the widow
Alice having renounced on the day previously, with a day for an
inventory. The bond entered into on that occasion is thus worded,
" Bond of John Haines of Kirdford, Gent., son and administrator
of the goods, &c., of Gregory Haines, late of Kirdford, Esqr
deceased, Willm Ireland of Wimbleton, Surrey, and George
Barrell of Chichester, innholder, in the sum of £1,600."[2]

---

[1] I believe he is given this title because named in an Act of Parliament (1733)
as Commissioner with other gentlemen of Sussex for the repair of the harbour of
Littlehampton called Port Arundel. (6 George II, cap. 12.)

[2] Chichester Administration Bonds.

Enlarged from impression of seal to
will (P.C.C.) of Mary (Haines)
Greenfield, Aug. 1755. The seal,
however, does not shew any tinctures of the crescents.

Impression of seal of General
Hezekiah Haynes from a letter to
Thurloe, 1655.

Bodl. Rawlinson, A 24,388.

Crest, coat and supporters of Sir Frederick Haines, G.C.B., etc., etc., etc.

CHAPTER XII.

FAMILY OF RICHARD HAINES'S BROTHER.

THE FAMILY OF GREGORY, YOUNGER BROTHER OF RICHARD HAINES.—Gregory was baptized at Shere in Surrey 24 May, 1636, and in 1654 his mother and brother assigned Sladeland to him. On 23 October, 1660, he married Margaret Lidbetter of Bramber, in Sussex. In his will[1] dated 24 February, 1670–1, he is described as of Blackchurst, in the parish of Warningcamp, yeoman. He leaves his lease of "Sladelands" (for the term of 9000 years), containing about 100 acres, to his son Gregory, and failing him to his daughter Mary, the latter to have £100 out of the profits of said lands at 20 years of age, Richard the brother of testator to administer the estate during the children's minority. To his wife he leaves an annuity of £4 out of the profits of same lands. Overseers of the will were the testator's two brothers-in-law, Richard Everenden of Horsham, gentleman, and Richard Carpenter, of Sompting. Witnesses were William Wheeler and Jane Beeding.

A codicil to the will leaves £100 out of the profits of Sladelands to "such soun as my wife is now with child of," to be reduced to £60 if the child proved to be a daughter. Four days later the testator was buried at Sullington. We have an inventory of his goods, "valewed and prised by John Duppa, Samuel Lover, and Richard Parham, 10 March, 1670–1." The silver bowl, mentioned in the inventory of his father's goods, appears here, and is again priced at 30s. The household effects come out at about £40, money in purse and wearing apparel £15. Farming produce and cattle[2] and implements total nearly £375, and the lease of Sladeland is valued at £500. Debts were due to him, £11 from William Gatlon of Arundel, and £3 from Richard Rogers.

Our ancestors seemed to have eschewed luxuries, not to say many things we consider essential to wellbeing and household comfort. No crockery of any sort appears in these inventories, no

[1] Chichester Consistory Court, XXXV. 32b.
[2] Among these were Dorsetshire and Hampshire ewes.

knives or forks, carpets or mats, and only occasionally any books, no pictures or knick-knacks, and only once a mirror. The total value of Gregory Haines's estate was given at £941 7s. 6d. His wife married again, as we learn from an entry in the Court Rolls of the manor of Pallingham under date 22 May, 1678. " John Jelly in right of his wife, late wife of Gregory Haines, held as above (leasehold land called Sladeland), amerced in 1s. for not doing service of court." In spite of this, in the marriage licence of her daughter dated 9 June, 1692, she is called Mrs. Margaret Haines, her husband John Jelly being at that time most probably still alive. She was apparently buried 4 April, 1694, at Sullington as Margaret Jelly.

Gregory the son, born 16 June, 1663, was baptized at Sullington. His marriage licence[1] dated 18 February, 1690-1, says, "which day appeared personally Gregory Haines of the parish of St. Saviour's, Southwark, draper, aged about 26 years, and a bachelor, and alleged that he intended to marry with Mrs. Elizabeth Champneys of ye same parish, aged about 30 years and a widow." Either through his inheritance or his business, Gregory became a rich man.[2] In 1712 (probably) he built the present house at Sladeland. In the walls of the cellar is the inscription, " Gregory Haines, 1712."

In 1716 (Trinity Term) he bought from George Lowes and Hannah his wife, 1 messuage, 1 barn, 1 garden, 16 acres of arable, 4 of meadow, 4 of pasture in Kirdford. In the same year he purchased the copyhold of Laneland in Kirdford parish from Richard Gratwick and others. He is described as gentleman in both cases.

In 1718, under an Act of Parliament dealing with the estates of Charles Eversfield, Esquire, Gregory Haines, gentleman, bought from the trustees of the above Charles Eversfield for £2,650, " lands and premises known as Wephurst, Spitweeks (Spitwick), Wild Strode, Giles Mead, and all that parcel of land thereunto adjoining called ' the Lane ' and ' the Hill ' in the pshes of Kirdford and Wisborough Green, and also all those lands and tenements known as Great Ford and Little Ford in the sd psh of Kirdford." Gregory Haines's signature was witnessed by Edward Shelley, John Jackson, and Thomas Parham.[3]   •

---

[1] Office of the Vicar-General.

[2] 9 Nov., 1710, Greg. Haines, of Southwark, woollen draper, bought from Charles and Mary Newington, of Merton, 91 acres of woodland, etc., in Wimbledon.

[3] The third of that name who witnessed documents of the family.

In 1722, Gregory Haines, gentleman, purchased of John Seyliard 1 messuage, 2 barns, 2 stables, 1 garden, 1 orchard, 40 acres of arable, 20 of meadow, 50 of pasture, 10 of woodland, 20 of furze and gorse in Kirdford.

In 1734 his name appears in the Poll Book for Sussex.[1]

No children seem to have been born to him, and his wife died 26 July, 1727, and was buried at Kirdford. Gregory himself died 28 November, 1749, aged 86, and was buried nine days later[2] beside his wife, leaving his sister Mary Greenfield his heir.

She had married, at the age of 23, Thomas Greenfield of Pulborough, yeoman, at St. Mary's, Aldermary, on 10 June, 1692. Her death took place 25 August, 1755, and she was buried, aged 87, five days later at Kirdford. Her will, made on 9 August, 1755, is a long and interesting document, and shows that she was possessed of a large amount of property.

Besides Sladeland, which is not mentioned, and went to John Haines, the residuary and universal legatee, she owned (1) Wephurst Farm and Wephurst Lands, which she left to John Haines her principal heir; (2) the farm called Rowlands with Rowlands lands and Garlands, also in the parish of Kirdford, which she gave to *her kinsman Gregory Haines,*[3] *farmer, son of William Haines of Devonshire*; (3) Croucham Farm, or Croucham lands, which she also left to the last-mentioned Gregory Haines; (4) farmhouse and lands in Ashington parish which she gave to Mrs. Hannah Batchellor,[4] widow of the Rev. Paul Batchellor, to go on her death to Gregory, son of William Haines of Broadwater, yeoman; (5) a farmhouse and lands called Nolderhead (Naldretts) in the parish of Wisborough Green which she left to William Mardiner of Sompting, farmer; (6) a farmhouse and lands in Wimbledon, at the time of her death in her own occupation, which she left to Hannah Seward, wife of John Seward[5] of Brewhouse Mill in parish of Wisboro' Green, charged with the sum of £100 to be paid to Coles Fortrie, linen-draper of Cheapside; (7) a farm and

[1] It is not found in the Poll Book for Knights of the Shire, 1705, now at Lewes.

[2] This points to his dying away from Kirdford—perhaps at Wimbledon, where he had property, as we have just seen.

[3] I cannot fit him into the pedigree; but he must have been a descendant of either William, brother of Richard of Wantley, or of one of the sons of Richard, perhaps of John, who married Sarah Seale.

[4] See pedigree.

[5] He was bondsman at the marriage licence of John Haines, 26 March, 1752.

lands, called Bleach Farm or Bleachlands Farm in the parishes of
Wiston and Ashington, which she left to Samuel Lidbetter
of Bramber, farmer; (8) a double house with malthouse and
garden in Petworth, which she left to [*blank*] Walls, son of
William Walls of New Shoreham by his wife Barbara, and in
case of failure of heirs to him, she left it to Ann Ford, widow of
James Ford of Ham in the parish of Angmering.

Money legacies are given to the following persons (among
others):

> to the said Ann Ford, widow, £100;
> to Bridger Lidbetter, brother of Ann Ford, £50;
> to Ann Brown, widow of Francis Brown, late purser of a man-
>   of-war, £100;
> to Thomas Mathews, servant to "my late cousin" Gregory
>   Haines, deceased, 40s.;
> to Thomas Durrant, servant to "my late cousin" Gregory
>   Haines, deceased, 40s.;
> to "my godson" Richard Boxall, £5;
> to John Fortrie, jun., son of the late Rev. Mr. Fortrie, £21;
> to Coles Fortrie the elder of Guildford, £21;
> to his sister Ruth Fortrie, spinster, £21;
> to "my cousins" John and Samuel Lidbetter, £50 each;
> to "my tenant" William Boxall and Sarah his wife and his
>   two daughters Elizabeth and Mary, £5 each;
> to Ann Fortrie, daughter of the late Rev. Mr. John Fortrie,
>   £10;
> to Rev. Mr. Copley, minister of Chiltington, and Sarah his
>   wife, £10 each;
> to Thomas Denyer, servant to "my late cousin" Gregory
>   Haines, deceased, £60;
> to Gregory, Love, Elizabeth, Thomas, and Mary, the 5 children
>   of Mr. William Haines of Broadwater, gent., £5 each;
> to Adam Martin of Steyning, £5;
> to his 3 children Thomas, Elizabeth and Mary, £10 each.

The will was proved 25 September, 1755, in London by the
executors William Mardiner, of Sompting, William Haines of
Broadwater, and William Mitford, Esq., of Petworth. The will
was sealed *with the Haines seal* and signed "Mary Grenfild" in
the presence of John Roberts, clerk, John Rowland, and Charles
Browne.

The possessions of the Haines family in this neighbourhood, as is abundantly clear from this will, were very considerable, and bear out the tradition which I heard at Kirdford that a man might walk eight miles without setting foot on any land not owned by this family.

CHAPTER XIII.

JOHN HAINES.

OUTSIDE the family of John Haines and their posterity, no descendants of Richard[1] Haines seem to have survived to the present time. To use an American expression, John is our "stock-father." Unfortunately no picture of him remains, though there is a miniature of at least one of his sons, viz., Thomas·Haines, my own great-grandfather. This represents a man of very florid complexion with round ruddy cheeks and a hooked nose, who had evidently been nurtured upon good old English beef and ale. Some such outward appearance we may attribute to his father John.

Where John was born we do not know, but we must suppose that it was in South Carolina. He entered the Royal Navy under the rating of able seaman. Whether he was pressed, or, if not, why he held no higher position, is matter for conjecture. He entered the service on board H.M.S. *Gloucester*, 50 guns, 24 January, 1744, and was discharged sick 30 November, 1747, as unserviceable. This was due to his losing his right arm on the 14 October, 1747, in battle against the French off the coast of France in latitude 47°.

Perhaps the log of H.M.S. *Gloucester*, under Capt. Durrell, for Wednesday, 14 October, 1747, will interest our readers.

LOG OF THE *Gloucester*.—" Winds S.S.E., S.W.B.W., W.S.W., S.W.,S.S.E. Course S c/47² Wᵗ. Distance in miles 42. Lat.47°28' N., Long. 10° 20' W. The Lizard N. 52° E. 88 Leagues. Moderate and clear Wʳ at 3 p.m. sent our boat on board the Admiral. Signalled dᵒ. Brought too in 1st, 2nd, and 3rd R. T. sˡˢ. At ½ past 6 a.m. we made ye signal of seeing 12 sail in the S.W. Qʳ. The Admiral made a signal for all the fleet to chace in that Qʳ if we discovered them to be a large Fleet. At ½ past 10 the Admiral made ye signal for the line ahead, 9 of the enemy's ships to windward Laying too in line aBreast, the merchant ships above 200

---

[1] This name does not appear again in the family, though I narrowly escaped being named Richard by a mistake of the officiating minister at my baptism, who misheard Reginald as Richard. Dr. Morehead, writing, 18 Aug. 1874, to my mother, says: "I nearly made him Richard, from which he was saved by your promptitude."
Query 47°.

sail crouding to the Westw^d. At ½ past 10 the Admiral made the signal for a general chase, the Having made sail (*sic*) and signal to engage. At ¾ past 11 our Headmst Ship began to engage. At noon we began to engage.

· "Thursday,[1] 15 October, 1747, Wind S.B.E., S.S.E., S.W. E^t. S.E. Course W.B.S., Distance in miles 21, 47° 24′ N. 10° 9′ W. The Lizard N.E.¼E. 88 Le^s. Moderate and Clear W^r. Continued in action till night. T^d and stood to another ship, the Admiral made the signal for a close engagement. We began to engage. The Admiral coming up the Enemy's ship struck. Left of engaging. But several of our ships astern was engaging till 10 at night. Brought too, our masts and Rigging being much damaged, the People employed in repairing the Rigging, found 6 men killed and 16 wounded. At 11 wore and Bro^t too. At 8 a.m. bore down to one of the French men of war that was much damaged. At 9 took her in tow and stood to ye Admiral, she called *Le Fougueux*. At noon 29 sail in sight 6 of which is French men of war that had struck. Bro^t too. Y^e Admiral made the signal for all Captains.

"17 October had the prize in tow.

"29 at noon anchored in P'mouth Sound.

"4 (*sic*) November. At noon fired 19 guns, it being the Anniversary of Gun powder Treason.

"The *Gloucester* took home the body of Capt. Saumarez of the *Nottingham*, who was killed in the battle."

The despatch[2] of "Edward Hawke Esqre, Rear Admiral of the White Squadron" dated 17 October, 1747, was as follows:—

"At seven in the morning of the 14 October, being in latitude 47° 49′ N. longitude from Cape Finisterre, 1° 2′ west, the *Edinburgh* made the signal for seven sail in the S.E. quarter. I immediately made the signal for all the fleet to chace. About 8 saw a great number of ships, but so crowded together that we could not count them. At 10 made the signal for line of battle ahead. The *Louise* (60 guns[3]) being the headmost and weathermost ship, made the signal for discovering eleven sail of the enemy's battleships. Half an hour after Capt. Fox in the *Kent* hailed us, and said they counted 12 very large ships. . . . Finding we lost time, in forming our line, while the enemy was

---

[1] Thursday in the log starts on Wedn. at noon.
[2] Written at sea on board the *Devonshire*.
[3] I have inserted the number of guns in each case.

standing away from us, at eleven I made the signal for the whole line
to chace. Half an hour after . . . I made the signal to engage,
which was immediately obeyed. The *Lyon* (60 guns) and *Princess
Louise* (60) began the engagement, and were followed by the rest
of the squadron as they could come up from rear to van. . . .
In passing on to the first ship we could get near, we received many
fires at a distance till we came close to the *Severne* of 50 guns,
whom we soon silenced and left to be taken up by the frigates
astern.   Then perceiving the *Eagle* (60) and *Edinburgh* (70), which
had lost her fore topmast, engaged, we kept on wind as close as
possible in order to assist them.   This attempt, of ours was
frustrated by the *Eagle* falling twice on board us, having had her
wheel shot to pieces, and all the men at it killed, and all her
braces and bowlings gone.   This drove us to leeward, and prevented
me attacking the *Monarque* of 74 and the *Tonant* of 80 guns,
within any distance to do execution ; however we attempted both,
especially the latter. . . . Capt. Harland in the *Tilbury* (60)
observing that she fired single guns at us, in order to dismast us,
stood on the other tack between her and the *Devonshire* (60, the
flagship) and gave her a very smart fire. . . . I was got almost
alongside the *Trident* (64), whom I engaged as soon as possible,
and silenced by as brisk a fire as I could make. . . . Seeing
some of our ships at that time not so closely engaged as I could
have wished, and not being well able to distinguish who they were,
I flung out the signal for coming to a closer engagement. Soon
after I got alongside within musket shot of the *Terrible* of 74 guns
and 700 men. Near 7 at night she called for quarter.

"Thus far I have been particular with regard to the share the
Devonshire bore in the action of that day. As to the other ships,
as far as fell within my notice, their commanding officers and
companies behaved with the greatest spirit and resolution, in every
respect like Englishmen. Only I . . . must except Capt.
Fox. . . .

"Having observed that 6 of the enemy's ships had struck, and
it being very dark and our own ships dispersed, I thought it best
to bring to for that night, and seeing a great firing a long way
astern of me, I was in hopes to have seen more of the enemy's
ships taken in the morning. But instead of that I received the
melancholy accounts of Capt. Saumarez being killed,[1] and that the

---

[1] He was taken home in the *Gloucester* and buried in Westminster Abbey.

Tonant had escaped in the night by the assistance of the *Intrépide*, who by having the wind of our ships had received no damage that I could perceive. Immediately I called a Council of War (copy enclosed).

" As to the French convoys escaping, it was not possible for me to detach any ships after them at first or during the action, except the frigates; and that I thought would have been imprudent, as I observed several large ships among them, and to confirm me in this opinion I have since learned that they had the *Content* of 64 guns and many frigates from 36 guns downwards. As the enemy's ships were large they took a great deal of drubing, and lost all their masts, except two who had their foremasts left. This has obliged me to lye by them two days past in order to put them into a condition to be brought into port, as well as our own which have suffered greatly."

A few days later the following ships were sent to Plymouth to refit: The *Monmouth*, 64 (Capt. Henry Harrison); the *Edinburgh*, 70 (Capt. Thomas Cotes); the *Princess Louise*, 60 (Capt. Charles Watson); the *Eagle*, 60 (Capt. George Brydges Rodney); the *Windsor*, 60 (Capt. Thomas Hanway); the *Gloucester*, 50 (Capt. Philip Durrell); the *Portland*, 50 (Capt. Charles Stevens); and the *Shoreham*; while the rest went to Portsmouth taking the prizes in tow, viz.: the *Devonshire*, 66 (Capt. John Moore); the *Yarmouth*, 64 (Capt. Charles Saunders); the *Kent*, 74 (Capt. Thomas Fox); the *Nottingham*, 60 (late Capt. Philip de Saumarez); the *Tilbury*, 60 (Capt. Robert Harland); the *Defiance*, 60 (Capt. John Bentley); and two fireships, *Vulcan* and another.

From some packets that were thrown into the sea from the *Fougueux* and *Severne* important information relative to the French fleet was gained and forwarded to the Admiralty.

The French ships taken were:—

  Le Monarque, 74, Capt. de la Bedoyère.

  Le Terrible, 74, Capt. du Guay.

  Neptune,   74, Capt. de Fromentières.

  Le Trident, 64, Capt. d'Amblimont.

  Le Fougueux, 64, Capt. de Vignault.

  Severne,   50, Capt. du Rouret.

But the *Tonant* (80), with the Admiral M. des Herbiers de l'Etenduère, and the *Intrépide* (74), Capt. De Vaudreuil, escaped, badly damaged, having been followed and engaged, on their own responsibility, by the *Yarmouth*, *Nottingham*, and *Eagle*, in the course of which action Capt. Saumarez was killed.[1] The *Content* (64), and some frigates were with the convoy.

The list of killed and wounded given on 4 November is :—

Devonshire, 12 killed ; 52 wounded.

Kent,	1	„	10	„
Yarmouth,	22	„	70	„
Defiance,	11	„	42	„
Lyon,	22	„	79	„
Tilbury,	6	„	13	„
Hector,	1	„	1	„

But this list is evidently incomplete, and we know that the *Gloucester* lost 6 killed and 16 wounded, of whom John Haines was one, as he tells us that he lost his right arm in the battle.

The total loss of the French is given at 800 killed and wounded, amongst them being Capt. de Fromentières, of the *Neptune*. The British loss is put at 154 killed, including Capt. Saumarez, and 558 wounded. The English had a decided but not overwhelming superiority—14 ships to 9, and 858 guns to 630.

The complement of the *Gloucester* was 300 to 315 men. From the pay book of that ship we learn the following particulars concerning John Haines :—

No. on ship's books	...	147.
Entry		24 January, 1744.
No. and letter of ticket		Q.L. 538.
Quality ... ...: ...		Able.
When discharged	...	30 November, 1747.
For what reason	...	Unserviceable.
When signed ...	...	6 January, 1747.
To whom delivered	...	Party.
Neglect	...	7s. 6d. and 2s. 6d.
Slopseller's clothes	...	£1 16s. 4d.
Tobacco	...,	£1 2s. 2d.
Chest	...	£1 17s. 3d.
Hospital... ...	...	18s. 8d.
Full wages ...	...	£44 12s. 3d. Net £38 7s. 10d.
When paid ...	...	31 March, 1748. Paid to party.

From the above we gather that John was a smoker, and that he recovered quickly from the loss of his arm. From the same pay book we find that there was a namesake of his on board

---

[1] See Clowes's *History of the Navy*, Chapter xxvii, p. 126.

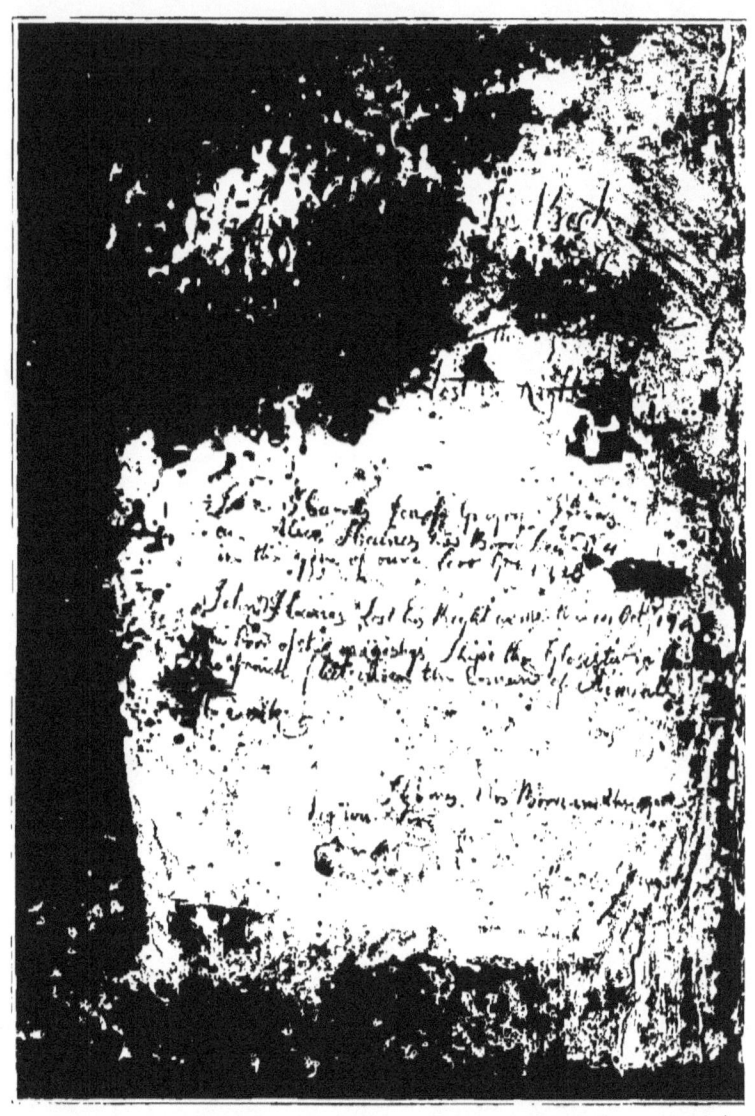

Photograph of the inside face of the upper cover of John Haines's Bible.

the same ship : Ticket No. 170—supernumerary, John Haynes, able seaman, 5 April, 1747, discharged 16 April, 1748, at Plymouth.[1]

We should never have known that John Haines was a sailor had it not been for the entry in his Bible.[2] This is in the possession of Mrs. Hare, of Southampton, his great grand-daughter, and I have had the two pages of writing photographed. The date of publication is 1683, so it *may* have belonged to Richard Haines, though I do not think this likely. The Bible was such a familiar book to him that he almost must have written something in it. No doubt he had a family Bible with much priceless information in it, which has not come down to us. I have turned over every page of the present book and find only one trace of writing except the above-mentioned entries on the insides of the cover. Above Chaps. II–III of Malachi are the words, written in a good hand, "Wo to the theife and cheator." There are imitations here and there through the book of capital letters on the margin, as if some one had been practising writing, and between the leaves three or four petals of a dried flower, striated like a lily.

On the inside of the upper cover is written :—

" John Haines his Book.

" Son to Grigry Ha   .   .   .   and Alice Haines.

" John Haines son of Grigry Haines and Alice Haines was Born Dec[br] y 4 in the yere of oure Lord God 1723.[3]

" John Haines Lost his Right arme the 14 Oct[br] 1747 one bord of his magestys Shipe the Glosester in Gaging the french fleet onder the Comand of Admirall Hawk.

" J. Haines wos Born in the yere of our
Lord   .   .   .
".   .   .   Augst 1748."

As the photograph of the inside of the lower cover is quite clear, I need not transcribe it. Judging from the only other authentic signature which we possess of John Haines,[4] the writing in the Bible appears to be by himself. If so, he cannot be said to have been a man of any education.

After being discharged as unserviceable, we may suppose that

<hr>

[1] Curiously enough, 43 years before there was a negro named John Haines on board the same ship. See P.C.C. Administration, 5 January, 1704-5.

[2] And, I should add, the Navy Warrants in the possession of Mr. Edwin Haines of Paddock Wood.

[3] Apparently altered from 1722.

[4] Witnessing the marriage, 15 May, 1758, of Edmund Tupper and Mary Puttock.

John Haines went home to Kirdford to recover. But within five
months he was again serving in the Navy. He was appointed
25 April, 1748, gunner on His Majesty's ship *Montague*. He is
thus described :—

"John Haines of good testimony, who has passed an
examination to be gunner of H.M.S. *Montague*, former (*sic*)
removed to the *Berwick*, together with such an allowance of wages
and victuals for himself and servant as is proper and usual for the
gunner of the s^d Ship." The warrant, which mentions the above
date as the date of appointment, is itself dated 27 September, 1748.

On the 7 February, 1748-9, he was appointed by warrant
(dated 15 February) to be gunner of the *Jason*, and on the
10 May, 1751, by warrant dated 19 June, appointed gunner of the
Preston. On the back this is endorsed *Mr.* John Haines, gunner.

The position of gunner at that time was rather above that of
warrant officer at the present day. The latter's duties have been
graphically described by Rudyard Kipling in his *A Fleet in Being*,
and I make no apology to my readers for transcribing the passage.

"His word is very much law forward. He knows his
men, if possible, better than the officers. He has seen, tried,
approved, and discarded hundreds of dodges and tricks in all
departments of the ship. At a pinch he can wring the last ounce
out of his subordinates by appeals unbefitting for an officer to
make, by thrusts at pride and vanity, which he has studied more
intimately than any one else. Hear him expounding his gospel to
a youth who does not yet realise that the Navy is his father and
his mother, and his only Aunt Jemima; go out with him when
he is in charge of a cutter; listen to him in the workshop; in the
flats forward; between the pauses of practice-firing, or up on the
booms taking stock of the boats, and you will concede that he is a
superior and an adequate person."

A naval certificate dated 5 May, 1767, tells us that John was
a pensioner to the chest at Chatham for a yearly pension of £8.
It is scheduled at the side, "Hurt on board the *Gloucester* the
14 day of October 1747.—To appear in 3 years."

He probably retired from the service on the death of his father
in 1752, if not before; for he was married at Bramber on 9 April,
1752, to Mary Lidbetter. The marriage licence was taken out on
26 March at Chichester. John Seward, of the parish of Green
(brother-in-law of Mary Lidbetter), was bondsman with John Haines.
In 1754 and 1755 John Haines was churchwarden of Kirdford.

Bramber Church, Sussex.

On the death of Mary Greenfield in 1755 John Haines succeeded to a large part of the estate as heir-at-law and residuary legatee. Thus he inherited Laneland, Spitwick, and Wephurst. In the latter he lived from his marriage till 1759 at least, but before his death he had taken up his abode at Sladeland. On 6 March, 1766, acting as executor, he proved the will of his friend Henry Osborne, of Kirdford. In 1762 he had purchased the copyhold estate of Bedland, and he either inherited or bought a property called Fordlands, for there is an entry in the Pallingham Manor Rolls, dated 12 October, 1769, stating that his ownership of the lands must be inquired into, before his heir is admitted.

In 1766 (17 April) a fine was levied for some lands in Kirdford,[1] consisting of " 1 mess. 1 barn 1 stable . . . 1 garden, 1 orchard 15 acres arable 10 of meadow 5 of wood . . . with appurts.," which he bought from Francis Gosden and Rebecca his wife and William Cowper, alias Steyning, and Mary his wife.

Some of the property left in 1755 by Mary Greenfield to Gregory Haines, son of William Haines of Devonshire, was sold[2] by said Gregory and his wife Jane in 1757 to John Nightingall the younger. It is described in the " Fine " as " 1 mess. 1 barn 1 garden 1 orchard 6 acres of arable 4 of meadow 4 of pasture and common of pasture with appurts in Kirdford." In the Manor Rolls of Pallingham under date 2 September, 1762, we find respecting the Rowlands property, which was a part of that left to Gregory Haines, that on 28 October, 1758, Penelope Woodyer, by William Whitaker, her attorney, surrendered it to John Haines, of Kirdford, gentleman.

In 1766[3] again, John Haines bought of John and Mary Lidbetter " 50 acres of wood with appurts. in Kirdford."

John Haines made his will on 10 July, 1769, perhaps because he was failing in health, and dying on 29 September, 1769, was buried 4 October following, in the 46th year of his age.[4]

By his will[5] he devised (1) to Gregory his son his leasehold farm and lands called Sladeland, his freehold farms called Foord Land, Mill Land, and Mill House and Wephurst Coppice in Kirdford and copyhold farm called Rowlands in Kirdford (manor of Pallingham), at the age of 22, charged with testamentary and

---

[1] Feet of Fines, Trin. 6 Geo. III.   [2] *Ibid.*, 31 Geo. II, Trin., 26 May.

[3] *Ibid.*, 6 George III, Easter Term, 26 March, 1766.

[4] His death may have been due to dropsy, consequent on the loss of his arm.

[5] P.C.C. 299 Jenner.

funeral expenses and subject to "user" of Sladeland house by wife Mary Haines at her pleasure, and subject to annuity of £25 till youngest child is 21 for their support, and after for own use, and charged further with legacy of £100 apiece to six younger children of testator, viz., Thomas, Mary, Samuel, Elizabeth, Hannah, and Jane, payable at respective ages of 22.

(2) To son John Haines farm and lands called Wephurst, Wildstrood, and Giles Mead in Kirdford and Wisborough Green, at age of 22; profits meanwhile to go to wife, and charged with testamentary and funeral expenses, and further subject to annuity of £25 to said wife, and charged with legacy of £100 apiece to testator's younger children, as above named, at 22.

(3) To wife Mary divers tenements and lands in Kirdford, now occupied by James Denyer, [*blank*] Cooper, widow, John Martin, and Arthur Randoll, for life, with reversion to eldest son Gregory Haines.

(4) To wife Mary copyhold premises in manors of Buckfold and Slinfold, and also copyholds in Kirdford called Bedland and Laneland, with freehold farm called Speedweek[1] in Kirdford subject to sale of same at majority of youngest child Jane. From the proceeds of sale £100 apiece to sons Thomas and Samuel, and residue equally between six younger children as above named.

(5) To wife all plate, linen, furniture, etc., and at her death to be divided among all the children. He made his wife sole executrix, and his brothers-in-law, John Ludbetter, of Thakeham, and Samuel Ludbetter, of Bramber, overseers. Witnesses to the will were Robert Holmes, John Allen, Elizabeth Johnson.

The will was proved 25 August, 1770, by Mary Haines, widow and relict.

CHILDREN OF JOHN HAINES.—Hannah Haines, the daughter mentioned in the above will, made her own will 16 December, 1789,[2] and died 3 June, 1790, aged 24, leaving property valued at less than £600. This she left to her brother Gregory and her kinsman Thomas Lidbetter, of Bramber, in trust for her "honoured" mother during her life. After her death the whole was to be converted into money and £100 each given to her sisters Mary and Jane, and the rest divided between her brothers and sisters, viz., Gregory, Thomas, Mary, John, Samuel, and Jane. The will was proved by the executors, Gregory Haines and Thomas Lidbetter, 8 May, 1791.

[1] Spitwick.　　　　[2] Chichester Consistory Court, XLIV, 330.

Photograph of inner face of the under cover of John Haines's Bible.

John Haines, the brother mentioned in the above will, made his will 13 September, 1813,[1] and died 8 October, 1813, aged 59. He left all his trinkets[2] to his nieces Elizabeth, Mary Ann, Hannah, and Jane, daughters of his brother Gregory; to his brothers Gregory and John Eldridge, of Kirdford, he left all his houses and lands in Kirdford and Wisborough Green in trust to sell the same, giving one-fifth of money realised to his brother Gregory, one-fifth to his brother Thomas, the remaining three-fifths to be invested, and the profits given one-fifth to sister Mary Clayton, the principal and interest to be divided at her death between all her children, another fifth to Samuel Haines his brother for life, with reversion to niece Susannah, wife of John Eldridge, and said Elizabeth, Mary Ann, Hannah, and Jane, daughters of Gregory Haines, equally; the remaining fifth to sister Jane for life, and at her death £100 to her daughter Jane, and remainder to above-mentioned nieces.

The will was proved by the executors, John Eldridge and Gregory Haines, 15 November, 1813.

Mary Haines, the mother, sold Laneland, Bedland, and, in conjunction with Gregory Haines, gentleman, first part, John Haines, Thos. Haines, surgeon, John Clayton and Mary his wife, Samuel Haines, Jane Haines, and Thos. Lidbetter, second part, sold Spitwick, to Richard Smyth in 1791, according to the terms of her husband's will. She died 13 April, 1798, aged 74, intestate; and on 10 October, 1798, administration of her goods (under £1,000) was granted to Gregory Haines her son.

Jane Haines, her last surviving child (except Samuel) made her will[3] 29 July, 1821. Her child Jane had died previously. She left her property in Kirdford to John Eldridge, of Plumpton, gentleman, and her nephew George Haines, of Kirdford, yeoman, in trust for Mary Ann Barnes, her niece, and at her death the interest equally between her children at 21; all her household goods and liquor to said niece Mary Ann Barnes and nephew Charles Haines equally; all her linen and plate to said Mary Ann Barnes and niece Jane Haines equally, and to the latter all her rings and trinkets; to niece Ann Clayton, wearing apparel and some furniture; to nephew George [Charman] Haines, of Godal-

[1] Chichester C. C., XLVIII, 521.

[2] He had a great many rings and jewels, and wore rings in his ears.

[3] Chichester C. C., XLIX, 44.

I

ming, surgeon, a pair of candlesticks,[1] snuffers and stand[2]; to niece and god-daughter Mary Clayton, one dozen silver teaspoons and one pair of silver sugar tongs. To said John Eldridge and George Haines £30 each upon trust for Harriett Downer, daughter of John and Rhoda Downer, at 21; to said John Eldridge and George Haines £10 apiece; the residue to said trustees for brother and sister, Samuel Haines and Mary Clayton, for their lives, and after their decease one-third to all the children of Gregory Haines, her nephews and nieces (except Mary Ann Barnes) equally, one-third to children of sister Mary Clayton equally, and one-third to children of brother Thomas Haines equally.

This will was proved 20 March, 1822, by John Eldridge and George Haines, executors, with power reserved for Mary Ann Barnes, the executrix. The effects were sworn under £1,500.

All connection with Kirdford seems to have ceased before the thirties. Local tradition just remembers the Haineses and no more. One old inhabitant, named Sopp, recollected Gregory Haines, afterwards Commissary General, as a keen huntsman and judge of a horse. The only other person I have met who could speak from personal recollection of the Kirdford Haineses is Mr. H. F. Napper of Laker's Lodge, Billingshurst. He remembers several of the children of John Haines. Samuel, the youngest son, he tells me, was lame with both legs, having broken both kneecaps. He lived at a farm called "Fountains."

---

[1] Now in possession of his grandson, the Rev. Percy Moline.
[2] Now in my own possession. They have I. H. on them.

Field-Marshal Sir Frederick Paul Haines,
G.C.B., G.C.S.I., C.I.E., etc.

CHAPTER XIV.

SIR FREDERICK HAINES.

As I have now brought down this family history to a generation whose grandchildren are in some cases alive, and as each branch of the descendants knows its own history so far back sufficiently well, I have not thought it necessary to attempt any detailed account of further generations.[1] I have made an exception in favour of my own immediate family, for which I ask the indulgence of those readers who are not concerned with it. Still I have felt that this memoir would not be complete without a fuller mention of Sir Frederick Haines, G.C.B., G.C.S.I., C.I.E., Field-Marshal of England, who may rightly be considered as the most distinguished of all the descendants of Richard Haines, our common ancestor.

What I have put down here about that distinguished soldier (except the opening sentence and the few lines from a private letter), is taken from public sources and has no further authority than they can give.

Frederick Paul Haines, great-grandson of John Haines, was born 10 August, 1819, at the Parsonage Farm, near Sladeland, in Kirdford parish, and baptized in Kirdford church 23 November, 1820. His father, Gregory Haines, C.B., was the Duke of Wellington's favourite Commissary General in the Peninsular War, and was present at the following battles:—Toulouse, Orthes, Nive, Nivelle, Pyrenees, Vittoria, Salamanca, Fuentes d'Onor, Busaco, Talavera, Corunna. There is a good-natured caricature of him, made by Commissary General Ibbetson (about 1826) in water-colours. He is supposed to be looking over the points of a horse, of which he was a good judge, being also a fine horseman. The son went to school at Midhurst till 1836, and three years later was gazetted Ensign 4th Foot, 21 June, 1839; Lieut. 4th Foot 15 December, 1840; Capt. 10th Foot, 16 May, 1846; Brevet-Maj. 7 June, 1849; Maj. 21st Foot, 15 June, 1854; Brevet Lieut.-

---

[1] The *pedigrees* are given separately.

Col. 2 August, 1850; Lieut.-Col. 8th Foot, 28 October, 1859; Maj.-Gen. 25 November, 1864; General, 1 October, 1877; Field-Marshal, 21 May, 1890; Regimental-Col. Royal Munster Fusiliers, 16 May, 1874; ditto Royal Scots Fusiliers, 5 October, 1890.

Staff Service.

A.D.C. to C. in C., East Indies....	20 Nov.,	1844, to	22 May,	1846
Military Secretary, Headquarters, East Indies	23 May,	1846, „	7 May,	1849.
Commandant, Balaclava	10 Dec.,	1854, „	17 Jan.,	1855.
A.A.G., Aldershot	20 June,	1855, „	31 Jan.,	1856.
Military Secretary, Madras	10 June,	1856, „	24 June,	1860.
Acting Brigadier-General, Aldershot....	28 Dec.,	1861, „	30 June,	1862.
D.A.G., Headquarters, Ireland	1 July,	1862, „	22 March,	1863.
Brigadier-General, Ireland	8 March,	1864, „	31 Dec.,	1864.
Major-General, Bengal	28 March,	1865, „	27 March,	1870.
Q.M.G., Headquarters, Army	1 Nov.,	1870, „	31 March,	1871.
Lieutenant-General, Madras	22 May,	1871, „	24 Dec.,	1875.
C. in C., East Indies	10 April,	1876, „	7 April,	1881.

War Service.

On the formation of the army of the Sutlej in 1845, he was appointed to officiate as Military Secretary to the C. in C. in India, Sir Hugh Gough, and was present in that capacity at the battles of Moodkee and Ferozeshah (medal and clasp); in the latter engagement he was severely wounded by a grapeshot in the thigh at the attack on the enemy's works, his horse being killed under him at the same moment. At the recommendation of Lord Gough he was promoted to a Company in the 10th Foot without purchase. As Military Secretary to Lord Gough he served in the Punjaub campaign of 1848–49 and was present at the disastrous affair of outposts at Ramnuggur 22 November, 1848, and subsequent operations resulting in the passage of the Chenab and the battles of Chillianwallah and Gujerat (medal with two clasps). He was mentioned in despatches in both these campaigns.

He served with the 21st Fusiliers in the Crimean War 1854–5 and was present at the battles of Alma, Balaclava, and Inkerman, where he was second in command of the right wing of the 21st under Col. Ainslie, and of course at the siege of Sevastopol (medal with four clasps, fifth class of the Medjidie, Turkish medal). He was mentioned in despatches and promoted to Lieut.-Colonel. In the Afghan War 1878–80 he directed the military operations between

September, 1879, and September, 1880, and received the thanks of both Houses of Parliament 4 August, 1879, and 5 May, 1881.

In his *History of the Crimean War* (Vol. V.) Kinglake devotes several paragraphs to the share taken by Col. Haines in the battle of Inkerman. He was in charge[1] at a point (in the fore-central part of the field) called "Main Picket Barrier," and while maintaining his position there, was able on occasion even to advance beyond it. With forty men of his own regiment (the 21st Fusiliers) and a few of the 63rd he pushed his way at one time to the trench across the Port Road.

"To be holding this singular post," says Kinglake, "under the fire of Shell Hill, and in very contact with the jaws of the Quarry Ravine, doubly garnished with infantry columns, was to stand grappling with Dannenberg's army, and that, too, on the central ground, where its main strength always stood gathered."[2] Here after the fall of Gen. Goldie, Col. Haines exercised an undivided command, and was successful in beating off successive attacks of the enemy, and was able to take the offensive so far as to drive off a Russian battery in front, though his few men did not take the guns.

Perhaps he will excuse me if I give a few of the particulars of his life furnished me by Sir Frederick Haines himself in 1893. "As a young man," he says, "my father had the forethought to give me a year in Brussels and a year in Dresden. This last was the most valuable part of my education. But then as now much of my thought was turned to Art. As opportunity offered I always returned to Dresden. Leaving it in 1837, I revisited it in 1850, after an absence of thirteen years, with the rank of Lieut.-Colonel. This in German eyes was a miracle of promotion in those days. In 1882 I was sent to St. Petersburg to attend the manœuvres."

In 1893 Sir Frederick had to undergo a severe operation, from which his wonderful vitality enabled him to recover completely.

His full title is: Field-Marshal Sir Frederick Paul Haines, G.C.B., G.C.S.I., C.I.E., Colonel Royal Munster Fusiliers and Royal Scots Fusiliers.

---

[1] By the death of Col. Ainslie, Col. Haines succeeded to the command of the right wing of the 21st, and after Gen. Goldie's death he was in command of all the forces in the fore-central part of the field.

[2] Kinglake, v. 369.

CHAPTER XV.

THE FAMILY OF THOMAS HAINES, SON OF JOHN HAINES.

"To the gods I am indebted for having good grandfathers, good parents,
good kinsmen and friends, nearly everything good."— M. Aurelius,
Thoughts, I, 17.

BEING the third son, Thomas did not inherit sufficient property
to enable him to live a life of leisure, and perhaps he disliked
the idea of farming. At all events he elected to earn his living
as a surgeon. He left the paternal nest and migrated to
Godalming in Surrey in 1781, where he made a fairly good living
as physician and surgeon. His practice was not confined to
Godalming, as I have found payments,[1] made to him, entered in
the parish accounts of Puttenham and Elstead. He is also
found acting as accoucheur during the early years of the century
near his native place, Kirdford. On 3 May, 1783, he leased from
John Upfold, of Godalming, blacksmith, a house and garden on
the south side of the High Street in Godalming,[2] of which he
was at the time in occupation, for seven years for the rent of £18 a
year, on condition that John Upfold built a stable. On the
death of John Upfold[3] in 1792 these premises, described in the
Manor Rolls of Godalming as "a tenement in two tenements,"
with an acre behind the house and about 2½ acres at Crumpets
(Crownpits), then in the occupation of Thomas Haines, surgeon,
and John White, were devised in trust for his great-nephew
Edward Walter (of Pinner, gent.). In 1795 (30 April) the said
Edward Walter sold to Thomas Haines the tenement in his
occupation, and the other to Richard Haydon, Thomas Haines
paying a quit rent of 1½*d*. On the death of Thomas Haines a
cow was seized for a heriot in respect of his portion of the
property, which consisted of a tenement with an acre behind
and 2½ acres at Crumpets. John Haines, his son and heir, then
held it, and on his death his brother and heir George C. Haines;

---

[1] In 1789-90-91.   [2] Opposite the King's Arms Inn.
[3] He made his will in 1784 (14 February), in which he refers to a niece, Mary
Haynes (wife of Robert Haynes, of Pinner, gent.).

and in 1829 Samuel Haines held the tenement opposite the King's Arms with an acre behind, and Robert Munroe the $2\frac{1}{2}$ acres at Crumpets.

Thomas Haines also held other property in the manor, subject to a quit rent of 6*d.* per annum, namely a tenement called Peter Atler's (described in the rental as adjoining Hackman's), which was sold by William Russell, of Aldershot, to Thomas Haines and descended to his heirs. This was opposite the Sun Inn.[1]

Thomas Haines was three times Warden (*i.e.*, Mayor) of Godalming—in 1786, 1794, and 1813. It was in the last of these years that the new Corn Market was built, and his name is inscribed thereon with the date 1814. I sincerely trust that he was no party to the act of vandalism by which the old picturesque building that stood on the same spot previously was pulled down and destroyed. He must have made his way among his fellow-townsmen very quickly for him to have been elected mayor before he was 30 and in five years from his first settlement in the town.

In appearance, judging from the miniature above mentioned, he was a very florid, square-faced man with a prominent nose, a double chin, and rather high-arched eyelids—not an intellectual face, but with a certain homely cheerful vigour about it. The testimony of his youngest child, Ann Pattison, was that " he was everything that was nice." " He had a wonderful memory and could repeat word for word anything he had heard only once or twice. He was short-sighted and would pass his own children in the street without knowing them. He was musical and could play the 'cello very well."[2]

On 18 July, 1784, he took out a licence (at Chichester) to marry Mary Charman, of Midhurst, maiden, aged 25 years, and married her there four days later. She is said to have been a very delightful person. Unfortunately, after bearing her husband five children, one of whom lived to be 86 and another 90, she died, apparently from the effects of her last confinement, and was buried 13 September, 1799. Very little more than a year later, rather to the scandal of his relations owing to the shortness of the

---

[1] The above particulars are from a document drawn up 9 August, 1856, by Messrs. Woods and Co., solicitors, of Godalming, in support of a claim for quit rent on the above-named premises, then in the occupation of A. T. Chandler.

[2] From Mrs. Richard Moline, his granddaughter.

time, he married a second wife, Catherine Isabella Thomegay,[1] widow of Richard Thomegay, of Swiss extraction, who had been buried at Godalming 28 June, 1793. She was of a Quaker family named Wakefield from Worthing, and was christened just before her second marriage. This wife was from all accounts very inferior to his first one, and as she survived her husband, she was able to get rid of many family relics and heirlooms that would have been of priceless interest to us now. In this way she parted with some valuable old china, and I cannot but put it down to her that we know so little about her predecessor, of whom no likeness or description remains. There were no children by this second marriage, and if a story that I have heard on good authority be true, she was not able to retain the affections of her husband.

Thomas Haines died of heart disease, perhaps fatty degeneration of the heart, 27 May, 1820, and was buried in Godalming churchyard on 2 June. He died intestate, and administration of his goods, which were valued at under £4,000, was granted 14 July, 1820, to his son George Charman Haines, the widow renouncing.

On 31 May, 1820, an agreement was made that the interest of £3,000 out of the personal estate of Thomas Haines should be paid to the widow for life, for support of Elizabeth and Ann, the daughters, and on her death each of the latter was to get two-fifths of the principal, and Samuel Haines, the third son, one-fifth.

On 1 June, 1821, George Charman Haines assigned the premises to his brother Samuel, and the next day Samuel mortgaged them for £600 to Richard Haydon, gent., and Benjamin Kidd, banker.

On 23 December, 1837, the mortgage was assigned to Henry Marshall, who reassigned it to Benjamin Kidd and George Charman Haines. The trust money under deed of 31 May, 1820, was now divided, and the property was on 12 January, 1841, fully vested in Samuel Haines.

On September 29, 1842, Samuel Haines, surgeon, for the sum of £1,350 assigned to Alfred Thomas Chandler, of Godalming, surgeon, "all that messuage or tenement curtilage outbuildings stable garden and land thereto belonging, 2 acres, in or near High Street Godalming." Samuel Haines was joint-executor, with his brother George Charman, to the will of their eldest brother John

---

[1] Sometimes spelt Thaumingay.

as far as his estate in England was concerned.[1]   John made his will at Rajamundry in the Madras Presidency, where he was assistant surgeon in the East India Company's service.   A codicil was added to his will 11 April, 1822, in consequence of the deaths meanwhile of his brother Robert and sister Mary Charman Daubeny.   His whole estate amounted to about £500, the only property of his in England being the £51 2s. 2d. due to him under the will of his brother Robert, who predeceased him.   He died on 20 May, 1822, at Rajamundry.

Administration of the goods of Robert Haines, his brother, was granted to Samuel Haines 12 January, 1825.   Robert, who was mate on board the merchant ship *Vittoria*, made his will on board in the river Thames 20 September, 1819.   He died 9 August, 1820, off Madras of yellow fever, and left £100 to his brother George Charman Haines, £400 to Samuel, and a share in the merchant ship *Albion*, worth £160 on sale, to Jane Matilda Beale, of Poplar, to whom no doubt he was engaged to be married. There were other small-dividends owing to him, but his estate was under £1,000 altogether.

A painted silhouette of Robert in his naval jacket, now in my possession, shows him with prominent lips and a peculiar " feather," or bunch, of hair on the forehead.[2]   This picture bears some resemblance to the photograph of the miniature of William Haines, his first cousin, above mentioned.   The only other fact about Robert Haines known to me is that he was an observer of birds.   In the *Letters of Rusticus*, a delightful book about old Godalming by Edward Newman, it is said that Robert Haines observed that rare bird " the nutcracker " in Peperharow Park.

Samuel Haines also administered the goods (under £1,500) of his sister Elizabeth (administration 7 September, 1829), and was also trustee, under the will of Anna Baptista White (proved 21 November, 1836), to Elizabeth Handford, a Godalming girl, testatrix's servant, who had an illegitimate daughter Maria Angela.

A miniature of Samuel Haines as a young man (recently married) exists, which shows him as a fresh-looking, rather dapper man, with a pleasing countenance and full lips.   Mr. H. F. Napper, of Laker's Lodge, describes him to me as " a tall slim wiry-looking

---

[1] William Haines, his first cousin, was the Indian executor.

[2] This, I am told by Mrs. Richard Moline, his niece, was inherited by my father.

man of the Don Quixote type, rather swarthy. Very outspoken in his opinions, he never hesitated to say what he thought." His niece, Mrs. Richard Moline, tells me he was a very kind man, but much inclined to be a hypochondriac, and always talking of his complaints. His patients liked him very much when they got to know him, but they would never send for him in the first place in preference to his brother George, but when once they had experienced his kindness and gentleness, they sometimes came to prefer him to his brother, who was generally regarded as the more able man. In his family he was the favourite brother, and his character must have been one that inspired trust, for he was on several occasions chosen trustee and executor, and certainly, from evidence in my possession, administered his trusts in a most conscientious and painstaking manner. Owing to some drug he took,[1] his complexion became a rather ghastly colour, and Henry Daubeny used to call him " our blue uncle." He was not a reading man, like his son, and time hung rather heavy on his hands, so that he seemed in a constant state of unrest. Sometimes, as one who knew him has told me, he would come into a room for the purpose merely, as it seemed, of walking out again. He was fond of whist and a superstitious player, anxious to change his seat when unlucky. He also played backgammon a great deal, but his favourite pursuit was shooting, in great contrast to his son, who was always poring over his books when his father and uncle were impatient to get to the coverts at Stroud House, near Witley. His niece, Mrs. Turner, tells me that he was, though rather quick in temper, a very kind-hearted man, devoted to his beautiful wife, whose early death from cholera in 1832 must have been a great shock to him.

He was very fond of his garden and grew a great many melons, and at the end of his garden were two paddocks where he kept some deer, pheasants, and hares, with clumps of furze and heather as a covert for them. But he sold this house near the Square,[2] and went into lodgings in the third house across the bridge at Godalming, where he died 20 April, 1848, aged 57. Latterly his health was not good and he suffered from bad headaches. He finally succumbed to some internal complaint which need not have proved fatal, but he had so often fancied himself seriously ill that his fellow-practitioners did not take

[1] Perhaps nitrate of silver, but there is no evidence of this.
[2] In 1842 to A. T. Chandler, Esq.

sufficient notice of his complaints on this occasion, and when his brother George came to take up the case it was too late—to the latter's extreme grief—to save his life.

The house in High Street near the King's Arms, now and for a long time past in the occupation of Arthur Jackson, saddler, and now the property of my brother Major Haines, was bought by Samuel Haines from his brother George Charman Haines 24 March, 1832, for £495. George Charman Haines had bought it in 1830, for £450. Curiously enough the property had been previously (14 February, 1784), left by John Upfold's will to his niece Mary Haynes, wife of Robert Haynes, of Chingford and of Pinner, officer of Excise. At the death of Samuel Haines in 1848 the house passed to his only child Robert, who was sole legatee and executor in his father's will (dated 22 June, 1841, proved 22 May, 1848).

CHAPTER XVI.

ROBERT HAINES

" In my father I observed mildness of temper, and unchangeable resolution
in the things which he had determined after due deliberation ; and no
vainglory in those things which men call honours, and a love of labour
and perseverance."—M. Aurelius, *Thoughts*, I, 16 (Long's translation).

ROBERT HAINES was born 8 June, 1821. He had rather an
unhappy school time, as I have heard my mother say. Latin he
learnt at home. At the age of sixteen, in 1837, he entered his
father's surgery as apprentice, and learnt practical pharmacy for
five years. He then went abroad,[1] visiting Paris and Boulogne,
and also took his degree of M.B., at the London University,[2]
obtaining an exhibition at the first examination for his degree,
and also the gold medal for chemistry.[3]

In 1845 (March) he became engaged to Anna Moline, niece to
the famous Dr. Prichard, descended on her mother's side from a
Quaker family, well known in Herefordshire, and on her father's
side of Dutch or Huguenot lineage, and of Kentish blood leading
back to the Scotch Kings and St. Margaret of Scotland.

Looking round for a practice for his son, Samuel Haines was
induced to buy the moiety of the practice of a certain Abraham
Wolff, of Shoreditch, London, which proved a complete disappoint-
ment, to use a mild term, and resulted in a loss of at least £800
to £1,000. At this time Robert Haines lived at 7, Finsbury
Circus. All this time he was working hard, and in 1848 he again
went abroad, visiting Paris[4] and Berlin, where he received valuable
introductions to Karl Ritter and others from his relation by
marriage, Dr. Prichard.

From his passport, 6 July, 1848, we learn that his height was

---

[1] Passport, 13 May, 1844.
[2] The first descendant of Richard Haines to take a degree.
[3] Now in possession of his third son, H. A. Haines.
[4] He was present at the Paris massacres and helped to tend the wounded.

5 feet 11½ inches, hair brown, eyes chestnut, nose long, chin round, and face oval.

Meanwhile he had learnt sufficient French and German to enable him to read and translate both languages with facility. Nor did he neglect the classics, for he was a fair Latin scholar, and left a translation of the *Epistles* of Pliny the younger behind him at his death. This was unfortunately destroyed about the year 1874. During his short and busy life he found time to amass an enormous amount of knowledge, and without any doubt he was the most learned and intellectually able of all the descendants of Richard Haines up to the present time. In chemistry his knowledge was especially profound, and had he lived there is no doubt that he would have come quite to the front in that science. Like his grandfather he was musical and played a great deal on the flute.

He was married on 1 August at Lee church in Kent, and sailed to India *via* the Cape in September, 1848, to take up a post in the Medical Establishment of the East India Company's forces, as superintending surgeon in Bombay, Sind, and the Punjaub on 25 January, 1849.[1] He was soon transferred for a time to the naval department, a duty which he cordially disliked, being a bad sailor. During the next ten or twelve years he held the following appointments at different times and for various periods—Superintendent of Vaccination, Concan Division ; surgeon of Jamsetjee Jejeebhoy Hospital, Bombay ; Acting Professor of Chemistry and Materia Medica in the Grant Medical College ; Professor of Chemistry and Natural History in the Elphinstone College ; Superintendent of Vaccination in the Northern Division of the Deccan ; Surgeon to the Jails[2] ; Acting Garrison surgeon ; Professor of Chemistry and Botany at the Grant Medical College ; Professor of the same and of Geology at the Elphinstone Institution ; Acting Chemical Analyzer to Government ; Secretary to Government in the Educational Department ; Acting Educational Inspector ; and surgeon to the Coroner.

He did not have an extensive private practice in Bombay, for which he did not lay himself out, but, says Mr. Bickersteth in a letter to me, " I can speak from personal experience as to his unremitting care and attention ; and the time he was willing to spend

---

[1] He was, I believe, attached to the Fusiliers and attained, before his death, to the rank of Surgeon-Major.

[2] It was then he was brought into contact with the Captain Haines above mentioned. See p. 2, *n.*

on serious cases was far more than is usual, or probably possible
for an ordinary practitioner."[1]

In applying for a post in 1855, Robert Haines claims for himself the following qualifications for it :—

"During the greater part of 1851, and the whole of 1852, I
undertook the whole of Dr. Giraud's classes, both at the Grant
Medical College and the Elphinstone Institution, in chemistry,
materia medica, botany, and geology, and I received the assurance of the perfect satisfaction of the Board of Education and of
the principals of those institutions.

"To mineralogy as a branch of chemistry, and to comparative
anatomy and its systematic development, zoology, as intimately
connected with and throwing light upon my professional studies,
I have devoted a good deal of time and labour ; and toward
geology, as that portion of natural history which comprehends
and requires for its elucidation the application of all the rest, I
have unavoidably felt great attraction. I would not say that I
have attained any absolutely high degree of proficiency in any of
these studies by making either of them so much the special object
of my attention as chemistry ; but I do not offer my services to
teach them, without feeling the wish, and I hope the ability, to
inspire those I would instruct with some portion of the interest
with which I regard them, and to lead them through the multi-
farious phenomena laid open in the study of nature on to the
appreciation of the unity of all science, and of the fundamental
truths which that conception involves—the ultimate object, as I
conceive it of all teaching and study."

From this time to his death Dr. Haines devoted himself to his
work, scarcely leaving Bombay except on duty, or during his
vaccination tours, and only for short visits to Mahableshwar or
Poona.

On 13 April, 1854, was born at Poorundhur, near Poona,
Bombay, his first child, a daughter—deprived of life by the very
act of birth. My mother, writing 17 April, 1854, to her mother,
says : "One of our servants waited up and watched on my
account day and night and thought no trouble too much for me—
the same who went the night our poor little babe was born to
make a grave for it. We sent him because he was a Christian."[2]

---

[1] J. P. Bickersteth, Esq., Grove Mill House, Watford, 29 November, 1898.

[2] I am glad to print this testimony. Some living Anglo-Indians deny that there
is such a thing as a trustworthy native Christian.

Three other children, all sons, were born in the three following years.

In 1865 on Dr. Giraud's retirement from the principalship of the Grant Medical College, the vacant appointment, one of the very highest in the medical service at Bombay and the duties of which he had been practically discharging for some time past, was bestowed on Dr. Haines. It seemed that the time had now come for taking the much-needed holiday to England, where his children had already gone. But it was not to be. On 3 January, 1866, the new principal read the year's report at the college, suggesting certain reforms. On April 13 he seemed particularly well,[1] and his heavy work for the year being now over, he might look forward to a short time for putting things in order before embarking for England. But on Monday, April 16, he was attacked with fever, and though everything was done that medical science could suggest, and though he was never left for a minute without one of his colleagues in the profession in attendance in his room, he succumbed on April 26, at 4.30 p.m. A MS. report of the case in my possession, evidently written by one of the doctors in attendance,[2] describes the illness as "an excellent example of the fever usually styled 'remittent,' accompanied with jaundice (which appeared on the night of the 22nd) . . . but (he adds) in Dr. Haines's case a striking feature was the absence of all delirium and coma. . . . Dr. Haines was perfectly sensible until a few minutes before his death."

One friend who was present describes the fever as malarial, and another says it was the first case recognised in India as exhibiting typhoid symptoms.[3] A third tells me that though an extraordinarily thin man, his liver was found at death to be abnormally large, and that death was due to enlargement of the liver. From the very first the patient lost all ·strength, and considered the attack to be very serious, and on the 20th April he made his will, leaving everything to his wife, with her and John Pares Bickersteth as executrix and executor and Thomas Benyan Ferguson as executor of the personal effects.[4] The will was signed in the presence of J. B. Lyon, assistant surgeon, and

---

[1] See letter from my mother to me, dated that day.

[2] Perhaps Sir W. Guyer Hunter.

[3] The death certificate described it, on what grounds I do not know, as typhoid.

[4] The estate was worth less than £2,500, and the widow thus became entitled to £60 pension under Lord Clive's fund.

J. P. Bickersteth, senior magistrate. The Rev. W. K. Fletcher says : " I saw him during his illness, and can testify to his patience under great suffering and the peace with which he met death, in the blessed hope of the resurrection to eternal life."

He was buried on April 27th at the Colaba cemetery, after a service held in the cathedral at 5 o'clock, 200 men of the 4th N.I. (Rifles) under Major Warden forming the funeral escort. The coffin was taken out of the hearse and carried on a litter by men of the 4th King's Own Royal Infantry, and the pall was borne by Drs. Leith, Stovell, Rogers, Joynt, Hunter, and Mr. Bickersteth. The Rev. W. K. Fletcher read the burial service.

The death of Robert Haines was regarded as a great loss not only by his friends, but by the whole European and native community of Bombay—as may be seen from the following tributes in the Bombay papers :—

" THE LATE DR. HAINES.

" Bombay has suffered in the death of Dr. Robert Haines a great, and indeed irreparable, loss. He was one of the most distinguished officers of the Bombay Medical Service, and as a scientific officer no one in the Medical Service of India can take his place. He was one of the most valued and ablest Fellows of the University of Bombay, and he was a philosophical chemist of the very first capacity, who had already acquired solid reputation in England, and who would have gained, had he lived, the highest eminence in this science. He was master of every branch of natural science; he was an accurate and accomplished scholar; he was full of all manner of out-of-the-way learning, and withal was a most admirable man of business. His was a mind of the highest order, obscured only by obscure service. His moral superiority could not be hid. By temperament he was indeed reserved almost to excess. ' No one word spake he more than was need'; and none but those who knew him in the intimacy of domestic life can possibly estimate the endearing virtue of his soul, and certainly it is not the pen of private friendship which attempts this tribute to the dead. But the most casual acquaintance with Dr. Haines revealed the impartiality, the perfect transparency, the wonderful unworldliness of his character. No one could ever have mixed with him in business without having carried away this impression of the man, and probably preserved it in

Robert Haines, M.B.,
late Principal of the Grant Medical College, Bombay.

some pointed anecdote. And it was these moral characteristics, joined to his wide and various knowledge, his shrewd sense and sound judgment, which made him so trusted, as well as admired, by others. In ordinary affairs of life he seemed still the man of science, who sought not victory but truth. In all public business, in which he was concerned, a wise and truthful solution of the question which might be in contention, was his single aim; and this always became so clear to the conscience of his colleagues or associates, that any debate in which Dr. Haines took part became at once an investigation. Victory so won could leave no sting. In a young University, and as Principal of a College, the value of such a man is past computing. Dr. Haines's favourite science was chemistry. He was singularly qualified to excel in this science, which requires for its successful cultivation some of the greatest powers of the mind. He added to it innumerable important analyses, and but for the exigencies of his official position he would have already gained that general recognition of his scientific merits, which in the end, had he lived, was certain. For many years he had been known in England as a philosophical and perfectly trustworthy chemist. Government and the High Court can replace his services as chemical analyzer only from England or Germany. The un-initiated can perhaps hardly understand the public loss, in this respect, in the death of Dr. Haines; but they may form some slight appreciation of it, when they know how a controversy between George Wilson and Professor Gregory concerning some infinitesimal decimal quantity in an analysis raged in Edinburgh for nearly 10 years. As an official Dr. Haines was singularly able. When some years ago he was for a time appointed Acting Registrar of the University, those who had known him before only as a man of great science and learning and unworldliness,—as a rapt student of atoms and forces—were taken by surprise by the thorough and absolutely brilliant manner in which he discharged the trying duties of the office. He was punctual and exact to the merest clerical detail, weighty in council, full of the right spirit of his office, and when the question for a seal and arms for the University turned up accidentally, he wrote a profound heraldic essay on the subject which excited the wonder of the Fellows and the admiration of the Garter King of Arms.[1] When again he succeeded to the Principalship of the Grant

[1] I have tried unsuccessfully to recover this from the Heralds' College.

Medical College, a doubt was felt as to how he might rule a college. He seemed to be rather a Grand Syndic of the mediæval type in very person, as if he had just walked out of a Vandyke canvas, than fitted to be Principal of a modern college. But the doubt was only for a moment. He at once succeeded in his new duties, and, as his colleagues know, with distinction. In fact Dr. Haines's proved extraordinary scientific capacity was but the sign, and not the full measure of his mind ; and such power joined to great goodness of soul, could not but be successful in everything, and so he proved equally master in the world and in the laboratory."

The *Bombay Gazette* for Saturday 28 April, 1866, says[1]: " In the death of Surgeon Robert Haines, M.B., Principal of the Grant Medical College, the Indian Medical Service has lost one of its brightest ornaments, and Bombay one of its best friends. . . . Apparently cut off in the prime of life and in the vigour of intelligence, when an extensive field of usefulness lay before him, his loss is mourned as the loss of one taken away ere his course was run and the aim of his existence accomplished. For many years Dr. Haines devoted himself closely to study, and his recreation seemed to have been sought in the laboratory and library, while the remainder of his time was taken up in hospital duties and in educational work.

"Too long in India without a change, too anxious to perform his duties with faithfulness, Dr. Haines thought not of leave to Europe, nor of leave in India, and he worked on to the end, yielding himself a victim to his own integrity. In the educational department of this presidency, Dr. Haines attained the highest rank both as a scholar and a teacher. His efficiency as a lecturer is known to the general public. As a practical chemist he was counted a man worthy of a European reputation. Native education stands largely indebted to him for valuable disinterested

---

[1] A later issue of a Bombay paper, speaking of the various Principals of the Grant Medical College, says : " The living enthusiasm, deep research, and high attainments of Dr. Giraud's successors are not likely soon to be equalled within the College walls." See *Life of Dr. Morehead*, by H. A. Haines, p. 42. The *Times of India*, February, 1871, says : " By the great earnestness and zeal with which they performed their task, by their sense of honour and their just and impartial decisions, by their sound practical instructions and their superior attainments, by the entire absence in them of pride or presumption, I say by the possession of these noble qualities, the names of Morehead, Peet, Ballingall and Haines will ever remain so dearly cherished in the hearts of all their pupils." *Ibid.*, p. 59.

services. In the University Senate he was a leading member. His eminence as a scholar was known to all but himself, for humility and unobtrusiveness were marked features in his character. . . .

"The general public have known Dr. Haines best as an eminent chemist, as Surgeon-in-Chief of the Jamsetjee Jejeebhoy Hospital, as Principal of the Grant Medical College, and as the Registrar of the Mortuary Returns of the city. Well may it be said that his life was spent in relieving the body as a physician, and opening up the mind as an educationist. Successful in both, if he laboured hard and rested little, if his toil and diligence were not relieved by ease and relaxation, if he bestowed upon others more than he himself received of praise and profit, he has earned for himself not only the respect and commendation of his fellow men, but that greater reward which the world can neither give nor take away."

The same copy of the *Gazette* contains a letter from one of his native pupils, the sincerity of which is only enhanced by its somewhat quaint phraseology. After stating that he was qualified to speak from a three-year acquaintance with the deceased as his pupil, and after speaking of his vigorous mind and upright character, he says :

"He was truly made to ' scorn delight and live laborious days.' His reading was never desultory or superficial, for he had been full and clear in his exposition of subjects ; he seemed to pursue it (*sic*) till he had mastered it. Withal he was upright, modest, and of an unassuming disposition." He ends his letter with the apostrophe—" ' But now that good heart bursts and he is at rest.' With that breath expired a soul who never indulged a passion unfit for the place he has gone to. Where now are thy plans of justice, of truth, of honour ? Poor were the expectations of the studious, the modest, and the good, if the rewards of their labours were only to be expected from man . . . while others with their talents were tormented with ambition, with vain glory, with envy, with emulation—how well didst thou turn thy mind to its own improvement in things out of the power of fortune.[1] . . . How silent thy passage, how private thy journey !

> "COWASJEE NOWROJEE,
>
> "*Graduate, Grant Medical College.*"

On the next Prize-giving day of the Grant Medical College,[2]

---

[1] This reads somewhat like a passage out of the *Thoughts* of Marcus Aurelius.
[2] 12 January, 1867.

Dr. Hunter[1] spoke of his predecessor's attainments, and stated that " had his life been spared he would [as a chemist] in all probability have taken rank among some of the foremost men in Europe," and in the course of his speech on the same occasion, the Hon. C. J. Erskine said, " There was something in the habit of his mind—I may say in the habit of his life—which most fitly associates itself with the retirement of a place of learning and study."

A resolution was passed at the meeting of the senate that—

> " The University of Bombay, in token of its regret for the untimely decease of Dr. Haines, and to show its appreciation of his many valuable services, as Fellow, Acting Registrar, Syndic, and Examiner, resolves to vote the sum of Rs. 1000 towards the proposed testimonial in honour of Dr. Haines's memory."

Many were the testimonies to his worth from friends in Bombay and elsewhere. One who knew him well during the last eight years of his life says he was " a kind and considerate friend, and a liberal host, a very keen but kindly critic of the men and women he met in society, incapable of the least intrigue or underhand dealing to get advantage for himself."

A colleague in the medical service calls him " one of the best of men," and another speaks of his loss as irreparable. His brother-in-law described him to me as one of the most gentlemanly men he ever met. The late Sir Bartle Frere bears testimony to his admirable service in the Educational Department in Bombay, adding that " from the first years of our acquaintance I had reason to admire both his ability and unselfish public-spirited devotion in promoting the cause of education in all its branches in Bombay." But the most striking tribute of all is the following letter from Sir Alexander Grant dated Mahableshewar 29 April, 1866.

" My dear Du Port,

" We are here filled with sorrow at the loss of our friend whom we admired and loved so much, and with whom we had lived in such intimate relations. Few human souls have ever impressed me more with a sort of sense of perfection. So wise he was, and calmly self-dependent, so pure and unselfish, so helpful to all, so above everything petty.

> " ' So many worlds, so much to do,
> So little done, such things to be,
> How know I what had need of thee,
> For thou wert strong, as thou wert true.'

[1] Now Sir Wm. Guyer Hunter.

The loss to us here both privately and publicly is irreparable, and the loss to his wife and boys is irreparable beyond expression. And it is a bitter thought that a little pause and relaxation—a journey to England some two or three years ago—might have saved this valuable existence for us. Well, God's will be done, and on Haines's tomb be it inscribed,

"'His life was noble and the elements so mixed in him, that Nature might stand up and say before the world, This was a man!'"

I feel broken-hearted to-day and cannot write more.

"Yours sincerely,

"A. GRANT."[1]

Another great friend, J. P. Bickersteth, Esq., describes him as of a very quiet and retiring disposition, and far more fond of reading and study than social life and amusements; and says that when called upon, as surgeon to the coroner, to give evidence in cases of murder and manslaughter, Dr. Haines, in giving his evidence, was "calm and deliberate to a degree, but always ready to give a reason for any statement that he had made or opinion he had expressed, and never put out or shaken by cross-examination, however severe it might be."

The same observer notes the great ability he showed in connection with the Bombay Army Medical Retiring Fund. This fund had been established on a basis financially unsound, and the junior contributors were in a fair way to lose their contributions to it. Dr. Haines was one of the few men in the service competent to deal with such a question, and he worked the matter out with infinite pains, and set the annuities on a sound basis.

He also left at his death statistical tables relating to the duration of life among the natives on which he had bestowed immense labour, and which he had nearly finished. During his last illness he advised that the work should be completed by an actuary and the annuity tables be calculated from them.

In their memorandum on these tables the Government of Bombay speak of him as "distinguished in an eminent degree both for high scientific attainments and for habits of the most careful and accurate observation."[2]

[1] Curiously enough, Sir A. Grant's son is named Ludovic, and among the signatories given above, p. 96 (of whom Gregory Haines is one) stands a Ludovic Grant.

[2] So says General Lester, another old Indian friend, who adds, " in his disposition and manner he was full of gentleness and kindness, and all who knew him must have liked him greatly." The son of Captain Stafford B. Haines (see p. 2 *n.*) says of my father that he " was a kind and good friend—*sans peur et sans reproche.*"

In a letter addressed to Dr. Haines's widow 25 February, 1867, the Government of Bombay inform her that 5,000 rupees had been paid in to her account in respect of the above mortuary tables, and concludes with assuring her how warmly the eminent services of Dr. Haines in this, as in so many other ways, were appreciated by Government, and how sincerely they lamented the loss of so valuable an officer.

Besides these tables of mortality printed by Samuel Brown, F.I.A.,[1] I only know of the following papers by my father:—

1. "Two Addresses delivered at the opening of a session of the Grant Medical College, 1856," and another, year unknown.

2. Paper on the "Volatile oil of Ptychotis Ajwan" in the *Chemical Soc. Journal*, VIII, 1856, pp. 289–291. Also *Prak. Chem.*, LXVIII, 1856, pp. 430–432.

3. "Report and analysis of various kinds of coal," *Bombay Medical Physical Soc. Trans.*, VI, 1860, pp. lix–lxii.

4. "Notes on the extraction and estimation of some of the crystalline principles of opium," *Bombay Med. Phys. Soc. Trans.*, VII, 1861, pp. 222–234.

5. "On the analysis of mineral waters and the arrangement of the results." *Chemical News*, 1861, pp. 29–31.

6. "On the presence of nitrate in mineral waters and in the production of saltpetre." *Chemical News*, IV, 1861, pp. 154, 155, 165–166, 194, 195.

7. "Notes on Nitrification." *Chem. News*, IV, 1861, pp. 245, 246, 259, 260.

8. "On the conversion of calomel into corrosive sublimate by ammoniacal salts." *Bombay Med. Phys. Soc. Trans.*, VIII, 1862, pp. 224–230.

9. "On the natural formation of carbonates of soda." *Pharmaceutical Journal*, V, 1864, pp. 26, 27.

10. R. Haines and Herbert Giraud.[2] "Analysis of the mineral springs and various well and river waters in the Bombay Presidency." *Bombay Med. Phys. Soc. Trans.*, V, 1859, pp. 242–263.

11. "Three articles on Heraldry," from the *Times of India*, September, 1863.

[1] *Journal of the Institute of Actuaries and Assurance Magazine*, Vol. XVI p. 187.

[2] A copy of this is in the British Museum.

Kirdford Church, Sussex, West Front, with brick tombs of the Haines Family in the foreground; those of Gregory of S. Carolina and his son John are the two to the immediate right of the tree on the left, and the tomb of Mary, wife of John, is just beyond the tree. The Sladeland pew was in the north aisle, and was formerly entered by a door with steps from the outside.

These are all the products of that busy and well-stored brain that remain to us.

In recognition of Dr. Haines's works, a sum of money was collected in Bombay for a marble bust to be placed in the Grant Medical College, and to provide a sum to be vested in the hands of trustees for the scientific and literary education of his eldest son.

The bust by Woolner now stands in the Grant Medical College, and a sum of £1,000 was collected for the second object. The inscription on the pedestal of the bust speaks of his "noble and devoted life."[1]

The tomb in Colaba Cemetery has the following inscription :—

In affectionate Remembrance
of
ROBERT HAINES, M.B.,
Surgeon in His Majesty's Indian Army,
Principal of the Grant Medical College,
Bombay.
He was born at Godalming in Surrey
on the 8th of June, 1821.
He died after 17 years of faithful service
on the 26th April, 1866,
at Mazagon, Bombay.

---

[1] The following testimony has come into my hands too late for insertion in its proper place :—

Edward L. Howard, barrister, of Bombay, writing to Dr. Haines's widow on 10 May, 1866, uses these remarkable expressions of her husband : "He seemed to me in the first place to be absolutely blameless — this was the more wonderful from his extraordinary acquirements and unceasing mental activity. He reminded me of the great men of a different age from this—of schoolmen without arrogance and saints without bigotry. If the next world is like the dream of Isaac Taylor, your dear husband was of all men I ever saw the fittest to enter it from this."

CHAPTER XVII.

THE ARMS OF HAINES.

THE earliest coat of arms, assigned to any one of the Haynes name, is that which was owned by Sir . . . Eynns, a knight of Shropshire in the reign of Edward I (1272–1307), viz. :

Arg. ; on a fesse gules three roundles.[1]

A pretty legend ascribes the origin of the fesse in heraldry to a "king at the close of a battle visiting one of his wounded warriors, dubbing him knight, and with his hand, dipt in the wounded hero's own blood, tracing a red stripe across his shield, and saying, that should be his device."

The roundles above mentioned probably represented bezants, or byzantine gold pieces, and in coat armour are generally taken to denote, as crescents also do, a crusader.

The old and genuine types of Haynes coats, such as are found "tricked" in the Heralds' Visitations, or for which the grants are recorded in the College of Arms, are chiefly three in number, viz., the coats with bezants (crest, an eagle),[2] the coats with crescents (heron, as crest), the coats with annulets.

1. ARMS SHOWING BEZANTS, AND OFTEN A GREYHOUND COURANT.—Recorded in the Visitation of Shropshire (1569) we find, under Heynes, or Eynns, of Stretton, a typical coat of this sort, as follows :

Or ; on a fesse gules 3 bezants, in chief a greyhound courant sable, collared of the second.

In the next visitation appears, as crest, an *eagle displayed azure, semée d'étoiles argent;* and in 1663, as a second crest, *an eagle displayed or, standing on a tortoise argent.*

Robson gives a coat Haynes,[3] co. Salop: *Arg. ; on a fesse gules 3 bezants between as many demi greyhounds azure.* These were the arms borne by a flourishing family of Haynes who resided at

---

[1] Brit. Mus. Harl. MS. 1068, f. 65. See a pamphlet by the late A. M. Haines of Galena, Illinois, U.S.A., on the Haines Arms.

[2] Mr. John Haines of 24, Hampton Place, Brighton, uses as arms the greyhound and bezant coat, *but the heron as crest.*

[3] Burke (? Robson too) gives demi-hinds, a probable error for *hounds.* See Notes on the Family of Haynes of Westbury-on-Trym, etc., by the Rev. F. J. Poynton. The Haines family of Painswick, Gloucestershire, use for arms: Arg.: on a chevron gu. 3 bezants between as many demi-hinds (? hounds) ramp. az.

Westbury-on-Trym, Wick and Abson in Gloucestershire from very early times. They do not appear in any Visitations nor is any grant discoverable. Atkyns in his *Gloucestershire* gives them with "hinds" not "hounds"; so also Bigland in his "Monumental Inscriptions," and Naylor in his "Plates of Arms."

With but slight difference the same arms as those of Heynes of Stretton are found ascribed to Hayne of Iberton and Dorchester,[1] and Hayne of Honiton, in co. Devon; and they were used by the famous General James Heane (pronounced Hayne) of a Gloucestershire family, who conquered Jersey for Cromwell and became its governor in 1652. He used the second eagle crest.[2] They were also granted or confirmed 4 September, 1607, to Thomas Hayne of Friar Waddon, co. Dorset,[3] who was of the family of Hayne of Iberton and Dorchester. Gideon Hayne, a descendant of the same family, stamped these arms on a token issued in the 17th century in co. Meath, Ireland. On 18 June, 1702, they were granted or confirmed to John Hayne, son of John Hayne, deceased, of Dartmouth, co. Devon[4]; and on 17 October, 1784, to John Haynes of Chelsea, principal registrar of the Province of Canterbury.[5] This coat is quartered by the Marquess of Bath, as descended from Thomas Thynne and Margaret Haynes of Stretton; and, impaled with that of Egerton, it is sculptured over the entrance of the Egerton family mansion at Ashridge, co. Bucks. It appears there through the marriage of the 7th Earl of Bridgewater with Charlotte Catherine Ann Haynes, a descendant of Hopton Haynes (from 1696–1749 officer of the Mint), who was probably from Gloucestershire or Wiltshire. The present family of Seale-Hayne of Devonshire use this coat,[6] and it was assumed before his death by the late lamented Mr. A. M. Haines of Galena, Illinois, his ancestor Samuel Haines having emigrated from Wiltshire to America in 1635.[7]

---

[1] Harl. MS. 1160. f. 19b.

[2] Geneal. Notes relating to the family of Heane by W. C. Heane, Esq.

[3] Harl. MSS. 1539. f. 107b.

[4] Used by the Rev. S. C. Haines, of Instow, Devon, and by Richard Haines, Esq., of West Bromwich, Staffordshire, and also by a family now settled in co. Cork, which emigrated to Ireland in the time of Cromwell.

[5] He died 1 February, 1750.

[6] Burke's *Landed Gentry*. Some Sussex family used it about 1775. See Burrell MSS. 5695, p. 628.

[7] See pamphlet by A. M. Haines of Illinois. An old altar tomb at Biddeston, Wilts, shows for Haynes: *Erm; on a fesse sa. between 3 torteaux a greyhound courant arg. collared or.*

2. THE COATS WITH CRESCENTS.—These are numerous, but their origin is not known, unless the crescents are but a variation for bezants or plates, as signifying the same thing.

On 10 June, 1578, William Heynes (or Haynes) and Nicholas Heynes, first and fourth sons of Richard Heynes of Reading, received from Robert Cooke, Clarencieux King of Arms, a confirmation of their arms, the grant to Nicholas being couched in the following terms :

> " being required by Nicholas Haynes of Hackney in Middlesex, fourthe son of Richard Haynes of Redinge in the county of Berkshire gentleman . . . . to make serche in ye Registers and Recordes of my office for the auntient arms and creast belonging to his name and family, I have made searche accordingly and doe fynde yt he may lawfully beare as his auncestors hertofore have borne these arms and creast heareafter followeinge That is to say ye first for Haynes ; *Argent, three crescents [paly]*[1] *undée azure and gules,* the second for Foxley ; gules two bares humité silver and so quarterly, and to his Creast uppon the healme *on a wreathe silver and gules a Heron volant the bodye in proper couller wynges silver legged and beaked goulde houldinge up one of his feet* mantelled gules doubled silver."

The coat confirmed[2] to William, brother of Nicholas, was in every respect similar, and it differed from their father's coat merely in having the heron's dexter foot lifted.[3]

Nicholas Haynes's family came to an end in the male line with the death of his son Richard, of Hackney, co. Middlesex, and Arundel, co. Sussex, 21 April, 1634.

The other brothers of Nicholas and William died childless, and judging from their wills, which only mention the children of Nicholas, probably William too died childless ; unless he was the same person as William Haynes, citizen and merchant tailor of All Hallows, Barking, who, by will dated 5 September, 1590, left charities to the poor of St. Dunstan's in the East. The identification is unlikely, as William, brother of Nicholas, was, like him, a

---

[1] Not in my copy of the grant, but the tricking shows that the crescents were paly of six [*not barry*]. The heron has a martlet sable on the body, as a mark of cadence for the fourth son.

[2] Harl. 1438. f. 10. Add. MS. 14,295. f. 10b. Camden's Grants (College of Arms, I, 15).

[3] Papworth, Robson and Berry give the arms of Haynes of Reading as *gu.* 3 *cresc. paly wavy, arg. and az.*

yeoman of the guard to Queen Elizabeth, yeoman of the toils, and purveyor of salmon and sea fish to Her Majesty. There is, however, at St. Dunstan's a side window, dated 1590, having these arms upon it, viz., 7th, Willm Haynes :

Arg.; 3 crescents paly of six gu. and az.[1]

But even if the two Williams were identical, it is probable that the family of William the merchant tailor, though at first flourishing, died out in the male line.[2] At all events Sir John Evelyn, husband of Thomazine Haynes, a grand-daughter of said William through another son than the grandchildren mentioned in the note, impales the Heynes arms thus :

Arg. ; a fesse wavy azure between 3 annulets gu.

Crest: *a stork or heron.*[3]

This is certainly puzzling, as it combines the crest of the crescent arms with the annulets. Again there is the fact that a William Haynes of Tower ward was taxed £150 for leaving London[4] to live at Croydon in 1590, and a window was found some years ago in Croydon Church behind Whitgift's monument, which could not have been opened since 1598, showing these arms :

Arg. ; a fesse nebulée azure between 3 annulets gules.

This coat, therefore, *may* have been the coat of William Haynes the citizen and merchant tailor.[5]

Arms identical with those of Nicholas are used by the Haynes family of Thimbleby Lodge, co. Yorks,[6] with the difference that the stork (=heron) holds in its beak a serpent. They are also used by a family of Haines, that migrated in 1647 from Hurst, near Maidenhead, Berks, to Barbadoes (being Royalists), and whose present representatives claim to be descended from the Reading family. If so, they must be descended from another branch than that of Richard of Reading, if, as is shown to be probably the case, William the eldest son had no children.

---

[1] Burke gives under Heynes of London *arg. ; 3 cresc. paly wavy of six gu. and az.* Similar arms appear without pedigree under Haynes of Surrey. Brit. Mus. Harl 1147. f. 170.

[2] This depends on whether Benedick and Henry, grandsons of said William, had any sons.

[3] Misc. Gen. et Her. 2 Ser. viii, 319. The tomb is at Godstone in Surrey, dated 1643.

I have mislaid the reference to this.

[5] Robson gives this coat for Haynes or Hayne and adds "another of the second."

[6] See Burke's *Landed Gentry*.

A similar, if not identical, coat was borne by a very ancient family of Haynes (now probably extinct in the male line) in Herts and Essex. The name is spelt with the "s" almost always from the very earliest times.[1] From this family descended a celebrated John Haynes, afterwards Governor of Massachusetts and of Connecticut. The constitution which he drew up for this latter state, was the first ever written in the New World. John Haynes was probably the richest settler that went out to America, and an estimate of his character describes him as "of a very large estate and larger affections, of a heavenly mind and spotless life, of rare sagacity and accurate but unassuming judgment, by nature tolerant and ever a friend to freedom."[2] His son Hezekiah (born 1619, died 1693) was one of Cromwell's right-hand men, and made by him Military Governor of the Eastern Counties. A letter from a Royalist[3] says, "Among the Major-Generals, only Haynes is firmly Cromwell's." He was imprisoned at the Restoration, but afterwards released. His portrait, painted by Kneller, now in the possession of J. C. Brown, Esq., Providence, R.I., shews him in armour.[4]

John Barlee, the husband of Mary, sister of Governor John Haynes, impaled the Haynes arms with his own arms, as seen upon his tomb (1633).

These appear, from Hezekiah's seal, affixed to a letter in the Bodleian Library,[5] to have been

Arg. ; 3 cresc. barry of six az. and gu.,

with a small crescent in the centre of the shield as a mark of cadence for the second son. In the copy of the seal which I have the bars are not wavy. These arms differ from those granted to Nicholas Haynes of Hackney only in having the crescents barry instead of paly. The heron too on Hezekiah's seal has its beak open and dexter foot held out. But in the Visitation of Essex, 1664,[6] the heron has its beak closed and both feet down.

In the Visitation of London 1687,[7] Thomas Haynes, citizen and mercer, son of Hezekiah, enters his pedigree, and produces, in proof of his arms and crest, a seal on a silver inkhorn, said to

---

[1] I have a great deal of information connected with this family.

[2] *Dictionary of National Biography.*

[3] 20 January, 1657. Bodl. Libr. State Papers, 711.

[4] The face might have stood for a portrait of Susannah, daughter of Gregory Haines and Susannah Peachey, so great was the resemblance.

[5] Rawlinson, A 24,388.

[6] College of Arms, D. 21, 14.   [7] *Ibid.*, K. G. 148.

belong to his father. These correspond to the arms and crest on Hezekiah's own seal. Hezekiah's motto was *Velis et remis*. A correspondent in *Notes and Queries*, writing in 1860 over the pseudonym "Spalatro," mentions a seal in his possession engraved as follows:

Arg. (no tincture engraved); *3 cresc. barry wavy of six az. and ar., a mullet for difference, surmounting an esquire's helmet.*

Crest : *on a wreath a stork, heron, or crane rising.*

Motto : *Velis et remis.*

This would seem to be another seal of the said Hezekiah. He really was the third son, but his elder brother John died young.[1]

How was it that Hezekiah's family used, and proved to the visiting heralds their right to, the same arms as had been confirmed to a Reading family? It seems probable that the Reading branch, which we cannot trace further back than Richard Heynes of Reading, was an off-shoot from the Essex and Herts family, of whom we have evidence that they resided in those parts from very early times. These arms only appear elsewhere, as borne by Haynes of Stutton,[2] Suffolk :

Arg.; 3 cresc. barry wavy or and gu.

Besides the Thomas Haynes above mentioned, there was another Middlesex family of Haynes, or Heynes, that recorded their pedigree and arms in the Visitation of London 1634. They lived at Hoxton, and their arms were[3] :

Arg.; on a fesse az. between 3 cresc. az. and gu. paly of six 3 fleurs-de-lys or.

These are said to have been found in Alderman Smith's house at London Stone, and are recorded in the funeral certificates at the College of Arms. They appear upon the shields of Cage and Hart, through the marriage of Anne Haynes, daughter of Richard Haynes of Hoxton, to Anthony Cage and subsequently to Sir John Hart, and through the former marriage they find a place in the 100 quarterings of the coat of Hastings, of Burham, co. Bucks.

Robson under Haines gives :

Arg.; on a fesse azure between 3 crescents of the last as many fleurs-de-lys of the first,

and adds for crest 3 moors' heads conjoined on one neck.

A Gloucestershire family, anciently settled at Daglingworth

---

[1] The crescents, however, are differently coloured.

[2] From the Sperling MSS., Armoury of Suffolk. Probably the coat of Hez. Haynes, grandson of the above Hezekiah.   [3] Harl. MS. 1476. f. 280b.

and Duntsborne, are known from tombs in those places, dating about 1700, to have used for arms :

Arg. ; 3 crescents per pale gu. and az.

The Rev. Percy N. Haines, son of the late John Poole Haines, uses these arms except that the crescents are az. and gu. The coat impales az. a lion rampant arg. between 3 fleurs-de-lys or.

In the Burrell MSS. on Sussex there is ascribed (in blazon) to Haynes of that county a similar coat :[1]

Gu. ; 3 crescents per pale arg. and azure.

Another Haines coat is given by Robson and Burke, but without locality, as follows :

Gu. ; 3 crescents paly wavy arg. and az.

Crest : on a crescent an arrow in pale ppr.

And lastly[2] a monumental inscription in St. Martin's Church, Worcester, to Francis Haines, Mayor of Worcester in 1683, who died 1717, aged 71, gives as his arms :

Arg. ; 3 crescents gu.

3. THE COATS WITH ANNULETS (generally combined with bezants).—Besides the arms in Croydon Church, and at Godstone, both mentioned above, an early instance of the annulet arms is afforded by a tomb in St. Dunstan's Church, London, where the coat of Crooke al's Heyne[3] appears thus :

Or ; a fesse wavy az. bezantée between 3 annulets of the second.

Robson and Burke assign this coat, with the field argent, to Haynes, or Haines, of Berks. The Burrell MSS. for Sussex give the blazon for arms of Hayne of Sussex as,

Arg. ; a fesse nebulée bezantée between 3 annulets gules.

Another Berkshire coat is given by Robson for Haynes :

Arg. ; a fesse wavy az. charged with 3 annulets or between 7 bezants.

And another Hayne, or Haynes, coat (no place mentioned).

Arg. ; on a fesse nebulée between 3 annulets gu. 6 bezants.

A monument in St. Martin's Church, Worcester (1687) to Thomas Haines, serjeant of His Majesty's Chapel Royal, who died in London and was buried at Worcester, has engraved upon it[4] :

---

[1] Brit. Mus. 5695, p. 626. Date about 1775.

[2] Guillim apparently gives as a Haynes coat—*Gu. ; 3 crescents or.*

[3] See Visitation of London, 1633; and *Church Notes on St. Dunstan's, London.*

[4] For his will see P.C.C. 94, Foot.

Arg.; on a fesse between 3 annulets gules as many ducal coronets or.

A tomb in Crofton Church, Hants, dated 7 May, 1849, to the Rev[nd]. David Haynes of St. John's College, Cambridge, shows the same arms exactly, with this crest: 2 batons in saltire enfiladed by a ducal coronet or.

An Irish coat, given by Robson, shows a combination of crescents and annulets, apparently the only one of the sort:

Arg.; on a fesse between 3 crescents az. as many annulets of the first.

Crest: *a lion sejant or, collared az.*

Lastly[1] a coat assigned to Haynes by Robson gives a combination of the crescents and the eagle crest:

Arg.; 2 palets vert between 3 crescents in chief gu.[2]

Crest: *an eagle preying on a tortoise.*

4. COATS WITHOUT CRESCENTS, ANNULETS, OR BEZANTS.—Simon Heynes (*ob.* 1552), one of the most distinguished men of the Haynes name, who took a prominent part in the great crisis of the Church in the 16th century, was one of the revisers of our Liturgy, eighth president of Queen's College, Cambridge, and Vice-Chancellor of that University in 1531, bore as arms,

Gules, a cinquefoil within an orle of crosslets or.

But Simon Heynes, probably his nephew, son and heir of John Heynes of Mildenhall, Suffolk, gentleman, received on 20 September, 1575, the following grant of arms[3]:

Or; a chevron between 3 brode arrows sa. On a chief embattled az. 3 mullets of the field. Crest: *on a wreath gold and az. an eagle's head erased arg., a crown about the neck az.*

A similar coat is assigned by Burke to Heynes of Turweston, Bucks; the crest however being

An eagle's head erased erm., ducally gorged or.

Three generations of Simon Heyneses, son, grandson, and great grandson of Simon, the president of Queen's College, lived at Turweston, and why they should have dropped their ancestral arms for the grant to Simon, son of John, I don't know.

This coat and crest are used by the family whose pedigree is

---

[1] Brit. Mus. Add. MS. 5524, for Heins of Essex, gives (apparently) 3 annulets, and for crest an arm holding a drawn sword. One Hannes of Oxford, father of Edward Hannes, physician to the Queen, has, in 1705, these arms: *per pale az. and gu., a fesse between 3 annulets or.*

[2] These arms are borne by Basil J. Haines, Esq. of Queen Charlton near Bristol.

[3] Misc. Geneal. et Herald., I, p. 251. Harl. MS, 1102. f. 53, etc.

given below, but though the ancestry of Thomas Haines (*ob.*
1705), whose name stands at the head of that pedigree, has not
been certainly traced, it is most likely that he came from
Washington, co. Sussex, or the immediate neighbourhood, and
that consequently he had no connection with the Suffolk family.

There is another ancient Haines coat in the west of England.
It is assigned in 1510 to Thomazine Haine of Devonshire [1]:

> *Arg. ; a chevron gu. between 3 martlets sa.*

A family of Hayne at Awborne and Kintbury (Wilts and
Berks) recorded their arms at the Visitation of Berks, 1664,
thus :

> *Az. ; a chevron between 3 martlets sa.*

The sister of the poet Lovelace married into this family and
the name Lovelace Hayne occurs subsequently.[2]

Robson gives these same arms, and as crest an eagle, with
wings expanded and distended, preying on a tortoise, all ppr., to
Hayne of Haddon, Jamaica, and Burderup Hall near Marlborough,
Wilts ; and a Mr. Hayne,[3] buried at Staines 16 August, 1678, has
the same escutcheon on his tomb.

Camden's Grants (*circa* 1644) give the coat of Sir Thomas
Hayns, knt., London, as

> *Quarterly 1 and 4 Or; a lion's head erased sa., semée of
> ermine spots.*
>
> *2 and 3 Arg. ; on a chief embattled   . .   3 martlets sa.*
>
> *Crest : a talbot passant.*

The crest of a greyhound is used by the Rev. Francis A.
Haines of Bosham, Sussex.   I also find a talbot or greyhound
sejant on the seal to a deed of George Haynes of Oldbury-on-
Severn, Gloucestershire, in 1666.   And it appears as the crest of
Hayne of Salop,[4] whose arms were—

> *Quarterly Arg. ; bugle and baldric sa.*

John Haynes, Receiver of Her Majesty's revenues in Wales
(*ob.* 27 May, 1591), had for arms :

> *Vert ; a lion rampant or ;*

and this appears as one of the 40 quarterings in the coat of
C. D. Cook of Wales.[5]

---

[1] Westcott's Views of Devon, 1630 ; Robson's British Herald ; Harl. MS. 1578.
f. 9b, under Hayne of Hayne, Devon.

[2] Very possibly descendants of this family, about which I have much information, still exist.

[3] Harl. MS. 1082 (? 1052), f. 97.   [4] Visitation of 1584.

[5] Burke's *Heraldic Illustrations*, Plate XVIII, p. 54.

Robson gives a coat for a Surrey Haynes or Heynes, which I cannot trace elsewhere:

Chequy or and gu., a canton ermine, over all on a bend az. a griffin's head erased between 2 falcons or.

THE ARMS AND CREST OF THE SLADELAND HAINESES AND THEIR DESCENDANTS.

There is no evidence that the Hayne or Haines family of Sullington, Storrington, and Kirdford, co. Sussex, was originally armigerous. No trace is to be found of any family of the name entering its pedigree, or arms, at any visitation of Sussex. The status of the family was that of substantial yeomen, and Richard Haines, the subject of this memoir, was the first to raise himself to a higher level. His sister married Richard Everenden, gentleman, of Horsham, and his wife was connected by marriage with Thomas Duppa, gentleman, of Storrington. He himself receives the title of gentleman in Patent Rolls in 1672 and 1684,[1] but this was very possibly a courtesy title. His burial in the Church of Christ Church, Newgate Street, shows that he was a person of some distinction. His nephew Gregory Haines, who built, or rebuilt, the present house at Sladeland in 1712, is called gentleman in deeds (dated 1718 and 1722) recording the purchase of lands at Kirdford. Richard's grandson Gregory is called Esquire in his burial register, while his uncle, the above-named Gregory, is at the same time styled gentleman. The title of Esquire may be due to his having been appointed, in 1733 with certain other gentlemen of the county, under an Act of Parliament to carry out improvements in the harbour of Littlehampton, co. Sussex, called Arundel Port. At least the Gregory Haines, Esquire, who appears in that Act, was probably the S. Carolina Gregory and not his uncle.

The earliest certain evidence we have of the use of arms by the family is in the will of Mary Greenfield, sister of the Gregory Haines, gentleman, above mentioned, which was signed and sealed on 9 August, 1755. The very seal which made that impression has recently come into the possession of my brother Major R. L. Haines, R.A. It was given him by William Pattison,

---

[1] And is called Gent. in the parish registers of Sullington, 1683, when acting as churchwarden.

Esq., of Plymouth, who found it among the effects of his mother Ann, *née* Haines, great grand-daughter of Gregory Haines, Esquire (of South Carolina). Since being used on that occasion the seal has become worn at the edges probably by being carried on a chain. The seal is of antique workmanship and has been variously dated by those authorities to whom it has been submitted. The dates given differ very considerably, but the most probable date is about 1680,[1] though it has been referred to as late a date as 1730. If the earlier date be correct, the seal was either discovered by, or manufactured for, Richard Haines himself. It is most probable that he would wish to assume arms. If the later date be correct, the first owner of the seal would be Gregory his nephew, or possibly Gregory of South Carolina, on his return to England, might feel a desire to appear armigerous. Whichever it was, we cannot tell whether he merely, in the way so common nowadays, appropriated the arms and crest of any other Haynes family which took his fancy, or whether he imagined himself, on good or bad grounds, to be really connected with such family, or whether finally he obtained a grant of arms in the proper way. I have not been able to discover any such grant, and, as the last visitation of Sussex was in 1662, there is no pedigree or arms entered in the visitations. Clan feeling naturally makes one wish and hope that the first assumer of a coat of arms assumed it in a legal and honourable fashion. Richard himself was a scrupulous man and I cannot believe without proof that he at all events used bogus arms.

The seal shows these arms and crest :

Arg.; 3 crescents 2 and 1 barry wavy of six.[2]

Crest : *a heron (or stork) rising with wings displayed, beak open and right foot uplifted.*

In fact it is identical in every respect with the seal of Hezekiah Haynes, excepting the mark of cadency, and differs from the coat granted to Nicholas Haynes in 1578 by having the crescents barry not paly, *and gules and azure, not azure and gules.* It seems certain, therefore, that if the arms were simply assumed by Richard Haines or his descendants, he or they took them from the famous General Hezekiah's arms and not from the long-forgotten

---

[1] This is the opinion of Mr. J. J. Howard, Maltravers Herald Extraordinary.

[2] The tincture of the crescents is not visible. Most probably it was gules and azure. The colours in the coat granted to Gregory Haines, C.B., are az. and or.

grant to Nicholas Haynes. Other evidence as to user of this coat by the Sladeland family is found in the fact, that the crest and arms appear on a silver salver,[1] of which the hall mark is 1733–4. A second silver salver, now in the possession of Mrs. Richard Moline, with similar crest and arms, is dated by its hall mark as made in 1757–8. Of course the arms and crest may be later than the salver in both cases, but the appearance of each leads one to the contrary conclusion.

Tradition informs us that before the opening of this century the above crest and arms, painted on wood, were displayed above the front door of Sladeland in Kirdford, and it was perhaps from this escutcheon that Sir William Burrell took his copy of the crest and arms which he blazons in his MS. Collections on Sussex, now in the British Museum.[2] The date of his voluntary " visitation " would be about 1775–1780.

---

[1] Viz.: $\frac{oz}{5} = \frac{dwt}{10} = \frac{gr}{5}$

[2] He gives the heron with beak closed and the crescents az. and gules. Mr. Fox Davies informs me that the church of Leighton, Salop, contains a tomb with arms similar to ours.

APPENDIX.

Heirlooms and Relics.

1. Old silver seal, with crest and arms, probable date about 1680, much worn, see p. 146 : Major R. L. Haines, R.A.

2. Silver salver, date of hall mark 1733, heron crest without crescent in its claw, see p. 147 : *ibid.*

3. Old silver fruit knife, mentioned in a letter of Ann (Haines) Pattison to A. M. Haines, 1867, as having been given by Gregory of South Carolina to his son John : dating between 1723 and 1752. See illustration, p. 148 : *ibid.*

4. Old silver salver dated by hall mark 1757–58, with the 3 crescents and the heron crest, but having the crescent in its claw. This crescent was perhaps added by mistake, since the old silver seal above mentioned *seems* to show a crescent under the outstretched claw of the heron, but in reality there is no crescent there. Perhaps the crescent was added as a mark of cadence. In the latter case most likely Thomas Haines, 3rd son of John, had the salver stamped. The crescents are apparently barry, but do not show any tinctures : Mrs. Richard Moline, Bath.

5. Old gold mourning ring with inscription now scarcely decipherable, "Mary Greenfield 1755": in possession of Mrs. Rutland of Bengeo, Herts.

6. Family Bible with entries (see above) which belonged to John Haines the sailor ; in possession of Mrs. Hare, St. Boniface, Westwood Park, Southampton.

7. Marriage certificate of Gregory Haines and Alice Hooke, attested in Charleston, South Carolina: see above. In possession of Edwin Haines, Esq., Beltring, Paddock Wood, Tunbridge Wells.

8. Three navy warrants appointing John Haines gunner on board the *Jason*, *Preston*, and *Montague*; also pension paper relating to same: *ibid.*

9. Miniature of Thomas Haines son of John Haines: now in possession of H. A. Haines, Esq., India Office, London.

10. A pair of sugar tongs of elegant make with initials M. L., probably M. Lidbetter *née* Edwards (see pedigrees): now in the possession of Mrs. Hare of Southampton.

INDEX.

The Index includes, I believe, all the names in the book except (1) those Haineses about whom the whole book is written; (2) the names of the English and French Captains in the sea fight (pp. 104-108); (3) the names of certain children baptized at Storrington (pp. 10 and 12).